The Net
Beneath Us

The

NET

Beneath

US

CAROL DUNBAR

A Tom Doherty Associates Book
New York

This is a work of fiction. All of the characters, organizations, and events portrayed in this novel are either products of the author's imagination or are used fictitiously.

THE NET BENEATH US

A Forge Book
Published by Tom Doherty Associates
120 Broadway
New York, NY 10271

www.tor-forge.com

Forge® is a registered trademark of Macmillan Publishing Group, LLC.

Library of Congress Cataloging-in-Publication Data

Names: Dunbar, Carol, 1970– author.
Title: The net beneath us / Carol Dunbar.
Description: First edition. | New York: Forge, 2022. |
"A Tom Doherty Associates Book". |
Identifiers: LCCN 2022008276 (print) | LCCN 2022008277 (ebook) |
ISBN 9781250826855 (hardcover) | ISBN 9781250826862 (ebook)
Subjects: LCSH: Bereavement—Fiction. | Outdoor life—Fiction. |
Wisconsin—Fiction. | LCGFT: Domestic fiction. | Novels.
Classification: LCC PS3604.U5176 N48 2022 (print) |
LCC PS3604.U5176 (ebook) | DDC 813/.6—dc23/eng/20220224
LC record available at https://lccn.loc.gov/2022008276
LC ebook record available at https://lccn.loc.gov/2022008277

Our books may be purchased in bulk for promotional,
educational, or business use. Please contact your local bookseller or
the Macmillan Corporate and Premium Sales Department
at 1-800-221-7945, extension 5442, or by email at
MacmillanSpecialMarkets@macmillan.com.

First Edition: 2022
Printed in the United States of America

0 9 8 7 6 5 4 3 2 1

For
Pickle E. Pie

The land knows you, even when you are lost.
—Robin Wall Kimmerer

FALL

Ethan Arnasson bent to fasten the chain to the skid cart as the saws buzzed in the distance and the horses behind him stirred in the leaves and forest funk. A root popped beneath his feet, a shift deep below ground that sent a tremor through his backbone and knees.

He straightened and looked out.

There across the woods, beneath a great white pine, stood what could only be the ghost of his younger brother.

Robby stood solid and strong in the way that he always stood, wearing an orange helmet, rumbling his saw; he hopped around that pine skinny and quick; smart-mouthed and smiley Robby who everybody liked, who died one summer even though he was younger, dead now twenty years, and yet there he stood not fifty feet away.

Ethan watched transfixed. Robby's saw churned out a bright cloud of blue exhaust, and the air shimmered between them, cross-hatched with dusty bars of light. The blade sank into the tree, dust spraying out in a thick white plume. The smell of wood chips and gasoline ripened; the noise crested to a shrill pitch, then cut out. Robby flipped his visor up, tipped his head back, and the ghost disappeared.

Ethan fell slack against the skid. His heart hammered under his work jacket and he took out a handkerchief from his back pocket. Of course, it was just Silas working over there, his nephew Silas wearing his helmet, holding his saw. Ethan wiped the sweat and dust from his worn-down eyes. It was uncanny how the boy moved so much like his father had, how he squinted up at that pine. Ethan still thought of Silas as the boy he was when his father died, but he'd grown now, hadn't he? Stepped up into the full sun of his life with the business he was running and the house he was building, married with a wife and kids; not a boy at all. This must be what parents meant when they said, *My, how time flies.*

Some things sneak up on you when you aren't even looking and spread themselves out across several years' time; other things change right away, inside the space of a single heartbeat.

Silas figured it out the moment before it happened. He stood back, peering up into the boughs of that pine. The saw idled, the horses chuffed. Ethan was only watching because he thought he saw a ghost, but then he knew it, too, the moment still and brightly lit as winter air.

Something was wrong with that pine.

1

Elsa Arnasson was making dirt. Wearing their son in a backpack carrier, with her long Nordic hair caught up loose and haphazard at her neck, she carried the empty compost container and walked up the hill away from the garden, crossing the field that was their front lawn and swinging her arms, because life in the country didn't mean you had to be content with the dirt you got. Nope. You could follow a recipe to make better dirt. New and improved dirt, because, she had discovered, everything about living in the country was about following a recipe.

Already she had made Christmas tree ornaments, vegetarian casseroles, and dyes made from onion skins and beets to color her own Easter eggs. That morning she'd made pancakes served with the wild blueberries she'd picked that summer by hand—berries so small they resembled capers, the mosquitoes so bad she thought she'd go mad. But she was starting to get the hang of it, life in the country, her body always in motion. And the recipe for dirt was simple: one shady patch of earth, a bushel of leaves, and scraps from your kitchen. Layer, water, repeat. She'd read that nearly a quarter of all household garbage could be used for compost, and now it was working, their first batch of topsoil, what gardeners called black gold, and she could turn it and touch it and crumble the dirt between her own two hands.

"We'll grow carrots and potatoes and mushrooms," she said to Finn as she went inside, everything a "we" with babies because experts agreed—explaining things helped them develop language skills. Their daughter in first grade could already read. Hester had asked for pancakes that morning and Elsa had made them—with whole wheat flour and yoghurt she'd cultured from raw milk. She'd made yoghurt! Her eyes adjusted to the dimness of the house they were building into the side of a hill—what she thought of with some affection as their cave.

"Squash and corn and pun'kins." She imitated a country twang, jerked her chin with a funky rocking motion, the baby riding along as she washed her hands at the kitchen sink. The water came not from the antique spigot but from the blue water jugs lining her countertop. And she'd never imagined it would take this long to build a house—they'd been living this way four years! But a person could get used to anything, she'd told Silas that morning, washing her hands in the pan of warm water she kept in the kitchen sink. She'd turned to him with a burst of affection.

He'd been sitting there with their two children, Silas, his back to her in a wooden chair, the sleeves of his plaid flannel rolled up. The muscles of his forearms tanned and strong as he tossed their daughter into the air. Hester's hair flew out like spokes around the sun and Finn banged away on his high chair tray. It was the picture of everything she'd always wanted—noise, color, mess. And love. Elsa could feel the love beaming out from every face.

It was never her dream to live this way—independent, not connected to the grid. She didn't grow up in the country, didn't grow up anywhere, and would never think of herself as a country woman even now. Before moving out here with Silas she hardly knew how to make her own toast let alone yoghurt, and gardening was something migrant workers did in a field. "We have a guy for that," her father always said. But Elsa met Silas during a time in her life when she needed something more to believe in, and Silas had ideals big enough for them both.

Drying her hands, she hefted up the laundry basket with its wet clothes and headed back outside.

In her tall brown boots she crossed the porch into the sun and squinted, stopping to adjust to the bright outdoors. A breeze blew down leaves in a dry gold rain. Finn in his backpack tugged at her hair, just the two of them in a clearing on a warm fall day. Leaves cartwheeled past her feet, past the fire pit Silas dug for them and the folding chairs he put out within hearing distance of the baby monitor, and past the spot where they'd spent two summers camping in a trailer. Silas, so respectful of the money she'd given to invest in their land—the last of her mother's inheritance, what she thought of as Winnie's legacy—he did everything the right way and he did it himself, the permits and digging, the gravel and concrete, septic tanks and inverters with wiring and insulation and the trees he felled and peeled by hand. Why buy new fixtures made in China from plastic when you can go to an auction fifty miles away and buy solid brass for three bucks? Why spend six gallons of water per flush when you can incinerate and compost the ashes? Why eat meat when there are so many different kinds of legumes? Why indeed. She never imagined it would take this long, thought they'd have the house finished before Finn was born. It was such a relief to finally move in, but the house was only a basement with cold cinder-block walls and windowless rooms. She'd opened boxes of cookware and dishes, the silver chest and wedding china from her grandmother, and she didn't know what to do with these things, her old life so different from how she lived now—surrounded by mortar and nail guns, chain saws and mauls, the spiders and snakes winding through the grass.

But for the first time in her life, she was starting to feel it: that she belonged. Not just because she'd made a family here, but because she felt it—a connection to something bigger than just herself, the rolling land, the rousing air.

It came out from the dark pines behind the garden: a puffball that floated in the breeze.

It came like the white fluff of a dandelion only larger, an airy jewel suspended in sunlight that seemed to glow although it was a hundred feet away. It moved on an invisible current and drifted through the trees, played peekaboo behind the boughs, bobbed in and out of shadow. It captured her full attention then because of how it crossed their field toward them, and then hovered, right in front of her, right at eye level—how friendly it seemed, interested, even! She wasn't imagining it—Finn in the backpack gurgled and kicked his legs.

She opened to the moment, forgot about the laundry basket in her hands, the baby on her back, and the house they were building. She forgot about everything and watched this puffball as a buzzing sensation moved through her, small at first, and then rising to fill her entire being, her whole body filled with a sense of rightness, a sense of peace so strong, she couldn't imagine feeling anything but good ever again. This beautiful day, this home they were building and the children they were raising, all of it exactly right, exactly as it should be. After getting so many things wrong, after losing her mom and leaving school and disappointing her dad, she was finally in the right place doing the right thing, and they would be okay.

She thought this, and the puffball whirled away, spinning off into the trees.

From out on the road came the honking of a car horn. It blasted through the trees as tires crunched along gravel, the horn blaring on and on, their driveway long and winding because Silas had wanted their house set way back from the road. Through the bare branches the sun flashed along the vehicle, and Elsa recognized the Jeep that belonged to Luvera Arnasson, Silas's aunt who lived eight miles up the road. She and Ethan had practically raised her husband on their small dairy farm, they'd lived here all their lives—and Luvera with her country know-how and thirty years' more life experience with *everything* would no doubt point out that she, Elsa, was doing something wrong.

But not even Luvera could get to her—everywhere under her skin still tingled and buzzed. Luvera turned the car around in the dirt lot with her window rolled down and her continuous honking, as if Elsa weren't standing right there.

"There's been an accident," Luvera shouted, almost barking. "Ethan and Silas. We have to get to the logging site. Now."

Her words had jagged edges, chaotic lines. Her hair tied back with bangs over her small, peering eyes.

"Elsa?" Luvera leaned forward. "Did you hear what I said? We have to go now. Get in the car."

"Yes." She looked around. This beautiful day, the house they were building. "I hear." She pulled out the plastic legs on the backpack—what she thought of as landing gear—and set her son down. Worked her shoulders free from the straps and turned to Finnegan Arnasson, nine months old. *An accident?* she thought, kissing his feet. *Did we have an oopsie-daisy accident?* She couldn't feel bad. Spilling a glass of milk at dinnertime was an accident, but nothing to get worked up over.

"I should get his diaper bag," she said, lifting out Finn. "I should run up to the house."

"Okay, fine. Leave him here." Luvera unbuckled her seat belt and hustled out of the car. "Do what you need to do but hurry. I'll get him buckled in."

Luvera took her little boy. Even though she had no children of her own, Luvera had purchased a used car seat and installed it in her Jeep. She kept an antique high chair in her kitchen and a children's Bible in the living room. She also canned her own jam and raised chickens and made her own soap from the goats she milked by hand.

"What are you still standing there for? Go go go!" she said. "And get enough diapers. We might be gone awhile."

We might be gone awhile. Elsa folded up the phrase like she folded up the diapers and clothes. She packed a bag in the cool, quiet house, while her thoughts floated like the puffball in the breeze. There were no problems, nothing had weight. *The logging site. An accident.*

She thought about the last time Silas had an accident, the summer they were living in the trailer. He was working at the sawmill on their back forty. It was hot, the night air filled with heat lightning and fireflies. She'd made dinner over an open campfire but he never came, and after getting Hester to sleep, she went back there into the woods by herself.

It was hard to see, the air hazy, cobwebbed with dusk. She found him working late, taking apart the whole sawmill, humming to himself.

"What happened?" She tried to sound amused but was actually horrified by the sight of things, the splintered logs, the jagged teeth of a crooked blade. She expected there to be blood on his hands but he only took the thermos she brought him and grinned.

"I know it's a mess," he laughed. "Broke the welds and everything but it's my fault, I was rushing." The saw had kicked back and torqued the carriage out of alignment, causing a massive jam, wrecking the blade.

"What are you going to do?" she said.

And he told her, as if it were obvious, "Keep on keeping on."

She came out of the house with the diaper bag on her shoulder, Luvera bent over in the back door of the car, the window rolled down, the engine still running.

"Luvera?"

"Oh, thank goodness." She backed out, shut the car door.

"Are they okay?"

Luvera straightened. "It's bad," she said to Elsa, sending the words down like a hammer to the pearl of her day.

2

Luvera Arnasson drove white-knuckled, clutching the steering wheel. Of all the women Silas could have fallen for, why did he pick this one? Elsa sat there tall and erect, almost lordly in the seat next to her—she didn't know a cattail from a cottonwood, but she had good posture. The car jostled over gravel and into pitted ruts. At the crossroads Luvera swung left and accelerated out onto blacktop.

The tires hummed along in the silence. They were on a county road now with nothing in front of them but ten minutes of empty road. No telephone poles or power lines, just miles of roadside ditches choked thick with shrubs and grasses, alder brush, and willow. A few dirt roads branched off to the left or right, driveways to hunting cabins or snowmobile trails or old logging roads closed by the county, but nothing else. Silas wanted it this way. She and Ethan had purchased this sixty-acre parcel for him when he graduated from his land management program at college—and they'd gotten a steal on it from a survivalist who'd been disappointed when after Y2K the world didn't end. But by then, he had already met Elsa.

"I think I'm in love!" he announced one August at the age of twenty-one, home to help with the harvest. Ethan had already gone to bed, Luvera in her bathrobe, but Silas followed her around the kitchen. "I mean, she's way out of my league, it'll probably never happen." His ears flushed rosy as peonies. "She's lived all over the place, Rhode Island, Switzerland, Texas. But we had this connection,

I mean, it was like we *recognized* each other. And when she reads me poetry, I think I actually understand it." He recited the poetry to her, right there by the kitchen sink. "'I have no name for what circles so perfectly, a secret turning in us, and what comes to rest in me, a turning night of stars.'" He read from a book Elsa had given him, a poet called Rumi; he'd never read poetry before.

The tires hummed along the tarmac. Elsa clung to the diaper bag as though it were a life raft. She didn't go to church; she went to poetry readings and wore crystals around her neck. She turned up her nose at the smell of the goats and recoiled from the unwashed eggs covered in green chicken poop. But she loved nature, she'd told Luvera, "And I've always loved trees."

Luvera had looked at her. "You know what Silas does, right? He comes from a family of loggers. After college, he plans to make a living by cutting trees down."

"Oh, yes, I know," she said. "Sustainable forestry management. He told me about his business plans, to harvest timber the slow way using draft horses and . . . skids?" She touched a napkin lightly to her lips. They were all sitting around the dining room table at the farmhouse, their first supper together, and Elsa had brought over a pie that she made herself, Luvera remembered, a raspberry pie that spilled juices dark red.

One year later, they married. Of course, Elsa was pretty, her skin pampered and smooth and her things of the highest quality, not like the women from around here. Luvera had never been to college, never been anyplace. Something about Elsa's face made her uncomfortable, as though she shouldn't be looking at it, just like she shouldn't walk into the house with muddy shoes after being in the barn. A silly thing to think, she knew. Elsa was just a young woman in the bloom of motherhood, and it became her, gave a soft fullness to her figure and face.

They were all surprised when the young couple announced it was time to start building on the land. Hester was only two, Elsa a new mom. They stayed with Ethan and Luvera at the farmhouse during that first winter, and once, while cleaning, Luvera noticed a pretty green bottle sitting out on the bathroom counter. La Mer, it was called, a "lifting eye serum," and what on earth that was, Luvera did not know. But later when she looked it up online, she discovered it cost two hundred and sixty dollars—for one tiny bottle! A world of things opened to her then, things she did not even know enough about to want. It intimidated her, that Elsa came from money, that she'd lived all over the world.

Beside her, the young woman swept up a few blond strands and tucked them by the side of her smooth dear cheek. Her demeanor aloof, her movements hesitant, stiff, as if at any moment she might change her mind and take the gesture back. It was difficult to be comfortable around her because she hardly seemed comfortable with herself. "Just give her a chance," Silas had said. "Just get to know her." But Elsa was hard to get to know. The things she said, it was never about practical matters, like what to make for dinner, but strange observations about inanimate objects, as if they had agendas. "I don't think my keys want to be found," she might say, because she always misplaced her keys, but of course it was never her fault, it was the keys that had "gone off somewhere."

And why, out of all the girls he could have had, why had Silas chosen this one with her head in the clouds?

"Luvera, what do you know?" Her voice came small and tremulous from beside her in the front seat, her first words since they'd been in the car.

Luvera flexed her fingers, gripped the wheel. "I'm not going to lie to you, Elsa. I'm sorry. Bob Westman called me from the site. He told me Silas got pinned under a tree and that it's bad. He said to come get you."

Out the window a cut field rolled by, stands of stubbed corn, stiff and pale against the black dirt. The clock on the dashboard read 11:40 A.M.

"And Ethan?"

"Ethan got run down by the skid cart. The team spooked, I guess. They found him first and they told me that he was okay."

"But not Silas."

"I'm sorry, Elsa. If it was me, I would want to be prepared." She glanced over, then back. How on earth could this young woman possibly be prepared? Only a handful of guests came for her on the day of the wedding, all of them from out of state. Her father did not come. It was Ethan who walked Elsa down the aisle, wearing a houndstooth jacket with his back ramrod straight, and the look on his face like he'd been waiting for that moment his whole entire life.

"Bob told me that it was bad and to come get you," Luvera repeated. "He told me to bring you right away to the site."

"To the site?" Elsa said. "Aren't they bringing him to the hospital? Why have us go all the way to the site if—" She inhaled, turned away.

Luvera kept her gaze on the road and her hands on the wheel. The car moved alone along the empty road and the two women stared out.

3

They pulled into the entrance of the Westman place and followed the dirt track lined with pine and birch, a road made back in the thirties and wide enough to fit a logging truck. Elsa had never met Bob Westman, but Silas talked about him, the retired cabinetmaker who owned a hundred and fifty acres on the west bank of the Brule River. To cushion his nest egg, he was logging off some of his bigger trees, but he didn't want to tear up his forest with heavy equipment crushing his saplings and compacting the ground. So, he hired Silas and his crew with their draft horses and skids.

Whips of red and blue light flashed through the trees and Elsa from the front seat recognized a few of the men who worked with her husband, moving in the distance through the woods. They wore brown Carhartt overalls with flannel shirts and moved among the trees alongside the medical technicians in their neon vests. The Jeep pulled up next to the emergency vehicles, all of the trucks and cruisers parked askew with back doors thrown open, the ambulance with its equipment and beds—arranged like the pictures she'd seen on boxed Lego building sets, The Emergency Vehicle and The Police and Rescue.

"I'll take Finn," Luvera said. "You go on ahead."

"Where should I go? What should I do?" She clutched the diaper bag, hugged it to her chest. "Oh my god, Hester."

"What?"

"I'm supposed to pick Hester up from school!"

"We'll get her on the way to the hospital."

"No, no we can't. She's on this field trip. They won't get back until three."

"We'll figure something out." Luvera lifted Finn, shut the door. "We'll call somebody at the school or someone will go get her."

The buzzing had left her body and she felt hollow, not connected to the ground. Finn's little face rode above Luvera's shoulder and Elsa followed. She heard her feet rustling below her in the leaves and smelled the forest must they stirred up, but they did not seem to belong to her, as if she were riding around inside her body like a passenger, gliding from here to there, past the ambulance, past the people. Inside her mind she was still talking to her son. *We're moving as if in a dream, aren't we? Yes, we are. Yes indeedy.*

"Why don't you go on ahead," Luvera said. "I see Silas over there."

"Where?" She didn't see him, Silas strong and outspoken and most comfortable when outdoors.

"Over there." Luvera lifted her chin.

He was lying down, strapped to a board, wearing the flannel shirt he'd put on that morning. His neck and head rested on a thick foam wedge and oxygen tubes branched into his nose, but his eyes were open, facing up. Elsa moved toward the EMTs who carried him. They picked their way carefully through the debris, their voices like the rustle of leaves as they stepped over downed limbs and branches. She arrived as they brought him to a waiting gurney.

"Silas!" she called, and reached out. A pair of hands landed on her shoulders. Someone said, "Please, don't touch him." Another said, "This is the wife."

The wheels of the gurney rolled out over the dirt and she walked beside him, holding her face above his. "Hold on," she told him.

"Just please hold on." She searched and strained, waiting for some glimmer, some sign that he knew she was there. The sky-shadows of the canopy drifted across the lenses of his eyes like clouds past the windows of a vacant house. She stopped. They went on, and he disappeared behind the ambulance.

A black dog appeared, wagging its tail. It licked the tops of her shoes, the cuffs of her pants. The smell of pine resin and sawdust filled her nose and the small bones of her face vibrated like glass about to shatter.

"Elsa, get in. They don't have room for us." Luvera hurried around the Jeep and buckled in Finn, the opening and closing of car doors. "We'll follow them out."

A fiery glaze of sweat on her skin. She had been doing laundry on a Tuesday, it was a beautiful day, and now she was here in these woods, as if someone or something had moved her here to this exact spot, set her down inside this body, this shell, where she would see things and feel things she never expected, while the world in turn waited, like the space just before breath, it waited, as if asking her, baiting her, *What will you do?*

Elsa turned, and the scene around her also turned, and then came the sensation of a spinning rope, and she, the weight at the end, holding on with all her might. It was a sensation that had haunted her all the early years of her life, in dreams, in nightmares. The people and trees and vehicles got farther away as she spun out, disconnected, her body flung to the outer edges alone.

The ground met her elbows and dirt filled her nose, a sandy shuffle of leaves, such a surprise to be on the ground, and when had she fallen? The whisper of nylon jackets and the hands who pulled her up—these men from the logging crew, Tommy whose voice sounded so young, "Are you all right?" And she said, "Why yes, thank you so much," as they floated her back to her feet.

The ambulance shuddered through the trees, the black dog

barked. Tommy closed the door after fastening her seat belt, and they moved out, the Jeep heading north up from the river in a convoy with the pickups and the cars and the emergency vehicles spinning out their sirens and lights.

4

Hester Arnasson came down from the school bus in a stream of little kids, a self-possessed first grader with fair hair from her mom and cinnamon eyes from her dad. She carried her pink coat and wore a backpack half zipped and fringed with the raggedy edges of papers poking out through the opening. At the sidewalk's edge she stood straight and alert, watching the clusters of parents and other kids with the posture of someone surveying their land.

"Hester! Over here!" Miss Cooper waved and called her name, purse slung over her shoulder, cell phone in hand. "You're coming with me today," she said, smiling with teeth showing. "I'll be driving you into town." Lip gloss pink with flints of glitter.

"What did you say?"

"I said you're coming with me today. Your mother called the school."

"Why did she do that?"

Brianna in her skirt and boots with matching leopard-print tights bounced between them, and the two girls hugged. Brianna took Hester's hands and hopped up and down. They crossed the parking lot, two young girls and one older, all with long hair gleaming in the sun.

"This is my car! You can sit by me!" Brianna clambered into the back seat, unzipped her backpack, and started taking things out. "I have stickers! I have smelly ones!"

Hester did not get in the car. She stood by it and watched the kids that followed their parents out across the parking lot. They followed like the baby ducks on her brother's toy, the one he pulled with a string. All the yellow ducks on wheels rolling out behind the mama duck, all of them shaking their heads, *quack, quack, quack.*

"It's all right," the teacher said. "You're going to meet your mom and dad in town, I promise. We don't want to be late or they'll worry." She smiled. "It's all right, Hester, get in the car."

Miss Cooper was a teacher's assistant at the school, but she was also Brianna's aunt. Hester had ridden inside Brianna's mother's car before, but not this one. It was smooth and clean with no stickers or toys or crumbs. A pine-tree air freshener swung from the rearview mirror and a Green Bay Packers bobblehead was stuck to the dashboard. Hester fastened her seat belt. Brianna held out some candy, but Hester shook her head, no. The bobble toy with no neck floated its head above its body as they turned out of the school parking lot onto County Road double B.

"Is Finn okay?" Hester said. "Did something happen with my brother?"

"Oh no," the teacher smiled. "Your brother is fine."

"He's okay?"

"He's with your mom and dad in town."

"My mom told you?"

"Yes." Miss Cooper's eyes flicked up from the road to meet Hester's in the rearview mirror. "He's fine."

They made another turn, right this time, and again the bobblehead swayed.

"Miss Cooper?"

"Yes?"

"This summer my brother picked all the cherry tomatoes when they were still green and bit them just one time and threw them on the ground. He's just a little bugaboo."

Everyone in the car laughed, even Miss Cooper. Brianna repeated, "Bugaboo," and couldn't stop laughing. Hester decided that it was all right to accept a piece of candy.

She sucked on a root beer drop as the view out the window flowed by. Trees crammed on the sides of the road opened out to bogs filled with spruce and tamarack. The needles of the tamaracks had changed to a color her mother called "ocher"—she had shown it to her from a tube of paint. Her father told her that the tamaracks were the confused conifers of the forest because they got tricked into thinking they ought to change colors, too, like the maples and the birch. So, every year they were the only evergreens to lose their needles in winter. They looked like they were dying, their poor needles dried up in the sun, some of them already naked with knobby branches twisted and bent. She felt sorry for them, getting tricked like that.

At the end of the long road Miss Cooper turned right. Sunlight streamed through the windows and Hester took off her coat. Black crows the size of bowling pins rose and flapped their wings and settled back down. It was almost four o'clock when they crossed the railroad tracks into town. Small houses on stamps of brown lawns held blow-up figures of ghosts and witches, with skeletons and bats that swung in the spindly branches of trees. The car turned in to a lot filled with rows of other cars. A wide building with stacked-up windows loomed and blotted out the sun.

"Okay, Hester. Get ready."

They drove under a little covered area, and inside the car turned ashen and cold. "What is this place?" Hester hugged her coat.

"Get your backpack and things. This is your stop."

"Where do I go?"

"Right through those doors. Your mother will be right there waiting for you."

Hester put on her coat, looked at the doors.

"I want to go inside!" Brianna said.

"No, honey, stay here. This is the emergency drop-off; I can't park here." Miss Cooper turned around in her seat. "Just go on through those doors and you'll see your mom. I'll wait here with Brianna just in case. If you don't see her, come back out."

Hester took her things and got out of the car. She stood alone on the hard, white sidewalk, while other people came and went. She looked back at the car.

"Go on," Miss Cooper smiled behind the window, her voice buzzy like a bumblebee in a jar. "I'll be right here. If you can't find her, I'll park and go in with you."

Hester walked toward the doors and they opened by themselves. Her feet stepped up onto a black mat that led through more doors. Once inside she stopped.

Rows of chairs filled a carpeted area and the air felt thick and heavy with moisture. Flat televisions hung on all the walls and hurt people sat in the chairs. An old woman in a wheelchair, a man with his hand in a big white bandage, and a boy her age with yellow-crusted eyes, curled on his mother's lap. Smells of bleach and vomit crowded together and the candy in her mouth turned into a hard, sour lump.

It was not her mother but Aunt Luvera who came toward her, from the rows of people in the chairs, both arms out, jacket flapping.

"Oh, Hester, thank goodness you're finally here." She hugged and patted and took Hester's hand. "Come on now. We have to go. They moved him to a different hospital. Your mother is already there."

"Where is she?"

"At the other hospital in Duluth."

"Why? Why is she there?"

"It's your papa, honey. He got hurt at work."

"Papa?" There was a twist in her stomach. "Papa got hurt?"

"They gave him a ride in a helicopter. Your mom is with him now."

"Papa?" She tried to stay still like the trees do to keep it from happening, but it was already too late. They were moving and everything was falling away, everything good and golden about her life drying up, and she had been tricked like one of the confused conifers of the forest.

5

E than Arnasson woke with a sense of urgency. They should have finished the job by mid-October, but the ground had been too wet, and so they were rushing to get it done. He clutched his blanket, searching the room. In his mind he heard the huff and jingle of the draft horses, the team that belonged to Silas, a pair of Percherons with hooves the size of salad bowls and fur that thickened during winter and shed during summer so always on those logging gigs he was fishing horsehair from his coffee. But he wasn't in the woods anymore. He was in a room with stark white walls and furniture sterile and smooth. His wife of forty years sat with her embroidery and those busy hands, Luvera Arnasson, her hair tied back in a ponytail like a young girl's.

"Luvey?"

"Ethan." She gathered up her things and came over. "How long have you been awake?" It was always she who worried about Silas and his family, how he would get the house finished and the well dug before winter, how he wouldn't have time to help them get the hay in, because that was his wife, always worried about the least likely, most terrible thing that could possibly go wrong. Well, now she finally got to be right.

"Is he awake?" he said.

She put a hand to his forehead. "How do you feel?" she said. "You're at the hospital in Sterling. Do you remember what happened?"

He tried to lift himself, but pain rippled through his torso, and

there was binding around his chest, the hairs there stuck to something adhesive that tugged at his skin.

"The doctor said you might have some memory loss," she said,
"but only temporarily."

Of course he remembered her, how she handed him the binoculars that day at Hawk Ridge, how she used to sing in church like a
bright-mouthed bird, her eyes teary from the music even when she
was young, and how that aliveness had changed over the years,
the darkening under her eyes, the tightening around her mouth.
She was always the strong one. When they lost Robby, and then five
years later when they lost the baby, it was always she who carried
on. He remembered who they used to be and who they were now,
an old farmer with a bushy gray head and his wife who sewed but
no longer sang; what they had been together and done together,
what they had not been and not done, and it seemed suddenly so
precious to him, all of it, even what they didn't get right, and he
wanted to hold her and thank her for it all.

"Luvey." He fumbled for her hand.

They wrapped their fingers around each other, hers strong but
cold. For a moment they just held hands and let everything be
there between them. He felt the privilege of that, of not having to
explain anything, the gift of having this one person here with him
who shared the people and circumstances of the last forty years of
his life.

"Your X-rays came back," she said. "There's been no puncture
to your spleen."

He squeezed her hands to let her know he heard.

"I knew you'd be fine because Dr. Olson said you have the
bones of a twenty-year-old. Remember when he said that? From
all that milk, I told him." She tried to let go, he held on.

"Did he wake up?"

She avoided his gaze. "Tommy Kroplin came over when you were
sleeping. He said not to worry about the milking or the feeding.

They got that covered. He'll rotate the grain with the hay the way you like. He and his brother will take shifts. Tommy knows the farm and Maggie won't bark at him or give him any trouble." Maggie was their golden retriever, and she would greet a bank robber with her tail wagging, but Ethan didn't argue. She gave his hand an extra squeeze, then walked around to pull the curtain closed on the window by his bed. The blinds were drawn, and he couldn't say whether it was night or day, morning or afternoon.

"It's two in the morning." Luvera read his mind, and he always liked the sound of her name, a name her mother had made up because she couldn't decide between Lavone and Vera. He looked at her; the lids of his eyes were heavy, but he didn't want to sleep. She read his mind again.

"You should sleep, Mr. Arnasson. You have two fractured ribs, some bruising, and a mild concussion to your head."

"Tell me about Silas."

"You don't want to know."

"I do want to know."

"I'll tell you in the morning, after you've had a good night's rest."

He laughed, a breathy huff. A trickle of spit slid down his throat and caught there, and he coughed but the tickle wouldn't go away. It sent him into a spasm of coughing where he couldn't stop, his torso convulsing as waves of pain beat and pounded off the inside walls of his chest. He gripped the bed rail, puffed air through his tear-streaked cheeks. The pain, it thundered.

"Here, here, have some water. Take a drink." Luvera shoved a Dixie cup into his face with a plastic straw sticking from the side, but he waved that away, trying to concentrate. His legs shook under the dry sheets and he coughed, his body brittle, tense. He was so tired, his eyelids, they seemed to weigh a thousand pounds, but he couldn't stop the itch in the back of his throat. Luvera held the cup to his mouth again and this time he accepted, working his lips around the straw like a newborn to the teat, leaking dribbles from the sides of his mouth. But the cough subsided. He lowered himself back onto his pillow.

"You need the nurse? She said to call if you needed anything. We can get more pain meds or more pillows."

"Quit hedging, Mrs. Arnasson. Just tell me. I need to know."

She set the cup on the bedside table. "Well, if you're going to be stubborn about it." She adjusted her sweater, tugged it down. "They moved him over to Angel of Mercy because of their trauma facility. All of us running back and forth across the bridge all day, it was just ridiculous."

"He isn't here?"

"You don't remember? The doctor spoke to us. They moved him to Duluth, but even if he was here you couldn't see him. He's in the ICU on a ventilator and they said we have to be—" She turned away and inhaled with a voiced breath, a kind of helpless yelp as she reached into her sweater pocket for a tissue. When she spoke again, the sounds came out high and thin like from some tortured animal. She used words she'd never used before, "spinal shock" and "crushed vertebrae," disgusting words, what she had learned to say, what he had made her say to explain why Silas would never be able to walk again, why he was on a ventilator, how the damage to his nerves along his spine was so severe, he might never breathe on his own again.

"He may never wake up." She turned to him now, her eyes red-shot and spilling. "They're worried about blood flow to the brain. Only five percent of all patients who get put on a breathing machine ever come back all the way." She swallowed, crumpled a tissue. "But the doctor said there's always those miracle cases. You just don't always know. Silas is young and strong and in the prime of his life. I called everyone from church. I talked to Father Martin. They're all praying. We're talking through Facebook. You'd be surprised at all the people who are showing up, people we haven't heard from in ages." She reached for the gold cross she wore around her neck and slid it back and forth along its chain. "A neurosurgeon will be there later today, and Dr. Olson is coming over from the clinic. Do you remember him? The one who said you had strong bones?" She plucked another tissue from its box.

Ethan closed his eyes. The plastic lid of the water pitcher flapped and fell into the bottom of the pitcher. "It's empty," she said. "I'll go fill it." In the bathroom the lid of the pitcher fell again and clattered into the sink, his wife the sort of person who couldn't go about anything quietly. But she closed the door. Behind the wall he heard the tap water run.

There must have been water in the sawdust. Silas must have felt it on that second cut because his pants were wet. Ethan noticed on the ride in the ambulance how his pants were soaked through, his thighs sprayed with wood chips black from rot. White pine can do that, those giants of the forest, and this one had to be over a hundred feet tall, three feet wide, the first seven feet hollow, its heartwood rotted out. Ethan saw the moment when Silas knew, held that knowing like a live thing warm in his arms and there wasn't one thing he could do with it to keep that boy safe.

Loggers called them widow-makers. All his life he'd heard his uncles talk about how pine can do that, blow apart in front of you, not tipping away, not falling sideways, but crumbling down, the whole thing on top of you thundering down in a mad dry cracking of rain. The boy tried to run. He left his saw in the tree as it cracked and shattered into splinters the size of doors that whipped through the air while he tried to get away, the debris falling, all that weight slamming down, and the boom-crack of thunder that broke the air.

The horses bolted—jumped and jerked the cart in a panic, throwing Ethan from his feet. They ran, yanking the eight-foot log over him as they took off in a blind jangle. He'd curled up into a fetal position as that pine rolled down and the ground shook with a thunder he could still feel in his spine.

When it was over, his insides felt scoured and dust choked the back of his throat. But the ground held him, and a warmth spilled over his body where he lay. He'd opened his eyes to see sun sprays churned up with the sawdust, and this one kindness—the warmth of the sun—came down to him through the rip in the canopy.

The team was found, tangled, but for the most part unhurt. After a while came the shouts that they found Silas, and the chain saws fired up, first one and then others.

Luvera opened the bathroom door and came back out into the room. Her hair tidy, her lipstick newly applied. She smoothed down her sweater and sat in the rocking chair, resumed her embroidery.

From the bed Ethan watched her, his chest pounding. He tried to contain his memories, to sort them out. He concentrated the way he had with his coughing to breathe around the pain. He studied her, his wife of forty years, how she sat there with her embroidery hoop, the girl he met and married, his wife wearing her good blouse and dangly gold earrings, her lipstick newly applied at two o'clock in the morning.

A bit of lipstick always stuck to her front tooth, the one that poked out on the upper left side. Whenever she smiled, he could see it. A little pink spark.

6

In the hospital waiting room, Elsa itemized apparel, what other people wore—an old habit and something she hadn't done in years, not since Hester was born and certainly not since they'd moved out to the land. She studied and listed, compared and judged, while the friends and relatives, teachers and families who knew Silas but did not know his wife kept her company and offered their kind words. Finn bounced on her lap or sat with Hester on the floor. Silas's relatives bought them little gifts. "Such beautiful children," they said. A stuffed animal for Hester, a balloon for Finn. "God willing," they said. Jeans with quilted vests and polar fleece.

In the hallway next to the vending machines, Tommy's wife chased a toddler. She must have come straight from work—a loose-fitting blouse, cream-colored with dots, her slacks too tight, with sling-backs in white. It was a month after Labor Day, did she not know the rule about wearing white? Elsa could hear herself, it was her mother's voice—oh, she'd been so horrible!—judging people based on what they wore.

"Canny," the boy said. He couldn't have been more than two. He patted the vending machine with sticky hands. Hester, next to him, peered into the case. They were at the Angel of Mercy trauma center in the middle of the night, waiting to hear if Silas would make it, or if his organs would shut down.

"Canny," the boy said again.

"No Tommy," his mother said. "That costs money. We have juice. Do you want your juice?"

"No, canny." The boy smacked his hands against the glass.

Elsa moved toward them. She wanted to let Tommy's wife know how much it meant to her that they had stayed. She couldn't remember Tommy's wife's name, but she saw her now in a way she had never seen other women before, as if all her life she'd known only their outer presentations, who they thought they were, or who they wanted to be, but looking at this woman now in the middle of the night with her tired curls loose around her face, Elsa saw a mother like herself who just wanted everything to be all right.

"I have some extra quarters." Elsa had the quarters in her hand. The machine took only change. She held them out.

Tommy's wife looked at her. "We have our own money." Her uncomfortable-looking shoes snapped hard against the floor as she hurried her son away.

Elsa closed her hand. The sting of it a surprise. They'd been living here four years.

"Just let them get to know you," Silas always said. She told him she felt like the lonely tree that grew out in the field by her grandmother's house. It stood there all alone with its perfect domed canopy, no other trees around. "Trees are actually very social beings," Silas explained. "They don't do as well on their own, they need each other to thrive."

The first time Silas took her to the back forty to move slabs of quarter-sawn wood, she'd worn sandals.

"Oh, you're wearing sandals," Silas noted.

"Yes," she said. "It's summer." Her mother taught her that women wear sandals in summer, but not without first painting their toes.

"You'll need to get your feet protected," he said, "before we move the wood."

It stung even coming from him, the familiar ache of getting it wrong after spending a lifetime trying so hard to get it right. It was always something different—some new fashion or climate zone or trend. She entered classrooms where she didn't know a single face and saw in their expressions how she had erred, sneakers instead of flip-flops, a stuffy cardigan instead of a shirt. She studied people, their clothing, their mannerisms and what they said. She learned to imitate them, to dress like them, to be someone they would like. Her habit and second nature, how hard she tried; she would crack the code, she would fit in.

Then, it would be time to move, again.

Hester chose Cheez-Its and they went back to the waiting room on the sixth floor with its couches for people who had loved ones in the ICU. Elsa smoothed down her soft autumn sweater and crossed her tall leather boots. The right length, a seasonal color. Her mother would be proud.

"Trees don't compete with each other," Silas had told her. "People always think that in a forest, their branches are up there fighting for the light, but they're not. They stretch out until their tips sense the leaves of another tree, and then they stop. A tree never wants to take anything from another tree."

Her mother never got to meet Silas, they met after Winnie died, but she would have liked him, Elsa knew. Her mother in a sleeveless salmon blouse. Elsa could see her sitting at the country club on a veranda during sunset while her father golfed. They were living in New Hampshire the summer before Winnie got sick. "Fix your blouse," she'd said. "Why didn't you wear that to the christening?" In the softness of air that brushed her mother's cheek, in the shifting of her slacks, the way light struck through the golden liquid in her glass, Elsa felt it, the loneliness of a life so centered on trivial things. Winnie only wanted to share those things with her, but Elsa was never able to enjoy those times. She missed her mother now with a ferocity that tugged like a current in her chest.

"Arnasson?" A doctor stood at the edge of the room. He carried a clipboard and spoke in a somber voice. Silas had made it through the critical first twenty-four-hour period. "His condition has stabilized," he said, "at least for now. Once the swelling goes down, we'll be able to get more imaging tests done." They could go see him, he said. The intensive care ward restricted visitors to immediate family and no more than two persons at a time in the room. "But we won't count the baby," he said. "If you want to follow me."

She hadn't seen Silas since they put him in the ambulance. She held Finn and swayed in the elevator. "Just let them get to know you," Silas always said. But she didn't know how to do that part. "We have our own money," said the voice of Tommy's wife in her head. She'd never thought to consider what his friends might think when she gave Silas that money to build on the land. They all had mortgages and loans and credit card debt. "Just give them a chance," he always said, and it sounded so reasonable, the way he said it. But had it never occurred to him that maybe they didn't want to get to know her?

Nurses orbited machines and monitors in a large open space with air ducts in the ceiling and a hard cement floor painted gray with red lines. Behind a curtain, Silas, lofted and cocked. Tubes twisted from his arms, the respirator covered his mouth, and a plastic neck collar obscured his face. He wore a hospital gown in soft white cotton dotted with chevrons in navy blue.

"I want to see, Mama. Can I see?" Hester tugged at her hand and hopped up and down. The Mylar cupcake balloon bobbed on its string.

She'd only known him ten years, but that was a record for her, by a lot. She'd failed to keep in touch with her other friends, the art students from the college in Providence and her coworkers from the restaurant in Minneapolis. They were all starting careers or going off to grad schools or seeing the world.

"I can't see, Mama, I want to see!"

She picked Hester up and stood with her two children, one on each hip. She was in that lonely space of early motherhood, with pockets of time at odd hours when no one else was up, and no time at all during the rest of the day.

Hester wrapped her legs around her and squeezed. Elsa wanted to yell, to shout at him like a crazy person, *What have you done! What were you thinking?* She wanted to ask him, *What do you want? What should I do?* She wanted to hold him and kiss him and throw herself on his bed, to sob herself to death.

She wanted to be alone with the one person who knew her, Silas, her best friend.

Driving home on Wednesday evening, the sun sinking below the horizon, Elsa thought about what Silas said that night back at the sawmill, *keep on keeping on,* and so she did. They went back to the house they were building into the side of a hill, the unfinished second story rising above with its posts and beams and roof joists, uncovered and unprotected like giant rib bones against the pines.

She carried Finn, who clutched his balloon, and Hester, who followed with her stuffed dog. Her children's eyes were wide and glazed and no one talked. Elsa turned on the lights. They flickered before they rose to a glow, but she did not get a reading on the batteries or go up the hill to start the generator. Instead, she cut up organic pears while still wearing her coat, slicing thin, delicate wedges and putting them into bowls. She stood in the kitchen and watched Hester and Finn, how they grabbed at the fruit, their chubby fingers, the innocent rise and fall of their voices, how juice dripped from their chins.

When she was ten and living in Switzerland, her mother signed her up for an adult art class for beginners. Elsa was the only kid in the room, and on that first day, the instructor took off his shoe and put it on the high table at the front of the room.

"Everybody take off your shoe and set it up in front of you. Today we're going to do our first still life."

Elsa had slipped off her tennis shoe with its laces still tied, and when the teacher came by her drawing of careful bow-tied loops, he took her sheet of paper and her shoe right to the front of the room. "What do we think of when we think of a shoe?" He drew a mock-up of her shoe on his easel, with its bow-tied loops. They looked silly and stereotypical and she was mortified, but also, it was the same mistake everybody made. "We draw what we see in our mind"—he tapped the side of his head—"not what we actually see here, in front of us." He started drawing her shoe right then and there, as it really was, narrating as he went, the folds of cloth, the bend of shadows.

She saw it, what was actually there: the laces as values of light and dark, not as she assumed them to be, or wanted them to be, but as they were. Her perspective shifted, right then, the moment snapped-to with a buzz-shot of excitement. After that, there wasn't anything she couldn't draw.

Living on the land with Silas was an opportunity to see the natural world the same way—as it really was. She would learn from it, wanted to connect to nature and herself, to deepen and grow as a person. They would raise their children, teach them about trees. She would learn how to do practical things like make yoghurt and grow peas. And someday, when she was ready, she would paint again. But for herself this time.

That was the hope, the long-term goal, the beautiful dream.

In the morning Bob Westman and his wife came to the house with two grocery bags of prepared food. They filled her table with Tupperware and aluminum pans—meatballs, a meat lasagna, sloppy joe filling and sauce. They had forgotten—or maybe they didn't know—that Silas was a vegetarian and so were his kids.

Their kindness hurt. She felt sick with it, heavy in her gut because she didn't know them very well, or what she could ever do to repay them, but Finn tried a meatball and liked it.

After they left she stood outside. She waited for it, but it did not come, that sense of peace. There were no puffballs in the air.

At the clothesline behind the house, she went alone at the end of the day with the laundry she had washed but not dried on Tuesday. Lumps of cold cloth stuck together in the basket but everything still smelled clean. Peeling apart the items one at a time, she pegged them to the line strung between the trees. She hung the laundry according to color, from light to dark, her hands knowing instinctively which article of clothing to reach for next. It felt good to be doing something useful, something that she knew how to do and that resulted in a pleasing picture, the progression of color stirring what was familiar and autonomous inside of her.

Her hand found his T-shirt, the one he had given her Tuesday morning balled up and dusty from the trunk of the car. "Would you mind washing this for me?" he had asked. His smile and how he handed it to her, so easy, so carefree.

"Sure." She'd taken the shirt and wondered how they'd ended up in these traditional roles, him going off to work, she home with the baby all day. She looked at the shirt and said something about how lucky he was to have her washing his clothes, would have said even more but he seemed so happy, the raspberry canes loopy behind him and the air a rose gold.

She wished she hadn't said that. Wished she had kissed him and told him that there was nothing more in the world she wanted than to take that shirt, felt special, even, that he had given it to her. Not because it was special, it was just a stupid shirt, but because he was, and he had chosen her.

She hadn't known it would be the last thing he would ever give her, his last words, their last moment together as who they were.

The sobs came hard and violent and her body contracted, as if she were giving birth to grief. She pulled his shirt to her chest and sank to the ground. It was the first time she'd cried since the accident. The power of all that had changed surged through her and she keened, bent over in the leaves beside the clothesline.

But she couldn't stay long with it; the kids were alone at the house. She had to be practical and brave and strong. She had to be what she was not.

Impulsively Elsa reached out for a tree. Wrapped her hand around its trunk and closed her eyes. Silas had taught her how to listen to the trees. At the time she had thought it corny and made fun of him, couldn't even do it without giggling. But she didn't laugh now.

The tree under her hand didn't move. Her palm pressed the rough, corrugated bark, the tree quiet and strong, all the things that she was not. She let herself rest there in that space, let her mind be empty. New thoughts rose up from a still pool. Silas was in the hospital and she was home. He was hurt but she was well. The children loved her and she loved them. All of those things were true. Right now, they were okay. If she went neither forward nor backward in her mind, they were okay.

She got to her feet, shook out his shirt, and pegged it to the line.

They fell into a routine—mornings spent doing chores, laundry, dishes, gathering kindling they foraged in the woods. Afternoons they drove to the hospital and stayed as late as they could before driving the hour home again. She kept Hester home from school; she needed her help with Finn. They were waiting for the testing to begin, and when it did begin, they were waiting for it to end.

"You should go home," Luvera said. "Take the kids and let them sleep all night in their beds." It was Saturday, late; they'd been at the hospital all day.

Elsa moved Finn to her other shoulder. They were in the family waiting room with its orange couches and chairs. Hester lay on the sofa with one elbow folded under her head, eyes glazed, watching a television screen in the corner of the room. "Hester, you can sleep," she called over to her daughter. "I promise you won't miss anything."

The girl didn't answer. She kept her eyes open, cheeks fevered. She hadn't eaten much of a dinner.

"Did you ask for more blankets?" Luvera pulled thread through her embroidery hoop. "They've also got pillows, you know."

"Thanks," she said. "I didn't know." Although she did. It was her habit to be the person who did not know, the one other people had to look out for and take care of because as the new girl, usually she didn't know. "Do you want to get home to Ethan?" she said.

"My sister's there," Luvera replied. "She and her husband arrived last night."

"Oh, that's nice." She pulled the blanket around Finn's head. "How's Ethan doing?"

"Oh, you know, well as can be expected. Every time he breathes it gives him pain."

Elsa laid Finn down on the other couch, folded up a second blanket and tucked it in along the side of his body to keep him from rolling off. His face was still and peaceful, and Hester also finally gave in to sleep, ten o'clock on a Saturday night. Elsa pulled the sleeves of her sweater down over her hands and stood by Luvera's chair.

"What?" Luvera said. "You're hovering like a predatory bird."

"I have something that I need to do."

"Okay. What is it?"

She inhaled, tightened her fists. "I want to spend some time with him, alone. If you wouldn't mind watching the kids. I want to say goodbye."

"Oh, Elsa."

"I was wondering, if you weren't going home yet, would you mind sitting with them for a bit?"

"Well of course I'll sit here with the kids, but Elsa . . ." She tapped the busywork on her lap. "Don't go jumping to conclusions before all the tests are in. We just don't know enough yet."

"I have this feeling. I mean, who are we kidding, right? They decided no surgery."

"But that's all preliminary, all the doctors said so. It will be days before we know what we're dealing with. Have a little faith."

She twisted the ends of her sweater sleeves. Silas wanted her to have faith in herself. "Trust yourself," he always said.

"I'm just trying to be realistic," she said now. "I have to be prepared, like you said. I have a lot to think about with the house and the kids and I have to figure out what we're going to do next."

"Did you get ahold of your father?" Luvera pulled at a thread.

Her father who didn't approve of her marrying "that hippie boy." Her father who didn't even come to the wedding and said she wouldn't last two months in the country. "Yes. We talked." They had their third conversation since Hester was born, the fourth time they'd spoken in the ten years since Winnie had died. Her father who now lived in Boston in a new house in the suburbs with a wife Elsa met only once, during Winnie's funeral.

"And?" Luvera said. "What did he say?"

"He said what he always says. 'Well, I'm not surprised.'"

When her mom got sick, she left their home in New Hampshire to go live with the nuns of the St. Peregrine ministry in the mountains of Idaho. They prayed. Elsa stayed with her father and they went to church and also prayed; Winnie's cancer went into remission—a miracle!, everyone said. But the cancer came back and spread to her brain. Elsa was sixteen when her mother was diagnosed, nineteen when she died.

She stepped into the white curtained space of the ICU and sat next to the shape of her husband. She found his hand under the sheet and held it, a hand unresponsive but strangely plump. The doctor told them that his body was on autopilot, in a comatose state. He said that sometimes, if you held their hand or talked to them, the sound of a voice or touch could cause them to sweat or increase their heart rate. And she wanted him to do that, to let her know that he was still there. But when she held his hand, nothing changed, and although she wanted to be with him when he woke up, she didn't believe anymore that he would wake up. Didn't she need to believe in order for a miracle to be possible? Wasn't some degree of faith required? Elsa could almost hear Silas laughing, how he always teased her for being so serious, her complicated search for what was real and true when he always just seemed to know.

Silas as a boy had gone to church with Ethan and Luvera, and he still went on occasion—they all did—Easter Sunday, Christmas Eve; Elsa dressed everyone up and they went to mass. But he wasn't religious, didn't believe what they believed. For spiritual guidance, he looked to the trees.

"Trees take care of each other," he said. "Their roots are connected for miles and miles underground in these intricate systems, they send each other signals, electrical impulses, they talk to each other and send each other food."

He told her this after sharing how his father had died, in a car accident after an asthma attack caused him to drive off the road.

"It's not random," he said of the trees. "Their root systems are the brains of the forest, they can distinguish between the roots of other species and those of their relatives and friends. When a family member gets sick, they take care of them, the weakest among them, they send out nourishment and support."

He and his mom were left with substantial debt after his dad died, they stood to lose everything—the farm, the equipment, and the house where they lived. It was Ethan and Luvera who stepped in and bought the farm so they could stay and not leave their home.

"When my mom got sick," Elsa said, "my dad had an affair."

They were lying on their backs in a park in Minneapolis while clouds scudded past. "While Winnie was off fighting cancer, he found someone else to love. They married three months after my mom died." A cloud brooded past like a barge. "In my family, we don't behave like trees. We get up and walk away and abandon the people we love. We do it all the time."

He had reached out across the grass. "I won't leave you, Elsa," he'd said, taking her hand. "You can count on me. Now that I've got you, I won't let go."

His hands now were placed on top of rolled towels to keep them from contracting into fists, and his pupils did not react to light. She held his hand and his face didn't change and his heart rate stayed the same.

"I'll try," she whispered. "I'll try to be strong like the trees." She felt self-conscious, hearing her voice in the room. Her eyes pooled and roved and dried up. She didn't feel him with her there at all. The numbers beeped on the screen and the nurses out in the halls chatted about their weekend, making their rounds. In her head, her father's voice, *Well, I'm not surprised.*

For the next several hours she sat in that chair, not surprised.

Late that same night, after they finally got home, Elsa went up to the clothesline by moonlight to take down another load of laundry. She approached slowly and set the basket on the ground. The line had broken, all the clothes fallen to the ground. Blue jeans and baby clothes at her feet. Pale onesies in the dirt. The two ends of the line were still tied to the trunks of the trees, but in the middle the line had been cut, broken clean through. A wind rolled dried leaves along the dark empty path.

In her mind she replayed the conversation she had with Silas last spring.

"That bear took down the clothesline again."

"It wasn't a bear."

"What do you mean, it wasn't a bear?" He had never revealed this information before. All the other times it happened, he just went out and retied a new line. "If it wasn't a bear, what was it?"

"Think about it."

She thought about it. There was something he wasn't telling her.

He laughed.

"What?"

"What exactly is it you envision that bear doing up at your clothesline?"

"Well I don't know. He just takes it down!"

"Why?"

"I don't know why a bear would do that but it happens every spring."

"Only in spring?"

She had thought so then but wasn't sure now.

"So, you imagine this old bear wakes up hungry from his hibernation and thinks, 'I'm gonna get me some nice tasty T-shirts'?"

Oh, she had laughed. And he had given her that look of his, like she was this bizarre creature, and how ever had she gotten here in his backyard? How indeed. With her Scandinavian heritage she had the same physical features as the majority of the local population; she looked like she belonged, but she'd never lived in this part of the country before, never gardened or hung clothes. Maybe it wasn't a bear taking her clothesline down, but she didn't have time to figure out what did; there were more pressing concerns.

The low temperature that night was thirty-six degrees, and by next week it would drop below freezing. It wasn't unheard-of for temperatures to sink below zero before Thanksgiving and she couldn't heat the house with only kindling. They needed wood.

At the bottom of the hill in front of their little, unfinished house, Silas had stacked eight-foot logs on wooden rails and covered them with a blue tarp. All summer long he talked about chainsawing those logs into stove-size lengths they could split for firewood, but when she pulled the tarp off, no logs were cut. No firewood split.

They had no running water, her clothesline was broken, and she didn't know how to use a chain saw, much less an ax.

The first time Tommy Kroplin came by was on a Saturday morning one week later, almost two weeks after the accident. His truck with its dented Wisconsin license plate pulled up with Bob Westman inside, and another truck behind it driven by a man named Anders who worked with them on the logging crew. They parked at the bottom of the hill. The sky pewter and overcast, all the trees bare.

Tommy Kroplin and Silas Arnasson had once been good friends. Growing up they went to the same schools and parties and traveled in the same circles. They both attended nearby colleges and over the years they kept in touch, even went to each other's weddings. But as they grew up, they grew apart. Their children didn't know each other and their wives had barely met. Outside of work they hardly saw each other at all.

But Tommy came early and arrived before Hester woke, after the baby was fed and dressed. He came with the men from the logging crew wearing his gloves and boots and Fire Hose work jacket, and he told her they were worried about the unfinished second story of the house. Tommy with his wide shoulders and quiet air, Anders with his gaunt, windburned face, and Bob Westman with his stained and knotted hands. Elsa stood in the doorway, holding the baby on her hip.

"It shouldn't take long," Tommy said. "We just got to wrap up those beams on the second story."

"They can't be left like that," Bob said. "Even with the roof."

"Why?" Elsa didn't understand. "What do you mean?"

"The wood will crack," Bob explained. "What happens is the snow comes in sideways, snow's going to melt even in the cold, and when water gets into your beams, it'll freeze, the wood will swell up, expand and contract, and then the beams won't be any good."

"Oh."

"We just got to get them wrapped," Tommy said. "They make house wrap for that. Keep the moisture out until you decide what you want to do."

"Okay," she said. "I see. Thank you."

The men looked down at their boots and shifted their feet. These men with their dirty jackets and beards, men she would have thought of as backwoods and provincial, if she thought about them at all. The only reason she fell for Silas was the timing, that's what people said. Once, she heard his friends talking before the wedding about how Silas had "caught her with a butterfly net." She'd been so charmed by the poetry of it, she hadn't thought at the time about what it meant.

"Those logs you have there." Tommy gestured to the stack of eight-foot logs at the bottom of the hill. "We can cut some of those up into firewood for you. Get them sized at least."

"I'll bring my wood splitter out here tomorrow," Anders said.

"We'll get a pile started," Tommy added.

Finn was fussing. Elsa bounced him on her hip and gave a nod. Kissed the top of his head.

"We also wanted to give you this." Westman held out an envelope. "It's payment for the job he did. What was owed." His hand shook a little, the pads of his fingers and cuticles stained dark from wood dye and oil. "There's a little extra there, too. What the men put together. We wanted to do it. Thought it might help."

She took the envelope, these men on her porch with their tired eyes and stained overalls. They were doing this for Silas. Her eyes shined up and the small bones in her face tingled, the feeling she got whenever she was about to cry.

"How's he doing?" Tommy said. "Last I heard, they were doing more tests."

She adjusted the baby on her hip. Behind the men out in the field a bird fluttered down, picked up a bit of dried grass in its beak, and flew away back up to its nest.

"They finished the testing," she said. "It's been confirmed, there's no activity in his brain. So, we have to make a decision."

Again the bird fluttered down, picked up another bit of dried grass, flew back. She was like that bird, these past two weeks—she moved back and forth, picked up this, then that. She went through the motions but felt disconnected from the things happening around her.

"And how are you doing?" Tommy said.

"I'm fine." She looked at Tommy, her words bits of dried grass. Tommy seemed to want more, she felt this from him, or maybe it was that she wanted to say more but didn't know how.

What she thought about was the day Silas's mother died, and he had hung up the phone and turned to her, his eyes wet but calm. His mother, Ivy, had passed away in her sleep. Ever since Silas left for college, she'd been living in Florida; she'd always been older than Silas's father by quite a lot, but after he'd died, the years went hard on her. An essential part of her seemed to have shut down. Whenever Silas tried to explain it, his voice would get quiet, with a look on his face like he had lost something back then, and still couldn't find it. But that day he had seemed almost proud. "That's the way to do it," he'd said. "Live each day to its fullest and then go quiet in your sleep." Both his parents had passed quickly, and those words had been coming back to her all week.

She washed the dishes and folded the clothes, while the men brought their tools and rolls of Tyvek up to the unfinished second story. The back of the house sat flush with the ground, so they didn't need a ladder. They hammered and nailed and banged around up there all morning, while Hester at the kitchen table drew butterflies and Finn in the living room pulled along his trains. Sometimes they watched the ceiling, hearing the footfalls of the men, and when they walked down the hill heading out to the car for the drive to the hospital, Hester called up to them, "Goodbye!"

It was Tommy Kroplin who stopped and stood and lifted a gloved hand in a silent wave.

7

Every morning on Hester's way to school they would drive along a county road past a clearing cut by loggers, where a solitary tree stood surrounded by mounds of debris and cut stumps. The loggers were supposed to leave clumps of seed trees, her papa had explained, not just so the trees could repopulate, but for wildlife habitat and better soil management. In this area they'd only left one, a smaller tree her papa had called a Norway pine. It stood on the eastern edge of the clearing, nearest the road, and Hester gave it a wave each morning on her way to school. She congratulated it privately in her mind for being brave, for standing out there all alone even though all its friends had gone.

They came up over the rise. The brave tree stood out there in the mist.

Bundles of needle-branched boughs held out like plates to the sky and she wanted to give it something, anything, because it had lost the hardest thing to lose. She thought it would need help to make it through the winter. Hester waved to it and wished it strength.

They wound past fields and cows and dilapidated barns, crept along the streets of Sterling and rolled by Hal's Feed Bin and up onto the bridge that crossed the St. Louis River. The steel beams batted shadows through the inside of the car, and they sat quiet, everybody lulled into silence by a drive so long so early in the day. This was the time she normally went to school, 7 A.M. on a Monday. She hadn't been to school in twelve days.

They curved around the exit into downtown Duluth, climbed the steep hill, and parked. Her mother carried Finn with the diaper bag on her other shoulder and they walked through the parking-ramp gloom, up the stairs, and into the skywalk.

The skywalk was a covered bridge made of glass that connected one building to another. They crossed the street without having to go outside, all the traffic flowing like water beneath while they moved inside this bright tube of sunlight with the busy doctors and nurses and other people who bustled across the bridge. At the end of the tube in a carpeted hallway they stopped at a bank of elevators, where her mother pushed the button.

"I wanted to do that!"

"What?"

"The button! You said that you would let me push the buttons today."

"Oh, Hester. I'm so sorry." Her mother adjusted her brother on her hip and studied the red light that marched through the numbers above the doors.

"Mama?"

"Yes."

"Will Papa be coming home with us today?"

Last week they had moved him into a room on a different floor with two beds and a window. Her papa's bed was not by the window, but yesterday the person in that bed went home and they pulled back the curtain so Papa could have the view.

The bell chimed, the door opened, they stepped inside the elevator. Hester watched her mother push the button for the top floor, then gasp and jump back. "I forgot to let you push the button!" she said.

"That's okay."

"No, no it's not!"

Hester watched her mother squeeze her hair and cover her face, her reaction too big, the elevator too quiet. The floor shuddered upward.

"Hester, I have to tell you something."

"Okay."

"I should have told you in the car. I just don't know how to say it."

"Just tell me." Hot tears pricked her eyes. "Is Papa dead?"

"Oh, honey. Oh, dear." Her mother took her and hugged her and the elevator stopped and the doors slid open. Hester started to go out, but her mother held her back. "No," she said. "Push that button. Let's go all the way back down and start over."

"Really?"

"Really."

Hester pushed the button. The doors closed.

"Do you remember when the doctor showed us the butterfly?"

"Yes. His wings got hurt."

"Yes, that was a diagram of your father's spinal cord. The top part of his wings that help his heart beat and the blood pump got pinched. But the bottom wings that control movement—like walking and talking—those got broken."

"So that's why he can't talk."

"Yes. That's right. But Hester." The elevator opened, the hall was empty, the doors closed. "There's not enough blood getting to his brain. So even though his heart is still beating and his blood is pumping, he can't wake up." The elevator lifted and the walls moaned. Her mother started to sway with Finn on her hip. "So even though your papa looks alive, inside his mind is quiet. The doctors have finished all the tests, and they know that there is nothing more they can do to help him. So, today, we are going to take him off the breathing machine."

The elevator opened and a tall boy got on by himself and pushed a different button. The doors closed. He took out a Fruit Roll-Up, tore the wrapper open, and peeled off a bright yellow and orange strip that looked like a piece of plastic. He folded the whole thing up into his mouth and chewed and swallowed before the elevator even opened its doors.

"Eat real food," her papa always said. He shared his orange slices with her, said they were "nature's candy" and knew how to peel one while driving the car, holding the steering wheel between his legs.

"Well, looky who's here," Ethan said. He sat in a wheelchair across from her father's bed, wearing a sling that kept his one arm hugged to his chest.

"Hello, Uncle Ethan, it's good to see you up and about." She'd heard a nurse say that to someone in the hall. Ethan smiled, but he looked older, his face bleached like the old leaves left all winter under the snow. She moved in through a doorway with its curtain pulled back, the colors of her father's room washed out like chalk on a sidewalk after a rain, but everything was clean and dry and hushed. Aunt Luvera's sister and a man who was her husband stood in the corner. Aunt Luvera sat next to Uncle Ethan and all their faces pointed at her father's bed.

Her papa lay all alone in a bed that was raised up. His face looked puffy with scratches and red patches creeping down the sides of his neck and into his beard that had gone thick and wild. There were tubes on both sides of the bed going into his body and a big plastic tube thick as a branch coming out from his open mouth. The machine clicked and huffed every few seconds, making his chest puff up in a little hiccup.

Finn fussed to get down. Her mother got him a snack from the hospital bag, a new orange food he'd never had before, bunny crackers that they got from the Co-op. Aunt Luvera came over and put an arm around Hester's shoulders.

"How're you doing, hon?"

Hester looked at her papa on his special mattress that wouldn't rub against his back so they didn't have to flip him over like they used to do in the olden days. Hester liked the nurses because they told her things when she asked questions and sometimes, they brought her and Finn Popsicles. They hadn't covered up her papa's foot. It stuck out from the bedsheet because they poked him there with needles and he didn't feel it.

"He wouldn't want this," Ethan said from his chair. Everybody turned to look at him. He hardly ever said anything, so when he did, they all listened. His lips twitched and his eyes leaked fluid like the runny part of an uncooked egg, but he said nothing more.

"Elsa," Luvera said quietly, "I talked with one of the nurses. She said she would stay with Hester in the family room when it's time."

"When what's time?" Hester said. "Time for what?"

Her mother answered, "When they take him off the machine, honey."

"No!" Hester cried. "I want to be here! I want to see!"

"Oh no, I don't think so," Luvera said. "That's not appropriate."

"You're not appropriate!"

"Hester!"

"I want to stay." Hester looked up to her mother. "Please? I need to see."

"You need to apologize to your aunt."

"I'm sorry," Hester said. "But if you make me go, I'll just come back."

Luvera looked to Ethan.

"Don't look at me," he said. "I'm in a wheelchair."

Luvera threw her hands up. "Do what you want then. What do I know, I'm not a parent."

Two nurses came in with the doctor and another man wearing a suit and tie, and her mother put Finn down in his own chair so she could sign some important papers. Finn sat up eating his orange crackers from a cup, and he accidentally dropped one on the floor. When he leaned forward to look at it, he tipped over the whole cup without meaning to and a bunch more crackers spilled out onto the floor. Hester waited for him to start crying, but he was looking at the cracker in his hand and didn't even know they had spilled. He still had some crackers left in his cup, and so he went back to eating, with no idea of how much he just lost.

"Take as much time as you need," the man with the tie said. One of the nurses pulled back the curtain across the doorway when they left. Last week people came and went from the room to see her father. Her teacher Mr. Silvernale had come, and a priest from church, but now it was just close family.

"Mama, Finn spilled his crackers."

"I know, honey. It's okay." Her mother reached out and put a hand on her back. "You can touch him if you want to. Hold his hand or kiss him goodbye."

His chest puffed up with the tubes coming out of his body and then his chest went back down. She was afraid to do anything. Afraid it would be like Finn with his crackers, where one small move would cause everything inside her to spill out. Her voice cramped up. Her words came in pieces like a hiccup.

"Is he . . . going to . . . die now?"

"They're going to take him off the ventilator."

"I don't want him to die!"

"I know, honey. But we talked about this."

"I know. The butterfly." Her cheeks flushed and she went to her father. She searched for a place to touch him that would be safe and settled on his elbow under the sheet. She whispered, "Thank you for being my papa. You did a good job." She patted him, kissed his arm, and moved away, quickly covering his foot with the blanket. Her mom nodded. She was crying but without making any noise, tears just spilling from her eyes, and Hester couldn't do that. When she cried it was with yelling and screaming, but she couldn't do that in here, so she squelched it all down in the back of her throat in a hard, hot lump.

After everyone had their turn to say goodbye, the doctors and nurses came back into the room. They shuffled across the floor, kicking and crushing Finn's crackers, which burst and crunched under the soles of their shoes, but nobody noticed. Soon the floor was littered everywhere with orange dust and Hester became agitated, worried about the mess, and Finn getting more crackers, while trying not to make any noise, and she missed the actual moment when they turned off the machine.

It was quiet; she looked up. All the tubes were gone from his face. He looked much better now, almost normal, and his chest was moving. She could see that, underneath the sheets, his chest was moving.

"He's breathing." She stood. "Mama, he's breathing!"

"Yes honey, he is."

They all watched in silence. His chest rose, filled with air, and went back down with a shudder like the elevator walls. They stood around the bed watching for a while. The doctor looked at the numbers on the screen by her father's bed and wrote something down. Then he looked at them and nodded and left the room.

"How come he didn't say anything?" Hester asked. "Doesn't he know? Didn't he notice?"

"Notice what, honey?"

"That he's still breathing!" She searched their faces, all of them wet, even Uncle Ethan. "What does it mean?"

"It means he can breathe on his own," her mother said.

"It means we have a miracle," Aunt Luvera said. "Praise God."

"It is not a miracle," her mother said. "It's a persistent functioning of the lower brain. The doctor said to expect that based on the MRI. We just don't know how long it will last."

"What if it lasts a year?"

"Hester . . ."

"What if his breathing wings aren't broken?"

Her mother made a small sound like her laugh got broken and Aunt Luvera took her hand.

"It's all right, hon," Luvera whispered. "It's going to be all right. Your papa just needs us to be strong and keep up with our prayers. With God, all things are possible. All things."

They watched her father lie there in the bed. His chest moved up, then down. It seemed they stood there for hours watching him do nothing but breathe. And yet she couldn't stop watching.

8

The nurse she had talked to allowed them the use of the empty bed so Elsa could get the baby to sleep. Luvera tucked her purse under her arm—her sister and brother-in-law had to leave, to go back to the city where they both had jobs. She left the room where Ethan sat with Hester, reading a book, and headed straight for the ladies' room. She was halfway down the hall when Elsa called out.

"Luvera!"

What now, she thought, composing her face. She'd gone to all the trouble of arranging a room for Hester to spare her the pain, because once you saw a thing, you could not unsee it. She'd learned this the hard way growing up on a farm, but what did she know? She hadn't gone to schools all over the world.

"Please don't give Hester false hope." Elsa closed the distance between them in her tall slender boots and stood next to Luvera, towering over her by a good six inches.

Luvera opened her mouth but did not know what to say.

"You saw the tests. You heard what the doctors said. There's no hope for a miracle so please don't say things like that." Her eyes shone like stones under water.

"What on earth are you accusing me of?"

"Nothing. I am not accusing you of anything. I just want to be realistic."

"Realistic? Didn't you see what just happened in there?"

"Yes. I see a man trying to die. Please, don't make this harder than it already is."

"Harder than it already is? Silas is in there fighting for his life! I hardly think there's anything I could do that would make this harder!" She clamped her purse to her side and continued down the hall, Elsa like an Amazon warrior following, this young woman from the city with her fancy boots and why did he marry her? When had she ever given him anything other than something else he had to worry about and take care of? Her nephew, the boy who was practically raised on her farm. The boy who chased the guinea hens and hugged the trees, stitched the words "love rocks" into the pot holder he made for her. What did Elsa know about hard? When had anything ever been hard for her? By the bathroom door Luvera turned back to face her.

"He needs us. Silas needs our help," she said. "We should get those antibiotics started up again and we should push the Medrol. The body wants to heal itself, it knows what to do but sometimes it needs a little help. I did some checking online. Medrol can reduce the swelling and prevent further damage to the nerves and even promote recovery. He could recover, Elsa. Don't you want him to heal?" She was trembling, fumbling with her words. "I've got an entire church praying for you. People are throwing their hearts and souls into your good cause and you should not underestimate the power of prayer. You shouldn't give up on him so soon. I'm surprised at you, disgusted, really."

Luvera pushed through the door on into the restroom.

She didn't know what she was saying, didn't do well with confrontation and now she couldn't think, all of it happening so fast. They'd only just talked about it, taking him off the machine. The doctor spoke of it on Friday and Ethan and Luvera had a conversation with each other while lying in bed. But Elsa didn't talk to them. She only told them what she had decided over the weekend, as if it were up to her alone. Luvera could hear her shuffling in the bathroom stall next to her. It was supposed to be a family decision, that's what was understood, even though it was Elsa who signed the papers, and she had assumed so much authority, seemed so comfortable with all that authority!, and Luvera would never have presumed so much.

She pulled out more toilet paper because she'd gone through all the tissues in her purse, and she wiped her face, drying her eyes. Tugged and straightened her top.

When she came back out, Elsa stood at the row of sinks, already washing her hands.

"I am not giving up on him," she said, their eyes meeting in the mirror. "I would never do that. I am not a person who does that. I will stand by him. Whatever else happens, I will stand by him." Elsa turned to get a paper towel, but the lever jammed, and though she pushed and pounded, nothing came out. She stepped aside and pressed the backs of her still-dripping hands to her eyes.

Luvera crossed the room, cranked out a length of towel, and left it there hanging while she went over to wash her own hands.

"Thanks," Elsa mumbled. Her skin shiny, her nose rimmed in red, and without any makeup on she looked so young. It occurred to Luvera that she probably wasn't getting much sleep, or eating properly, and she wondered again about her parents, a mother who died young and a father, supposedly wealthy, who lived just outside of Boston.

"Elsa, do you have anybody in town who you can stay with, a friend or somebody, at least until this is over?"

"When is this going to be over?"

"Well, I don't know, but you have to start thinking about winter." She paused. "Have you thought about moving into town? Getting an apartment, maybe?"

"I've been thinking about a lot of things."

"And? Is it the money? I know medical expenses can really pile up. If it's the money, we can help. We can't pay for everything, of course, but I know Ethan will want to help."

"My dad is not going to give me any money."

"I didn't say that he would."

"Yes, but that's what you were thinking. Everybody always thinks *Daddy can bail her out.*" Her arms jerked woodenly by her sides. She blew her nose on the scratchy paper towel and her nose glowed red. "He won't bail me out. He made it very clear when I moved out here that I was on my own now and anyway, I would never ask." She threw the paper towel away.

"Does he understand what things are like for you here?"

"I don't know what we're going to do."

"I know, hon. I know. But sometimes we have to swallow our pride. It's okay to ask for help, you know. God is in control, not us. He's the man with the plan. If He means to keep Silas alive, then it's up to us to do whatever we can to help him."

Elsa didn't say anything.

"I think we should go back in there and talk to the doctor about our options."

A woman entered the restroom, went into a stall, and closed the door.

Luvera lowered her voice. "Can you deny him food and medication when there's still a chance he might survive? Can you do that to him?"

"No." Her lips trembled, she whispered, "I can't do any of this."

"But you can." She took Elsa's hands into her own. "This is all a test, and all you have to do is pray. God never gives any of us more than we can handle."

Elsa laughed and broke away. "That is such a load of crap. People get more than they can handle all the time, every day, and it's up to us to do something about it. We're the ones who have to be there for each other, not God. I will not have Hester thinking that this is her fault, that God is testing her and that she isn't good enough, because he's going to die, and then we'll all feel like shit, right? What kind of God does that? Putting us through this just to see if we're worthy of His love? I'm sorry, but if that's how your God works, then your God sucks." She stopped, seeing Luvera's face. "Shit." She pressed her fists to her eyes. "I am so sorry."

Elsa left, and in the silence Luvera heard the shuffle of the woman in the stall behind her followed by the roar of the toilet's flush.

9

Elsa drove, glassy-eyed and numb, both hands on the steering wheel, the papers from the hospital next to her on the front seat. In the back, Finn sat buckled in his car seat with Hester quietly riding beside him, head turned toward the window. They followed an empty county road winding south away from the Great Lake. They passed fields and farmland, rolled hay bales and horses and small houses with large garages, all of it backlit by the last of the sun. In the low light, things that were broken or worn looked washed and new and golden.

Her eyes drooped and her head nodded, then jerked up; she tightened her hands on the wheel. She imagined drifting off the side of the road, just taking her hands off the wheel—let go and let God, was that it? She slapped at her face and sat up straighter in her seat.

They took Silas off the breathing machine, but he was still breathing on his own. She didn't understand why. He lasted the whole night and into the day, and he hadn't woken, but neither was he dead. His cerebrum—the center for consciousness, for thoughts and feelings—showed no signs of activity, but his brain stem was still functioning. "Breath is a primitive reflex," the doctor had said, "it's the last thing to go." Luvera still thought there was a chance, that a miracle was possible. She prayed over Silas alone and in groups with her church friends in a circle around his bed.

And Elsa had finally said yes. She'd changed her mind about the Medrol, they put Silas back on the feeding tube and the antibiotic. He was still breathing when she left.

Outside the red in the sky darkened like blood seeping into cotton.

The first time she ever saw Silas was out in the prairie grass of the Hoenettle Sculpture Park in Scandia, Minnesota. Silas at twenty-two stood looking out across a field, his hands in the pockets of his pale blue jeans. He wore a white T-shirt and a tan he arrived at by working outside, his body relaxed as a summer sky. Elsa at nineteen had never met a country boy before, and it wasn't just his wholesome good looks and long hair that caught her attention. It was how happy he seemed.

That summer she was living in the warehouse district of Minneapolis, working a restaurant job with no family and no plans. It had been five weeks since her mother had died. She went to the hot pour at the sculpture park with a group of work friends, then realized she didn't want to talk about art. She'd wandered off, and somewhere between the bonfire and the band she had crossed a field and found him, Silas Arnasson, the farthest thing possible from a tortured soul. In one look, she knew. He was like a song that she'd been humming secretly to herself for her entire life. He brought the missing notes.

"What do you think of this?" he asked. He stood in front of a sculpture, an installation of glass panels planted in diagonal rows like a crop.

"I don't know." She stood next to him, arms crossed. "What do you think?"

"Oh, I work here," he said. "I see this stuff all the time."

"And?"

"I think I would have preferred just the field."

The car drifted again over the center line and Elsa caught herself on the edge of sleep. Jerking the wheel, she corrected the vehicle, sitting up straighter in her seat.

"Mama, what was that? What happened?"

"Nothing, Hester, sorry. It's nothing. I wasn't paying attention." She lightly smacked her face. "Is Finn all right?"

"Yes, Mama. He's still sleeping."

In the rearview mirror Hester's face glowed in the back seat like a moon. Her daughter who always wanted to know the truth, and she and Silas had decided as parents that they would always tell the truth, but what could you say when there was more than one truth? She had asked the neurosurgeon, "Is my husband dead?" He told her that the medically accepted definition of death had been rewritten several times. "Your husband has slipped into a gray area," he said, "and medical definitions don't take into account personal beliefs, or the existence of a soul."

The Christian faith believed that a soul inhabited the body as long as there was a heartbeat. Orthodox Jews believed breath signified life. Buddhists honored a period of days between life and death when the consciousness of the deceased still lingered even after the physical moment of separation. The surgeon told her he'd seen cases where patients diagnosed as brain-dead went on to live for years. He'd even seen one case where the brain repaired itself and restored some of its functioning.

"And then what happened?" she asked.

"In every case the body eventually dies, usually from pneumonia or infection. Even if life can be sustained by an individual organ, an organ functioning as a subsystem, apart from the whole, eventually disintegrates."

"And how long does that take?"

"If there's no intervention, usually the heart stops beating within ten days."

At the top of the hill by the signal towers the temperature dropped and the windows of her car turned white. As if there existed an invisible line somewhere in the dark, dividing hot and cold, north and south. And we pretended that the same line divided right from wrong, end from beginning, when really, it was just miles and miles of gray.

Elsa rolled down the window. Air came thumping against her

ears like a wooden heart, *widow widow widow widow*. And it wasn't true, not yet, but the word preyed on her stomach, its black name beating in the wind, *widow widow widow widow*.

She must be clear about what was real and not real. She must keep her feet on the ground and make decisions based on reality because Hester and Finn were depending on her. Right now, reality was medical science and paperwork and lack of insurance. They didn't qualify for Medicaid and there was no advance care directive because they'd never talked about this. They put Silas on medications intended for recovery, so now he was no longer eligible for hospice. Luvera knew they didn't have the seven thousand dollars a day to keep him at the hospital, so how would she pay for this? By selling a half-finished house? Going into debt, into bankruptcy? Mortgaging the rest of their lives, the futures of their children, when Silas hadn't even been willing to get a loan to build their house?

She rolled up the window. The sun slipped below the horizon and the sky glowed bruised and hushed.

"Mama?"

"Yes, Hester?"

"I miss Papa."

"I know, sweetheart. I do, too."

"Can he come home?"

"Well now, that's a good question."

Those were his words, what Silas always said whenever he didn't know what to say. *Well now, that's a good question.* Stalling, buying time. The girl had a birthday coming up in a few days. What would they do to celebrate? And how would she prepare her daughter for what came next? *Usually the heart stops beating within ten days.*

Outside, the first of the stars pinned up their light. Fog drifted across the road in translucent bands and the windows clouded up again from the warming air. This time Elsa turned on the defrost. In the rearview she saw Hester wave at a seed tree left alone by the loggers in a clear-cut tract of land.

Once, Silas told her about this tree in Germany along the Belgium border, a stump that was over four hundred years old. The biologist who found it thought at first it was a ring of stones because the wood was so hard, but when he scraped away the moss, he discovered green wood. The stump had reserves of chlorophyll. While the tree's heartwood had long ago rotted out, its sapwood was viable and strong—it was living without branches or leaves because it was being nourished, kept alive by the other trees on a kind of underground life support. This one tree, out of all the other trees in the forest, because, the biologist speculated, it was beloved.

She thought of that when they were disconnecting the feeding tube and the IVs attached to Silas, she thought about how the trees take care of their family, how they needed each other, and what Luvera had said about not giving up when there was still a chance. Really, she was so afraid! She wanted to do the right thing, to honor him, take care of him the way he always took care of them. He was still breathing on his own by some mystery of synaptic nerve endings. When a spinal cord is damaged, healthy cells at a distance begin to die, and this was happening all along her husband's spine and scientists didn't know why. New corticosteroids like Medrol claimed to prevent this from happening. Like the Dutch elms strung along a boulevard, all sharing the same horrible disease, those trees talked to one another and somehow, the elms at the very end of the line developed a resistance to the disease. Sometimes, those trees lived.

Her eyes drooped, her head bobbed. The car drifted over the center line.

A large animal lurched up from the ditch and shot out across the road.

Hester cried out and Elsa came to and stomped on the brake. Her seat belt clenched, the tires squealed, and the animal loomed before her enormous and bright. It filled the windshield, blotted out her entire view. The car slid forward, she closed her eyes for the impact, but the moment sailed past and there was no crash. Elsa opened her eyes. They were stopped in the middle of the road, steam rising from the dark tarmac.

"Mama? What was it?"

"Are you all right? Everybody all right?"

"I'm all right. Why was that deer white?"

"You saw it?"

"Uh-huh. I think it had antlers. I think it could fly."

Elsa unbuckled her seat belt and scrambled out of the car. The engine hummed and the headlights cut into the dark. She stared at the bumper of the car. The autumn fog hung damp and thick with the smell of burnt rubber. Finn awake now, working up a cry. The animal they had come so close to hitting was gone. As if it had been made out of air.

She went back around to her son in the back seat of the car, unbuckled him from the harness, and lifted his little body. Pressing her face to him, Elsa breathed in the scent of him, their little boy; she kissed him and whispered, "It's all right, Finn. Mama's got you. I got you now." Purposeful, grateful, as if she had achieved all that was significant just by keeping what she already had.

Adrenaline coursed through her and she was wide-awake now, strong and buzzing with life. Holding Finn, she looked out across the road at the dried grasses in the ditch, the bracken and cattails and the pale tamarack, all of it shrouded in fog. She knew what to do. It was so obvious to her now she almost laughed.

She would bring Silas home. She would take care of him here. If tomorrow he was still breathing, then she would sign the papers and have him released because this was where he would want to be, and this was where he belonged. They were a part of the natural world with its mysteries and miracles and things that couldn't always be explained. What Elsa could believe was that love was enough. Whether her love or God's love or Luvera and her church, it didn't matter. Love was what she could do for Silas because she didn't want to let him go, not yet.

She wasn't ready to live without him, and if he was still in there, holding on, well then, she would hold on, too.

WINTER

10

On a Thursday in the first week of November, Luvera Arnasson pulled up to the unfinished house with the hot dish still warm on the seat. The sky white, voided of blue, and she had a bad feeling about this. The house seemed to breathe up there in the side of the hill, the entire second story a skeleton of rooms wrapped in Tyvek. The walls expanded with the wind, swelled out and then crinkled and moaned as they fell back in.

"I don't think she knows what she is in for," she'd told Ethan that morning, stirring milk into the menagerie of diced-up vegetables. "How in the world is she going to take care of him in that house with no running water?"

And Ethan looked at her with an expression like one of the cows and said one of his rare, fully formed sentences. "She's not taking care of him, Luvey. She's giving him a place to die in peace."

All week Silas had held on, breathing quietly in his hospital bed. Elsa had agreed to put him back on the antibiotics and to restart the Medrol, but then she'd announced she was bringing him home. "There's nothing more we can do for him but keep him comfortable," she said, "and I know home is where he would want to be." Luvera felt blindsided. Elsa with her head in the clouds, she wasn't the kind of woman who knew how to administer to the sick! She was the kind of woman who walked into a room, held up a scrap of fabric, and said, "I need a dress," and within seconds, someone was there to make her a dress. People just did things for her. She'd seen the way men doted on her. Maybe she didn't know what she was in for because she'd never had to ask for help, but even more to the point in this case, she was absolutely clueless as to how much help she would need.

City folks had such funny expectations of nature. They didn't want it to be ugly or unclean. They thought life in the country simple. They thought it quaint.

From out on the road came the low hum of car engines. Luvera pressed the hot dish against her coat, all the leaves gone now from the trees, the sky threatening to release snow. Winter in northern Wisconsin always came a full month before what it said on anybody's calendar, and it seemed cruel, to thrust a family still hurting into this maw of cold. She heard the tires on the gravel, one hospital transport vehicle without flashing lights followed by the small family car.

The girl was out first, running around to the back where they drew out his bed. Silas lay there in a neck brace, the first few flakes turning slow and lazy through the air and landing in his beard. Elsa stood by her daughter, Finn hooked to her hip.

"Elsa"—Luvera couldn't help herself—"are you sure you can do this? Take care of him out here all on your own?"

"Oh, I'm not on my own." Elsa patted Hester's head. "I have my daughter and my son and there's a nurse who will be coming four times a week." She hefted the baby on her hip, while the aide cranked up the bed. Silas lay motionless on top, the snow turning his beard white.

In a procession they wheeled the bed and the IV pole up the long, grassless walkway, onto the temporary porch, and into the house. Inside was nicer than she'd remembered—she'd forgotten how much Silas had fixed things in preparation for the baby. They didn't have the upstairs done, but downstairs had a carpet and a kitchen table with four wooden chairs. Heat emanated from the woodstove; everything was tidy and clean.

The home care nurse, a short, sturdy woman in colorful scrubs who apparently thought lavender an appropriate color to dye her hair, laid out several boxes of medical supplies. She explained things to Elsa, how to handle the catheter and switch out the enteral feeding bags with their concoction of protein, vitamins, minerals, and fats. The medics moved around to get Silas settled in the bedroom, and everything was done in a loving way, how they spoke to each other, how they cared for him. There were hydrocolloid patches for his sores, foam cushions to go under his heels and elbows, and a harness to help with the turning—he had to be moved six times a day. They had to watch for pneumonia and bedsores and uncontrolled muscle spasms. They could adjust the flow of his morphine drip and keep him clean with dry bathing. Elsa went into the bedroom but Luvera stayed out in the living room. There were framed paintings hung on the walls, all of them mountain views and signed by someone named Winnie.

Outside it had stopped snowing.

"I don't want those people to be here," Hester said, glancing sourly at the knot of people in her parents' room.

"Well, it doesn't always matter what we want, does it?" Luvera said. "You have to be strong. If you want to cry, do it at night when you are by yourself. That's what I always do." Luvera turned away, pinched her gold cross between thumb and forefinger and slid it across its chain. Guilt squiggled up her spine. Maybe she had been wrong to insist on the medication. She'd been wrong about the baby. Her daughter, had she lived, would be sixteen years old next spring, but she'd been born too early and without a tongue. There were abnormalities, the doctor said, and she'd been too afraid after that to try again.

"Life is hard on everyone," she said to Hester. "We all suffer. That's why God created heaven. So we can have a purpose to our lives."

"Is Papa in heaven?"

The thought flickered in her like a candle—it occurred to her just then that Elsa could have brought Silas to the farmhouse. They had plenty of room there. She and Ethan could have helped Elsa with the kids.

"Aunt Luvera?"

"Yes?"

"Where is he?"

"Your father? He's right there in the bedroom." Luvera pinched her cross. Of course, it was too late now. Hester kept looking at her like she expected something more and Luvera slid the cross back and forth across its chain. "You just keep praying," she whispered. "It's the prayers of little children that matter the most. It says so right in the Bible. God listens to those with pure hearts."

11

Hester stood next to her mother's car on Friday morning, the only other car in the school parking lot besides her teacher's old turquoise rambler. She traced the dewdrops on the hood with a finger while her mother got Finn out from the back. In the woods around the school the fog drifted in cottony bands that caught and tore in the trees. The brick schoolhouse sprawled across a grassy field, and Hester knew her teacher Mr. Silvernale was already there inside. He drove in early with his two boys, Ben and Owen, and they got to play outside until the other kids arrived.

"Okay, let's go." Her mother held Finn wrapped in a thick yellow blanket. "It's okay, Hester. Your teacher knows we're coming."

They trekked across the lot and in through the front entrance, past the benches in the lobby where she used to wait after school on the days her papa picked her up because he was always running late. She would swing her legs out and under the bench and talk to her teacher or the latchkey kids who stayed after school. He always breezed in covered in sawdust with a smile on his face. "Hester Pester!" he would say. She walked down the hallway now with her mother and in the doorway of the classroom they stopped. Mr. Silvernale glanced up from his desk.

"Hester Pester!" His face broke into a smile. "We've missed you!" He gestured emphatically. "Come on in, come in."

Hester wore her favorite sweater with her hair tied in braids as if it were a regular school day. She passed by the empty tables that smelled of crayons and used books and dried glue.

"Thank you for meeting with us early," her mother said.

"Well, sure. Have a seat." His voice bobbed like floating bath toys. As a teacher he was always like that, never sinking, always popping right back up to look at things on the bright side. He pulled down the glasses from the top of his head. He had a beard like her papa's, only darker, it looked like dirt. Her mother shifted on the little kid's chair, balancing Finn on her lap. Hester stood behind them.

"I don't want you to call me that anymore," she said.

"I'm sorry, what's that?"

"Just call me Hester, please."

"Oh. All right." He nodded. "Hester, as you are."

"Are Ben and Owen outside?"

"Yes. I believe they're in the ball field."

"Can I go outside?" She looked to her mother, who looked to Mr. Silvernale, who looked up at the clock.

"You have about twenty minutes before the buses start pulling up. Ben has a watch, so don't let him fool you. I expect you back here on time." He said this with a smile on his face.

She hurried out through the side door across the old playground and went over to the sandbox first thing. She wanted to check on the grasshoppers. It was a project she and Brianna had, to find grasshoppers during recess and keep them in a secret place dug into the sand. Every day they freed the ones from the day before and got new bugs, lined the holes with fresh pulled grass. "Grasshoppers don't eat grass," Brianna had said. And they constructed little rooms across which they laid sticks and large leaves so the sand wouldn't cave in while keeping them hidden and safe. And the next day, when Hester opened up the roof and peered in, there in the hole was a grasshopper munching on grass. She saw the bite marks, tiny half-moon nibbles.

Hester knelt in the corner of their secret spot and pushed back the sand. Inside the earthen bowl were three grasshoppers from recess the last time she was at school. Their bodies inert, wings crispy, legs oddly bent.

Out across the field the fog had cleared. The sun pushed up behind the tree line, revealing a broad blue sky. Hester stood. The two boys Ben and Owen threw a football back and forth, their hair so light it looked clear in the sunlight. Hester's shoes sank into the soft ground as she walked toward them, and Ben snapped the football back into his hands and called out, "Hey, you want to throw the ball around?" He was tall and lanky and two years older than Hester, but only one grade ahead.

"No," she said. "I'm not going to school today."

Ben wrinkled his nose. It was scattered with freckles she'd never noticed before, small brown dots in the morning light. At the far end of the field Ben's younger brother, Owen, came lumbering toward them. Owen was in Hester's class. His hair bounced off his square head, and he moved differently than Ben, his body wide and close to the ground, but still, you could tell they were brothers.

"Sorry about your dad," Ben said. "We made you a card."

"Oh. That's nice."

Ben threw up the football, caught it back in his hands.

"I'm going to be homeschooled," she said. "So I can help my mom with taking care of him."

"Wait." He held the football still. "I thought he was dead."

Her stomach flooded with heat like she'd done something wrong.

"We going to play color tag?" Owen arrived breathless, his voice husky. He swiped a hand across his face and sniffed.

"She's not here to play," Ben said. "She's leaving."

Owen's eyes widened. "You're moving? Where?"

"Don't be stupid."

"I'm not stupid."

"I'm going to be homeschooled," she said.

"Oh."

"Just until my dad gets better."

"I thought he already died," Owen said. She heard it like she was at the bottom of a pit. "What?" he said to his brother. "That's what Gigi said. You heard it, too." He hacked up saliva and spit.

That first night when they brought Papa home, they stood around his bed and her mother spoke to him. "You're home now. You're on the land." She kept saying that and wiping his brow. Hester felt embarrassed for her, talking to him like that while he lay there in his neck brace with the tubes going into his nose and the feeding pump that used up all the electricity. She felt embarrassed for him, too, lying helpless and trapped like the shells of her dead bugs.

"He's still breathing," Hester said. She wanted to tell them, wanted to tell someone. "The doctor said he couldn't breathe on his own without a machine but then he did. He's really strong." The cuffs of her jeans were stained with dew and her socks wet from the water in the field that had soaked through. "But inside his mind it's quiet, so he can't eat or talk."

"That's really creepy," Owen said.

"Shut up," said Ben.

"Well it is."

"Do you always have to be such an idiot?"

"I'm not an idiot!"

Owen punched his brother's arm and Ben punched him back.

"I have to go," Hester said. "My mom's waiting."

She left the two boys standing side by side in the field not playing football, turning away before the tears came, and when they did, she started to run to get as far away as possible, but still it was there, what they said.

Hester sat in the rocking chair across from the woodstove. They were having what she thought of as a romantic weekend because all the lights were off and the candles lit. They were conserving electricity because the generator ran out of gas, and her mama didn't want to go anywhere and leave Papa alone. Her mom stacked logs into the woodstove and waited for the flames to catch. The fire crackled and popped and the orange light lapped and waved across her mother's face.

Tipping the ant farm she got for her birthday, Hester watched the gel ooze. The ant farm came from a catalog, but it didn't come with the ants; you had to buy them separately. Her mom didn't know. All it was: a thin, clear, rectangular box filled with blue gel, or probably it was clear gel made blue by the lights. It was ant space food, she thought, turning the light switch on then off. She wondered would the ants like it in there and would it be mean to make them live in there with gel instead of dirt with miles and miles to roam.

"Mama? Do ants breathe?"

"Just give me a minute," her mom said. "I'm almost done."

The door to Papa's bedroom was open so he could hear their voices. That night after Finn went to sleep, she helped her mom turn him. She held on to his head and the plastic collar around his neck, while her mom pulled the strap. Her papa rolled and a smell rose up from behind his back.

"Did you pick your book?" her mother said. She didn't sleep with Papa anymore. She slept on the bottom bunk bed while Hester slept on the top. Finn also slept in Hester's room, her mother had moved the crib when they brought Papa home, so now everybody was crammed in her bedroom. Hester heard them breathing at night. Finn always went to bed early. He didn't have to read twenty minutes every night for school.

"*Days with Frog and Toad,*" her mother said. She smelled of woodsmoke and leaf litter and Hester sat on her lap and adjusted to the shape of her. She was soft and squishy like a pillow, and Hester liked having this time when she got to sit with her mama, just her all to herself. Her mother read softly, the door to the room where Finn slept was not closed, it was *ajar,* her mother said, because they couldn't waste electricity on the baby monitor with the feeding pump on all day. So, they had to be quiet.

But her mother was being hasty. That's what Uncle Ethan would say, "Let's not be hasty, now," whenever they were in the barn with the animals. You had to be certain and calm for the animals, but her mother did not feel certain or calm. Her words came out as just sounds, disconnected from the story. When the sap popped from a log in the woodstove, she jumped, and the book tumbled from her lap and clapped on the floor.

"Oh, my goodness," she said, and Hester had to get down so her mother could get up. The door of the woodstove creaked. Firelight lit only parts of her face as she peered in, the shadows pulling under her cheekbones and eyes so Hester understood the shape of her skull.

"Mama, is Papa dead?"

Her mother held on to the door of the woodstove; firelight lapped her face. "I don't know." She looked shy and sad. "That's a good question." She poked at the fire with a stick, moved around the logs. "I brought him home because I thought this was where he would want to be, where he would feel the most at peace. I like to think he knows he's here. I like to think his spirit is with us." She closed and latched the door.

The flames in the woodstove made a *whomp-whomp* sound like a helicopter taking off, while her mother settled back in the rocking chair. The cast-iron knobs of the stove were left opened to let the air in, and the fire winked behind them like two glowing eyes.

"Mama, what's spirit?"

Wind shuttled down through the chimney and tendrils of smoke curled out through the knobs like steam from a dragon's nostrils.

"It's the part of a person that you can't see, like their soul or inner essence. It's the part of you that goes on living even after you die." The smoke kept coming out through the vents, and her mother picked up the book and sat. "Some people don't believe in a soul, and we can't prove that it exists. We all get to decide for ourselves what we want to believe, but I like to think that anything is possible, that there's more to this world than what we can see."

The smoke detector beeped. It blasted sound through the small house and her mom leapt up, took it off the wall, yanked open the door, and banished the detector outside. Cold air swooped into the room and her mother flapped the door like a giant wing to move the fresh air in. The alarm finally stopped honking, but Finn could be heard crying in their bedroom.

"Oh dear." Her mother shut the door. "Hester, I am so sorry. You'll have to finish reading your book tonight while I deal with this fire and get Finn down again."

The eyes of the woodstove still glowed but the flames inside were quiet and the cast-iron box crackled with heat. Hester sat alone in the rocking chair next to the door that was ajar. "When is a door not a door? When it's a jar! Hahaha." Her papa always joked. She remembered when he tended the fire at night. He had turned the dials so the eyes were closed, but they were hot, and she didn't want to touch them.

A thin screen of smoke still hung in the room as she tried to read her book. The words had no meaning, they were just black ants on a page, the pictures squiggles and shapes.

An awareness of movement crept in from the corner of Hester's mind. She lifted her eyes, and there was the Mylar balloon, the blue cupcake her brother had gotten from the hospital. It shimmied and bobbed, dangling its curly blue string. It floated out across the floor through the smoky room. Hester laughed. She couldn't help it—it felt good to laugh, and it looked so funny.

When her mother came out holding Finn to see why Hester was laughing, she saw the balloon and slapped a hand to her chest.

"My goodness, what's that thing doing out here?" Hester threw back her head and laughed again. It was so funny! She couldn't explain why it tickled her funny bone, but it did. Her mom grabbed the balloon and stuffed it back into the bedroom where she disappeared with Finn, but afterward, sitting alone, Hester still felt good.

Hester felt happy, if she didn't think too much about it, if she didn't move anywhere else in her mind, didn't feel sorry for herself or worry about the smoke that still drifted through the room, or the firebox that glowed red from its two evil eyes. She could be happy, for a little while. She could think about her papa's spirit and feel glad.

12

Late in the afternoon Elsa loaded the blue water jugs and the yellow gas cans into the back of the car. She buckled in Finn and closed his door and drove away from the house that sat breathing in the side of the hill. Day seven, Sunday. She didn't want it to be ten days. The car buzzed north.

She thought he would pass on the weekend. Ethan and Luvera came over that morning with a priest from their church and they all stood in the bedroom and prayed. When she decided to bring Silas home, this was what she imagined: him surrounded by family, their freshly laundered marriage quilt laid across the bed with sunlight spilling over his head—it was senseless, the room had no windows.

She felt feverish. Pain like the edge of a saw blade snagged at the back of her throat, but it was a small pain; she was probably just dehydrated. They were out of water, but she didn't want to go all the way into town. She drove to the corner gas station fifteen miles away. She thought if she bought drinking water and filled up the gas cans, they would let her fill the blue water jugs from the store spigot outside. She inserted the pump nozzle into the mouth of the gas can and set the lever and waited for it to fill. If it had to be ten days, then she would just have to hold on for ten days.

But then what?

Luvera offered to let them live at the farmhouse. Elsa glanced at her children in the back of the car, their little heads bobbing. They loved going to the farmhouse, especially in the spring when there were baby goats and chicks. But she felt separate from them, from Ethan and Luvera and the rest of the world, detached, isolated, stuck inside this wormhole of time. Everything on hold, frozen; she was waiting in the space that came between breaths—she'd never noticed before how long it took for the inhale after the exhale, how in that space a quiet stretched on while she waited at the edge of some chasm and could not think one solid thought about what she would do next.

Gasoline burst from the can in a geyser and sprayed all over Elsa's clothes, her shoes, her hands. She hung up the pump, it hadn't shut off like it was supposed to. Stepping away, she looked around to see if anybody else had seen, but the parking lot was empty. Fumes stung her nose, watered her eyes.

A string of geese moved overhead, gently honking in a giant check mark across the sky.

She hadn't realized how much Silas did, how much there was to do. All the nights she thought she had it hard because filling up the bathtub was difficult. Pay for the gas, get more drinking water, refill the blue jugs—*check, check, check.* She knelt by the spigot beside the ice machine outside and rinsed the fuel from her pants. Lift the water jugs, lug them to the car, load them into the trunk with the gasoline and gallons of spring water except for one jug that she kept on her lap and chugged.

Back at the house she unloaded the gas cans and Finn into the wagon and hauled everything up the hill to the generator shed. Hester followed to help push, the wagon bumping over tree roots and uneven dips, the hill steep, the wagon heavy, the fuel sloshing.

They had set aside money for a well. Silas installed the plumbing and wired the electricity to the inverter, set up their small solar array and two backup generators with deep-cycle batteries to hold the charge. When they got the phone line installed, he was going to call the well digger, was going to have him come out that summer after Finn was born, but she said no. Said it was good exercise to haul water around, and it didn't cost very much to fill up the jugs at the Co-op. She could do it a little longer, she said, for the rest of the summer if she had to, because, she said, what she really wanted was something else.

He'd smiled and tilted his head. "And what is it you need, my dear? What do you want?"

"Skylights," she'd said. "As many as we can afford." She wanted to fall asleep at night among the stars. Wanted her children to know that they were part of the Universe, this living consciousness; she wanted them to experience God, not in a church, but in the world.

Back at the car with the wagon, the generator rumbling in the distance, she unloaded the five-gallon blue jugs weighing forty pounds each, and the one-gallon drinking jugs weighing eight pounds each, and she put them into the wagon with Finn, who weighed twenty-two pounds, and hauled everything up the hill to the house.

Silas put off digging the well and ordered skylights. They were expensive and he got six of them, stacked all together in the trailer where he stored his tools and building supplies. He went against what he thought best to please her, went against his better, more practical judgment because she had been so certain that's what would make a real difference in their children's lives.

Skylights. Not water. She wanted to cry.

If there was a punitive God and she was undergoing a test like Luvera had said, then her crime was being silly and naïve. *Carrying water is good exercise.* What a stupid idiot. *Whatever you need, my dear. Whatever you want.* She unloaded the water jugs and took Finn inside and gave him a snack, then went back down to the car with the wagon and loaded up and hauled some more.

Monday, day eight since they took him off the machine, Elsa emptied Silas's catheter bag and the smell of his urine watered her eyes. She dry-bathed him the way the nurse had shown her, patting the cloth over the weeping sores around the gavage tube in his nose that forced food into his stomach twenty-four hours a day.

Why was he holding on? What did it mean, that he wouldn't let go?

She wanted to lie down. The nurse said it was normal to feel tired and that she should feel good about caring for him. "When it gets hard," she said, "just think about how it will get you into heaven." That sent a small burst through her body. She wasn't doing it to get into heaven; she was doing it for Silas, for all he'd done for them.

She thought about their last morning together, the T-shirt from the car. "Would you mind washing this for me?" And she'd taken it, grudgingly. Had he noticed? She didn't like that he was going off to work while she was staying home to care for the kids and wash his clothes; it wasn't how she'd imagined her life would be.

Sometimes she played this game in her head, *What would I be doing now?* It was just what she thought about while hauling around water or pegging up clothes. She wondered what her life would have been like if she'd never left art school, if her mom hadn't died. She asked herself, *What would I be doing now?* And she saw it in her mind—the people and places and circumstances of her old life. She compared—her old life versus her new. And nine times out of ten, she was happier here.

But every so often, she wasn't. Sometimes she missed her old life, especially on the hard days when Silas was building and extension cords threaded like tentacles through the house with generators chugging and power drills shrilling, her babies underfoot around the screwdrivers and nails. Her father had been adamant— "You won't last two months in the country." And he'd been wrong. But now, she had to answer it, the question, what came next? She couldn't imagine her life without Silas.

Her drawing professor at college had said, "There's something special about the way you see the world." And Elsa thought that everyone must have their own way of seeing the world; indeed, she'd been hearing about it all week from the people who called. Concerned citizens, she thought of them. Luvera with her news reports about the recent rise in home invasions. "Make sure you lock your door," she said, "even during the day." Her stepmother in Boston who also called although they'd met only once. "I heard about the bear attacks in your area," she said. "What that bear did to that poor man's dog."

The sun sank below the treetops. They had no streetlamps or porch lights, and night fell with a prehistoric obscurity and the windows by the kitchen table turned black. The days were getting shorter, the nights colder. The pile of splits made by Tommy and his men wouldn't last at the rate she was burning it, and maybe she should ration the wood, but she couldn't stand the thought of the children being cold. Silas always talked about banking the coals, and maybe she should try that, whatever that meant.

"Mama?" Hester's voice called to her from the top bunk. Elsa lay half awake underneath. All the lights off except the night-light, and if she turned it off, she wouldn't be able to see her own hand in front of her face. "Mama, can you hear that?"

From the wall beside them came the scratching, scuttling, shifting of little rodent feet. Mice, moving inside the walls. *What would I be doing now?*

"Go away!" Hester banged on the wall with the flat of her hand. "Cut it out!"

"Shhh, Hester, please don't do that. You'll wake up Finn. Go back to sleep."

"I can't go back to sleep. They're too loud."

"I know, honey. It's okay." She thought about what Silas would say. "It's just the mice moving around because it's getting cold. They're preparing for the winter, settling in." It was only natural, he'd said. They were living in a hobbit home dug into the dirt. Once they finished the second story, it wouldn't be a problem anymore because the bedrooms would be upstairs.

"I want them to go away now," Hester said.

"I know."

"It sounds like they want to be in here."

"Don't worry. I won't let them come into the house."

That was another thing Silas always took care of. Their first winter in the house they lost their lights when a mouse chewed through one of their wires. Silas had to go around to all the outlets, figure out where the breach was, lower in a new wire that he attached to the switch box. Later, he went around the house setting out poison and traps.

One morning she got up to pee and a mouse walked out across her floor. It sat in the middle of the kitchen looking up at her with round open ears and meek blinking eyes. She turned on the light; the mouse scurried away. But there on the countertop under the steel bar of a trap a mouse lay with its body limp as a used tea bag. Another mouse in a trap on the floor by the stove, another with its black eyes bulged shiny as beads.

"Why are there so many?" Elsa had been horrified. "Do you have to do that?" She thought she would have nightmares, all those mice with broken backs. They scuttled and scratched in the walls, keeping her awake, too. But that winter, pregnant with Finn, she felt the baby inside her thumping along her stomach walls while the mice behind their bedroom walls scurried and flitted, and it had seemed symbiotic, somehow, a kind of graceful syncopation. She imagined they were sharing the warmth because they had so much; she believed it was understood—they had an arrangement—the mice could stay as long as they didn't come into her kitchen or cross her counters or floors.

"It bothers me, too," Silas said. "But we can't have them overrun the house."

A week later, the walls were silent.

She could be living with Santiago the sculptor from Madrid. She could be living in Providence, or Spain. She didn't want to live with Ethan and Luvera at the farmhouse. Did that make her a snob? Silas always put his faith in family. "Just give them a chance," he'd said. But they'd lived two winters at the farmhouse and always she felt judged. Luvera sniffed and commented about her "expensive" things and Ethan remarked every morning she slept past eight.

What would I be doing now? She wouldn't be listening to the mice in the walls. Would she be painting? Would she have a gallery showing in New York City?

The year her mother's cancer returned Elsa took airplanes back and forth between the hospice in Idaho and the university in Rhode Island. The stress of keeping up with the rigors of a curriculum got to her head. Her mother died in May; Elsa had finals in June. It was a competitive arts program. She didn't talk to anybody about what was going on, not to Santiago, not even her friends. Elsa kept to herself like she always did. "This family is toxic," her mother had said. "You need to get away." Her mother who spent her entire life in a battle between who she was and who she thought she was supposed to be. Her mother who wore painter smocks over her dresses and pumps, and once worked on a painting in a fervor minutes before guests arrived for their annual Christmas party. Elsa remembered because at the time she thought her mother was being a bitch—all the screeching and hysterics, her mother yelling at her when she came in to get approval for her dress, her mother yelling at the caterers, and fighting with Dad. Now, Elsa understood that what she saw was a woman desperate for her own autonomy. Nothing Winnie ever painted got finished to her liking. She would never have considered herself an artist, although later, in the mountains, that was how she lived.

"Promise me you'll get away," Winnie had said, lying in her hospice bed. Elsa remembered the collapsed look in her mother's eyes and the smallness of her hand, but it was her dying words that bothered Elsa the most: "I wish I was more myself."

Elsa got away. She left her friends and boyfriend, left the arts program and the college where her mother had always wanted to go; she left an open bucket of gesso and her easel and canvas boards stacked in her room. Her father had to go back to her apartment when the lease expired and get everything out. He did that for her. Packed everything up and put it in storage and she never explained. *I wish I was more myself.*

She was lying on the couch half asleep on a Tuesday, day nine, three weeks after the accident.

Finn was napping on her chest with one hand on her cheek, Hester with her laptop wearing headphones on the couch, legs swung over her mother's knees. Elsa felt like a stuffed animal, worn out, overtouched. And that's why she was hot, she thought, it wasn't a fever, it was just that she was always being patted at, pulled on, pawed.

"And the long vowel says ee, ee, ee, ee-eagle." The enthused voice came through the headphones, Elsa could hear it, a muted singing from the computer. "Choose the object whose name begins with a long *e*." Elsa listened for the sound that would indicate whether Hester chose correctly. When it was a happy ping, she mumbled, "Good job, Hester," and moved back into sleep. The sun, a white thumbprint, whorled behind clouds and the flames inside the woodstove thumped. She needed to get more wood, needed to start the generator, needed to put on a pair of clean pants.

"Mama, there's a man."

"And the short vowel says uh, uh, uh, uh-umbrella."

"There's a man walking up to our house." Hester's voice always louder and high-pitched when she spoke wearing headphones.

Elsa sat up and slid away from Finn.

"Choose the object whose name begins with a short *u*."

Disoriented, the warmth receding from her face, blood rushing to her head. Out the window a man ambled up the dirt path. He wore a red flannel shirt and a pair of Carhartts with boots, and Elsa recognized Tommy Kroplin from the logging crew.

"Yoo, yoo, yoo, yoo-unicorn."

He paused to look out at all the trees, the same way Silas had always done. She stumbled to the left, to the right. Raked her fingers through her hair and smoothed down her top. She was wearing the yoga pants she'd slept in and a long-sleeved T-shirt and a sweater with no bra. She'd worn these same clothes for the last three days. She found a jacket and slipped it on. "I'll be right back," she said, and her throat still hurt but only when she swallowed. "Stay here with Finn." From the laptop came the happy ping.

Sunlight even though it was behind clouds struck her sensitive eyes. Elsa winced and held up a hand to block the daylight. Tommy took it as a wave and raised his hand in a gesture of greeting. He wore work gloves, and there was a dog with him she recognized, the black dog that had licked her shoes. It came up to her wagging and bashed its tail into her calves.

"Hope you don't mind," he said. "I brought Kong."

She reached down, petted Kong, and racked her brain. What was he doing here? Had they talked?

"I brought my chain saw. Figured you could use more wood."

"Oh."

"I noticed you're running out of splits."

When had he noticed this?

"Do you have a wood splitter?" he said. "I'm coming straight from work."

"Um." She felt aware of the distance between them and stepped back. He leaned forward, or maybe it was she who was falling toward him. What was it Silas said about Tommy, the reason they grew apart? She felt unsteady, off balance; she was still waking up. "We don't have a wood splitter," she said. And the way his eyes found her face and rested there, it was like he wanted something from her, but she couldn't think of what he could want, she was still trying to work out why he was there.

"Do you have a maul?" he said.

"Uh, yeah." She moved and the dog stuck to her like a magnet to the fridge. She didn't know why dogs did that; she'd always wanted a dog but when she was a child they'd moved too much and when she was an adult Silas was allergic. Tommy followed her to the old trailer where they stored the tools they wanted to keep dry and all the skylights Silas bought for her. Tommy with his dark hair and beard, he was the same age as her husband. "It's in here," she said, opening the door. Tommy ducked into the space, and Elsa smelled the musk of his sweat and the pleasant odor of pine resin and sawdust in the wool. He smelled like Silas, they were both from here, this place that made them alike, and when he moved away with his back to her, for a split second he could have been Silas, his wide shoulders and quiet air, the stoop of his flanneled back. She wanted to press herself there, to feel the safety and protection and warmth of his girth. But then he turned, his body ponderous, heavy, and he wasn't Silas and never would be.

"Got it." He hefted the ax. "This'll do."

He went back outside and she followed him down. The sound of a gunshot cracked the air. It shattered the silence and another round of bullets spackled the air in a quick succession followed by a rally of barking dogs. It was so near; she pressed a hand to her chest, wrapped up tighter in her jacket.

"Hunters," Tommy said. "Season just opened up."

She nodded, rubbing her arms as if cold. He held her gaze a moment too long and she let him.

Wednesday, day ten. Finn woke early and they rose together as they did every day while the windows of the house were still dark. He sat in the living room hooting softly, rolling along his toy trains, Hester asleep in her room. Elsa went into her husband's bedroom and turned on the light.

He was still. His chest beneath the blankets did not move. The blanket she had folded in the middle of the night after turning him sat motionless across his chest, no movement. She waited, held still, waited some more. The sorrow and loss and even the joy—a dawning of such pain filled her, and then, almost as if in response, his chest did move. It shuddered with a rasp as it filled.

A garbled moan escaped her throat.

Finn from the living room turned his head.

She rushed from the bedroom, her every movement, every sound, sharp and exact as the prick of a pin.

"Mum," said Finn.

"Mama's going outside." Elsa flinched at the sound of her own voice, punched her hands into the sleeves of her coat. "I'll be right back." She opened the door and shut it firm behind.

Down the hill and out across the field, she inhaled and lifted out from herself as though separating from her body in a dream, watched herself listing sideways in her dark coat hung from her body like a bell. She screamed, a harrowing cry that sent up a spray of black birds from a nearby pine.

The sound plucked a string, a primal cord that vibrated inside her; she heard Finn cry from inside the house, as if he'd felt it. They were tied together, she and her son—connected by some invisible thread.

It was that thread she followed back into the house. Blindly, dutifully, it led her back to him, to Hester, to herself.

Gunshots rang in the air as Elsa took down clothes from the line. Out along the dirt road that went by her house the pickups filled with men in blaze orange jostled past, their hunting dogs hanging out the windows. Sometimes they parked along the side of the road and hunted on the county land that bordered her property. Sometimes the lathered barking of dogs reverberated through the hardwoods as they cornered their prey.

Tommy came by again that morning, Thursday, day eleven. It was early, still dark. Elsa was in the kitchen feeding Finn when a pair of headlights cast their cones of sharp light up their walkway at 6:30 A.M. A heightened awareness clutched her chest. She knew who it was.

His dark silhouette moved in and out of headlights and through the churned haze of exhaust. He left his engine running. Elsa stayed in the house. His chain saw droned from high to low as he sawed up the remaining eight-foot poles into stove-size lengths. He worked at the bottom of the hill and never came up to the house. She didn't want him to.

Hovering by the front door, she felt sick. She should go down there, say hello. She thought about how Silas trusted him enough to work with him on the logging crew but not enough to call him when his mother died. She couldn't remember the reason he and Tommy were never close, something Silas had said. But then the truck was leaving, its brake lights flushing red through the trees, and anyway it didn't matter because they needed the wood.

When she closed her eyes, strange things crept in from the shadows of her mind. Gray-faced men with bony hands that curled into branchlike claws. She didn't like that Tommy was coming over, that he could show up at any time. She didn't like the awkward quiet between them, the canted way he stood before her as though falling.

Elsa built a fire and stacked the wood inside the woodstove so the air circulated around the logs without smoking them out. She boiled water for tea—her throat hadn't gotten better but neither was it worse. Thursday evening, the children in bed. Her father sent an email, telling her to come to Boston. They had plenty of room, he said, they could stay for as long as they wanted, she and the kids. "Don't be foolish," he wrote. "Admit you made a mistake and come home. For once in your life be practical and think of your family."

Her laptop screen glowed blue in the dark and its little cooling fan hummed. They didn't have running water, but they had internet. Silas had set up the dial-up connection for one reason: so that she could communicate with her dad. Family is important, he said. It was his hope that she and her father would make amends.

Staring at the blinking cursor on her screen, Elsa wondered which part of all of this her father thought was her mistake. Bringing Silas home? Or living out here in the first place? It was interesting that he would call Boston her home when she'd never once lived there, and that he implored her to "think of family."

She tried to imagine living out East, but the thought of going back there made her physically ill. She couldn't uproot her children at a time when they needed stability the most. What was familiar to them was this place: Ethan and Luvera and their home among the trees, everything Silas had worked so hard to build.

The woodstove flickered, its firelight casting orange waves across the wood floor while everywhere else an oily darkness pooled. In her mind she thought of all the things she might say to her father, the hurt feelings still there. But he had reached out to her, offered help. She went through it all in her head until she landed on the one thing she really wanted to know, and this, in the end, was what she asked him.

"How?" She typed it out. "How do you give up on such a beautiful dream?" She hit send. Waited for their poky dial-up connection, her face washed in blue from the screen.

From across the kitchen under the cookstove came a shuffle. The scratch-scratch of little rodent claws. *It's just the mice in the walls,* she told herself, but a moment later, a sooty shadow smeared across the floor. The woodstove flickered; steam rose from her cup. She waited. A black ball of fur rolled out from under the stove across her floor and slipped beneath the fridge.

Elsa stood, grabbed her headlamp, and shined it across the room. More shuffling came from underneath the refrigerator, and the black creature reemerged, slipping back beneath the stove.

That was no mouse. It wasn't cute or brown and it had no ears. She waited for it to come back out again so she could get a better look. She swept her light under the fridge, across the room. The third time it crept as if sensing her there and raised its snout into the air. She saw its shrewlike nose, black fur, two slits for eyes, and a stub for a tail. It turned and scuttled back under the stove.

Voles. These were the voles! Silas always hated the voles, said they were almost impossible to get rid of once they came into the house—they had babies at alarming rates, built tunnels, chewed holes.

Elsa flipped on the kitchen lights and threw open the top cupboard doors. Somewhere up high Silas kept the poison. Boxes of blue-green pellets that she poured onto jar lids, the way she had seen him do, and these she slid under the stove, under the fridge. When it was done, she washed her hands and turned off the lights. Behind her rib bones, up under her sternum, something dark and slippery began to squirm.

It wasn't a mistake, bringing him home. This was where he felt most at peace, this land among the trees. They were part of it, she was part of it, and she wanted to be here. She wanted him to know how much she wanted to be here! All her life she'd been the person who had to leave, the one who couldn't stay. But moving out here was the best thing she'd ever done, and she'd made a commitment, not just to Silas, but to this place. What would happen if she left now, in the middle of winter, all the snow and vermin and disrepair?

From across the kitchen underneath the cookstove came the rasping scrabble of the poison as it shifted in the jar lids. The vole didn't come out again to cross the floor.

A new email blipped onto her screen. Her father's reply. His answer to her question—How do you give up on a dream?—in four words.

"Get a new one."

Elsa grabbed her coat and a headlamp and gusted outside. Under the hard bright stars she soldiered down to the woodpile and rustled under the tarp. White breath boiled out from her nose, and rays of light battled out from the band around her head. She threw down the cut logs and every sound made her jump, her footsteps, her breath, the thud of wood hitting the frozen ground and the crackle of the tarp. Each sounded close even if its source was far, the clatter of bare branches from the trees overhead, the sharp snap of sticks, every noise a predator just behind her head.

Lifting the ax, she widened her stance. Skittish, afraid of getting hurt, she tapped the log and jumped back. It fell off the chopping stump, unmarked, to the ground. Righting it, Elsa lifted the ax again. She would learn how to split wood. She would learn how to stay. She didn't want a new dream; she wanted this one. Her father didn't understand, how could he? When Winnie left, he did nothing and called it surrender. Luvera wanted Silas put on every medication possible and called it faith. But there had to be some part of it that was her responsibility, some part, however small, that she alone could affect.

She knocked over another log, which rolled and nicked her shins. In the shifting rays of her headlamp she stood up the logs on the ground and worked her ax, brandishing her blade. She would thank her father for the offer of a place to stay and tell him that she would for once in her life be practical. She would invest in her land. She would split the wood. She would use the money Silas had given his life to earn and she would get the well dug, put up the drywall. She would finish the second story, their home, the beautiful dream, with or without Silas.

If she couldn't hold on to him, she could at least hold on to everything that he held dear.

13

Ethan drummed his fingers along the kitchen counter, his other hand gripped around the phone. Maggie beside him on the kitchen floor lifted her head, waiting for him to go back outside and finish the chores. He punched the number into the phone. It rang and he paced across the kitchen, his boots tracking bits of hay and mud. Luvera would be cross with him, but she was still asleep upstairs.

"What are you doing?"

He jumped and turned around. His wife, in her slippers and robe. The phone, ringing in his hand. He looked at it as though surprised to find it there.

"You didn't take your boots off," she said, noticing the floor.

"I was just making a quick call." He hung up the phone. "No one there." It was early, not yet 7 A.M. "I thought you were still in bed."

"This darn cold, I can't stay another minute in bed." She filled the teakettle, lit the burner on the stove. "I know what you were doing," she said. "You shouldn't be bothering her." Luvera rattled around in the cupboard for the mugs.

"Tell me again what she said."

"Meddling, that's what you're doing. You're a meddler."

"I'm concerned. There's a storm moving in. Why is she so against staying here with us? Did we do something wrong?"

Luvera took down the box with the tea. "This isn't an easy thing, Ethan. No matter what we do or don't do and no matter where she goes, it's going to be hard."

He pondered this and knew it to be true. Some mornings, if he was honest about it, he didn't want to get out of bed. The kettle on the stove let out an aggrieved moan.

"It makes sense if you think about it," Luvera said, pouring water for her tea. "She has no mortgage to pay, no job other than taking care of those kids. Might be nice for her to take the winter and figure out what's next."

"She also has no running water."

"People have gotten by with less." She crossed to the table and he was surprised to see that she'd also made him a cup of tea. His wife was like that—she didn't do anything just for herself without also thinking of the other person.

"We have to start bringing her water," he said, accepting the tea. "Every few days."

"Silas used to fill up those blue jugs using the spigot behind the barn."

"I can do that."

"When you're better," she said. "Doc said no heavy lifting for six weeks."

"Those aren't much."

"She can also come over here to do laundry and take a shower."

"Good. I'll tell her."

"I already did." She dunked her tea bag up and down. "We have to stop calling over there, Ethan. Remember how upset she got with us before Finn was born? She said she would call us when there's something we need to know." She blew on her tea, took a sip.

He thought about last winter before Finn was born. He thought about the argument he overheard out in the barn. Elsa had been eight months pregnant with Finn, and she and Silas were talking about the house, which they were building up from scratch. Elsa with her background was a certain kind of woman and Silas was sensitive to that. He wanted her to be comfortable, to be happy.

"I can have the toilet done by the weekend," Silas had explained. "I've got the plans and the lumber set aside."

"A toilet in the house?"

"In the house."

"A wooden toilet?"

"A compost toilet. Doesn't use one drop of water and it's totally earth friendly." Silas took his time explaining. Ethan couldn't see them, but Elsa at eight months pregnant was an imposing figure; her height matched Silas's and she must have weighed nearly the same as he did, even with his lumberjack arms. Silas went on with his bunny-rabbit enthusiasm about how he would build a simple wooden bench with a hole cut in the top and a bucket underneath, with room for two more buckets beneath. Once you were done with your business, he explained, you scooped sawdust from one bucket and put it on top of what you just did in the other bucket until the bucket got full.

"You what?"

Ethan wished he could have seen her face.

"When it's full, you just haul it out and empty it on the compost pile. Few scoops of lime, few bales of hay, and in three years' time—ta-da—you have your own fertilizer. Humanure."

"That's a word?"

"You bet. It's good for the environment. Doesn't use one drop of water, and we have plenty of access to all the hay we could possibly want, and everything gets used in the garden, and that's the beauty of it."

"That's disgusting."

"It's perfectly safe and natural."

"Silas, I'm not doing that."

"Elsa, look. I already have the lumber set aside. I can have it done this weekend."

"No way."

"I can have it finished and installed and in the house."

"You promised me the _house_ would be finished before the baby comes."

"I know and I'm sorry. I'm doing everything I can."

"And I'm having this baby. If the house isn't going to be done and we're staying here, then you have to at least get me a toilet."

"That's what I'm trying to do."

"No, Silas, a real toilet. A proper toilet! Not this business of me hauling shit buckets out to the garden and then growing food in it!"

After she left, Ethan came around the corner to find Silas in the padlock humming away, brushing a curry comb through his horse. That was his way of dealing with stress—he would hum a tune. Ethan asked him, "What are you going to do?"

Silas looked over his shoulder and did not look happy to see him.

"If you want my opinion," Ethan said, "I think you'd better get that woman a toilet."

Silas wasn't too happy about that, either. "I can't do that. She knows I can't do that! The ground is frozen solid, there's over two feet of snow. I can't get a well put in before the baby comes." He exchanged the rubber curry comb for a finishing brush. That horse never had such a good grooming.

"What about waterless tanks. Have you looked into those?"

"That's what this is."

"No, I'm talking about incineration."

"That uses electricity."

"Not all of them. Some use propane or natural gas."

"Those are really expensive! We're talking two thousand dollars or more!"

"Sounds to me like a small price to pay."

He didn't have to say anything more. By the end of the week, Elsa had her nonelectric, two-thousand-dollar waterless throne, and two weeks after that, Finnegan Arnasson came into the world.

Silas would have figured out how to get his wife a hot tub if it would have made her happy.

"Maybe I'll just go over there and try talking to her again." Ethan was at the door now; he had his hand on the knob and was wearing his coat. Luvera chased around him with a mop.

"Absolutely not," she said. "You leave that poor woman alone. She made it perfectly clear that she doesn't want us around and anyway she isn't feeling well. She'll call us when she needs us. Let her have her space."

"It can't be long now."

"No. I wouldn't think so." The mop squeaked and streaked. "If you ask me, the mistake was bringing him home. He should have gone into a nursing home, that's what I think."

Ethan knew what she thought; she'd made no small show of it. He didn't understand how two women could be so strong-willed and yet see things so differently. His wife was a worrier who needed a plan, and that made Elsa nervous, he supposed, because in her experience things just worked out. Luvera said things worked out for her because Elsa never thought ahead, and people always jumped in to save her.

Well, that's what he wanted to do now. He wanted to save her from all of it, save himself and Luvera, too. But he couldn't. There was no saving any of them.

14

Hester stood with her brother at the bottom of the hill in front of their little, unfinished house. They wore jackets and snow pants and watched as their mother stepped around the logs, tugging and pulling at the tarp. The snow that fell during the morning melted by the end of the day and collected in small pools that froze at night, binding the tarp. Her mother broke the ice with the back of her ax. It shattered like glass. She yanked and stabbed and tugged. "Stand back," she told them, "both of you, stay back!" She tossed out the cut lengths of red oak, poplar, birch.

"But Mama, I want to help."

"Take care of Finn. That is a help. Please keep him safe."

"But Mama, I'm not afraid."

"I want you to be afraid. I could throw the ax by mistake, or chip off a splinter, or stab somebody's foot. You have got to stay away from me."

Her mother picked up a log, put it on the chopping stump, and raised her ax. She swung, but the ax only tapped the log and knocked it off the stump. It fell unsplit to the ground. She repeated this several times, standing the log up, lifting the ax, knocking the log down. Sometimes she yelled at the log, called it a dirty bastard or told it to "open up goddamnit." Finally, she left the log on the ground and got out a different log, a better log, one that was straighter and without knots. Again and again she raised and lowered her ax, and the logs fell over, sometimes before she even brought the ax down.

They would be getting more snow. Her mother wanted to bring

firewood up to the porch. Hester thought about the brave tree standing alone out there, getting piled on by snow. She worried about the tree now that she didn't see it every day on her way to and from school. "Why do you do that?" her mother had asked her one day when they were driving home and she saw Hester waving out the window to the tree.

"That's the brave tree," she said. "It lost all its friends." She didn't have to explain. After that, her mom started waving to the tree, too.

Hester called out helpfully, "Sometimes Papa didn't use the chopping stump."

Her mother wrinkled her nose and looked at the stump. She went over to one of the logs on the ground, righted it, raised the ax. She brought it down, and the blade stuck into the log without the log falling over.

"Yee-i," her brother said, looking to his sister. At first, she thought he was making a comment about her mother, who was still trying to pry her ax out of the log. But Finn waved his hand around and said it again, "Yee-i." He was trying to make the hand sign for "water." Finn had perfectly good ears, but their mother taught him sign language so that he wouldn't become frustrated before he could talk. Her mother was a good teacher and Hester remembered a lot of the signs she had learned, too. Her brother wasn't even close to doing this one right. She put up three fingers and tapped them on her chin.

"Water. You want some water?"

"Yee-i," her brother agreed.

"Wah—ter?" she exaggerated.

"Yee-i." He nodded, bobbing up and down. Hester sighed. His new word sounded nothing at all like "water," but he had no idea.

Hugging him around his waist, she carried him up to the house, his pudgy legs dangling and dragged down by his boots. Past the wind chimes and onto the porch, she set him down on his puffy bottom. "You stay right here."

He looked up at her and smiled, two apples in his cheeks from the cold, and there were so many things about which her brother had no idea.

Inside the house she inhaled the must and woodsmoke she had come to associate with warmth and safety. She made her way into the kitchen, where the water jugs sat. The blue jugs were for washing and the clear jugs were for drinking. She found one for drinking that was open and brought that along with a cup over to the kitchen table. She pushed back the cardboard boxes of medical supplies and important papers, unscrewed the cap, tipped the jug. The water splashed into the cup and from her dad's bedroom came a loud thump. She jerked, spilling the water.

"Papa?" The house went still. Water snaked and dripped off the table's edge. Hester grabbed a towel and moved the papers. Outside her brother babbled and smacked his hands in the snow blown across the floorboards. From the bottom of the hill came the thud of her mother's ax.

Hester went to the door of her father's bedroom. It was closed. "Papa, would you like some water?"

There came another thump against the wall.

She pushed open the door and entered. With no windows the room was dark and moist like the inside of a boot. It was her first time being alone in his room without her mother. The smell of his body rushed into her like pain and she felt sick and embarrassed for him. But she wouldn't leave. He always told her to face her fears, and she had turned seven that fall. She waited, allowed for the outline of his shape to appear.

There was something shiny in the bed with him, two bright spots shining up near his head. She waited to see what those shining spots would be. And then all at once she understood.

Those spots were her father's eyes. He lay on his back looking up at the ceiling, but he was not seeing, not blinking, not even knowing she was there. Hester stood without moving as knowledge crept like a taproot and set itself deep. His chest moved up then down. His eyes, two iced coins, offered up their empty glare.

Outside the wind chime struck a single note, over and over, the same note repeated, a simple, pure, singular song.

Gone. Gone. Gone.

15

Elsa marched up the hill behind the house through the woods, looking down and trying not to swallow. If she didn't swallow, it didn't hurt, and that meant it was nothing serious. She walked up the hill with the baby strapped to her back, Hester following in her snowsuit. The second week of November, day twelve, and they were having their first storm. The flakes laced doilies she obliterated with her boots, the last she would see of the ground until spring, twelve to eighteen inches followed by a hard freeze.

"Mama will be right back." She stopped before they reached the generator shed. "I'll come back as soon as I get the engine started."

Hester trailed behind, her posture sluggish; she wasn't even looking at the snow.

"Hester? Hurry up. I need you to watch Finn."

All week Hester had been asking questions about Silas. How was Papa and where had he gone? They kept the door to his bedroom closed now, because of the smell, she thought, and Hester didn't go in there anymore to help turn him after Finn had gone to bed. It was harder to get her to focus on schoolwork, she didn't want to do any reading on her own, and at night she cried softly in her bed, calling, "Papa? Papa?" Hester worried about her father, but Elsa worried about them.

All week she had been denying the pain in the back of her throat. She couldn't get sick, could not get the children sick. She pulled their hands off her and tried to get them to fall asleep on their own, but they clung to her, fearful, needy, their world falling apart. And what if it was? What if she couldn't hold it together? What if she had made a mistake?

She felt it, that dark quickening inside her like a worm. They should never have put Silas on medication, they should never have started the antibiotics or reinserted the gavage. That was the mistake. She did it for Ethan and Luvera out of respect for their faith, she did it because she wanted to believe. It was in her nature to believe. If only it was about how much she wanted to believe!

Taking her headphones from the nail on the outside of the generator shed, she put them on and tried not to swallow. In her mind she circled the image of her bedridden husband like a shark. *What should I do? What should I do? What should I do?* The question her mantra, her prayer. It haunted her every breath and muddied her sleep because the more he took from her, the less she had for the kids, the less she had for herself, and it only hurt when she swallowed, so that meant it wasn't serious. When your throat hurt all the time, even without swallowing, then you knew you had a problem.

The concrete floor of the shed was cold and soaked with oil from the slow leak in the backup generator, what they called Number Two. Leaves had blown in and pasted themselves to the concrete and she could smell them but mostly there was just the cold. She passed between the two engines and got a second reading from the inverter mounted in the back and the number was lower than she'd hoped. She would have to stay up late to get the charge up; would have to come back here at night, in a snowstorm, in the dark.

Twice now her hand had lingered on the plug in the alone hours during the night. Her husband who twitched in the bed and jerked under the sheets, his anima trapped like the rodents in the walls. To starve him seemed ruthless and cruel, but the cold, she read somewhere, was like going to sleep. Eskimos put their sick and dying on ice floes and sent them off into the night.

She stepped over the bag of tools Silas left on the floor the last time he was in there and approached Number One: an old Lister Petter that had once been used to make electricity on the caboose of a train. Silas found the generators at an auction, mounted them on cement pads so the levers were easy to reach. With her gloved hands, she opened the throttle, switched back the compression lever, and pushed the button. The belt turned with a whine, spun to its full speed, and there came a terrible sound, like pebbles grinding through a blender. She took her hand off the button, switched the lever back, pulled off her gloves.

"Gaaah!" She kicked the bag of tools across the floor. She didn't know how to fix a generator!

She dug through his tool bag, pushed aside the wrenches and C-clamps and power-drill bits. Silas had shown her how to do this once, before leaving for an out-of-town gig that lasted two weeks. He made sure she understood how sometimes the brushes got stuck on the starting motor, and they had to be banged back into place. And it made sense to her that he would hold on, he was always like that, so dedicated and diligent. They talked about her doing these things, how she would learn how to change the oil, start the snowblower, run a chain saw. But she'd been so busy with the kids and being pregnant, and she couldn't very well walk around holding a chain saw with her belly in the way.

She wrapped her hand around the hammer; it happened the same way it had happened with the T-shirt, the things he touched, the energy contained in them and the love-surge that brought her every time to her knees. The memory of everything she had lost, rushing back. She fell against the cement pad among the rubber-coated wires and sobbed.

Did Silas know? How happy she'd been? Because she didn't tell him, not often enough. She played that stupid game, *What would I be doing now?* And he knew she thought about it, he asked her once, "Elsa, are you happy, with me, here?"

And she'd told him yes and then gave him the money to prove it. But in her mind, she'd still played that game.

She wiped her face on the sleeves of her coat. The kids were waiting for her at the bottom of the hill. She couldn't stay long. She put on her gloves, gripped the hammer, and stood.

Along the cold cylinder of the starter she banged the hammer, leaned in between the wires and switches, nicking the plate so bits of gold paint flecked off, bang bang bang, *die die die,* she knocked the brushes she couldn't see back into place so they would make contact like they should and build a charge like they should, bang bang bang, *die die die,* she banged and pounded and flung the hammer into the corner of the room, walked around to the other side of the engine, kicked his tool bag out of the way, flipped the compression lever, pressed the start button, and the belt turned and the sound was good. She flipped the compression lever back again and the motor caught, roaring to life. It filled the room with a sound that crashed and banged off the walls. Back outside, back into the cold, she stumbled down the hill as the echoes shifted and shattered through the snow-filled woods.

The game started when they were still living in their apartment in Minneapolis, Silas working construction jobs to learn the trade, but he spent nearly every weekend on the land. She often came with and brought Hester. They camped in the small pop-up trailer, where she was always bumping her head.

The invitation came to the apartment, addressed to Elsa Oldare.

"Santiago is getting married." A wedding in New York City. She fingered the embossed script, the gold foil and thin sheet of vellum. That winter Hester had turned two.

"They make a handsome couple," Silas said, peering over her shoulder. Santiago had a dark, brooding jawline and rich chestnut hair. He was marrying Janelle Papaquet, a wispy collage artist who did three-dimensional abstracts in multimedia forms, wood, paper, clay.

"He was my first Rhode Island friend." He'd also been her lover and her muse. Everyone who got into that program was handsome; they had charisma and accents and highly eccentric clothes. It was a prestigious program. Elsa had only gained admission with her mother's help. Winnie instructed her on which images to include, influenced the drawings and sketches and progression of ideas for the portfolio Elsa had submitted for review.

"Did you sleep with him?" Silas had his back to her. It didn't sound like him. He was fussing with his knapsack behind the couch, she was kneeling by the coffee table on the floor, and Hester had just gone down for her nap.

"Is that what you really want to know?"

"I'm just kidding." He grinned, turned around. "You should go, if you want to go."

"Of course I want to go. We should both go. You would love Janelle, and Christmastime in New York City is a magical place."

"What about Hester?"

"We can leave her with Ethan and Luvera. They would love it."

"They would."

"So let's do it."

"Naw. Can't afford it." He went into the kitchen, where he took his bike down from off the wall.

"I'll buy the plane tickets," she offered. "I have my mother's money."

His bike helmet dangled from his arm. "If that's what you want to use it for"—the gears clacked as he rolled it toward the door—"sure, I'll go."

But he hadn't really wanted to go. He was like an elk in Manhattan, bumping into things, easily startled. He wore a tweed blazer and rumpled slacks and didn't know anybody there, the wedding venue on the top floor of a building with an aerial view of the city that gave him vertigo, he said. The raw oysters and tapas weren't enough for his dinner, the live jazz was too loud, the open bar too crowded, and he wanted to leave an hour into the reception and probably would have if he'd known how to flag down a cab.

She wore a black off-the-shoulder with her lacquered Louboutins. She saw her old friends and the current students and art professors who were doing shows, developing their brand; she met a gallery owner who gave her his card and said he'd "give her work a look" if ever she was in town. They were on top of the world, the windows ceiling to floor. She could have gone back—if she wanted to. It was what she had hoped.

But five years had passed, and things looked different. It was the champagne and having a baby and feeling her body change. It was wanting to be herself again, who she was without a child in her arms, who she'd been at art school before her mother died. It was her mother's dying words: "I wish I was more myself."

Silas grabbed her arm out there on the dance floor, his fingers cold on her bare flesh. "Are you going to save a dance for me?" He smiled, but there was an uncertainty she'd never seen before in the backs of his eyes, a vulnerability, a shifting doubt. He was seeing this other side of her for the first time.

"Of course!" She laughed like it was all a frivolity. "Let's dance now!" She tossed her hair and rolled her hips and pressed her body into the pulsing, throbbing crowd. She lost him as she went deeper in. Her old friends who had gallery openings and followings, they were being written up in *The New York Times*. She hadn't known it would feel this way, it overcame her, and she lost herself. The man behind her put his hands on her hips and they were grinding, gyrating, they had no inhibitions, none! It was a party, Christmastime in New York.

Silas left her out there on the dance floor. He somehow found his way back to the hotel and when she woke the next morning, he wasn't in the bed. That had scared her. She'd never seen him behave this way before, but also, she was defensive, arguing in her head—it had been a party for chrissakes, couldn't he let loose for one night? She flopped around in the sheets, sullen, morose, her stomach filled with lead.

When he returned, he acted like nothing was wrong, hummed and whistled and joked around with the checkout clerk, but he wouldn't meet her eyes.

Their plane landed in the dark. They had a ninety-minute drive out to the farmhouse to pick up Hester. That was when he asked her—not angry, but sober, with concern. The heater whirred between them and the car smelled of wet wool and snow, they were driving on a back county road and still hadn't talked about what had happened at the party.

He said, "Elsa, are you happy, with me, here?"

That was when she gave him the money. She gave him all the rest of her inheritance, what was supposed to be her college tuition, her gallery showing, her *whatever* to launch her career. She gave it to Silas instead, this boy who had a dream to build a house using the trees he felled by hand. The money to say what she couldn't say, what she didn't know how to express: *I'm with you, I need you, and I'm afraid of who I would be without you.*

Elsa woke to a cold black house that smelled of ash. Silas thumped the walls and when she flipped on the lights, they flashed. She had left the generator running and had forgotten to change his catheter and build a fire. Her breath whited the air as the lights blinked on then off because the batteries had overcharged. In his room, she held him down with her body and waited for the spasm to end.

It was like holding down the lever on the generator, the same feeling of an engine that wouldn't quit, how it wanted to run on and on, mindless, forever, and what had she done? What had she done!

Outside, down the hill, she stumbled through the haze as the snow pecked at her face. The generator was off but her mind still ran. What if he couldn't die? What if he was bound here to this place, to her, the right combination of fluids and drugs and she was keeping him stuck here forever in this limbo like an engine that couldn't quit and never would?

Back at the house under the cover of their temporary porch, she loaded her arms with wood. A layer of sweat coated the top of her skin, and her teeth chattered as she brought the wood into the house and came back out.

She reached out for a support beam to steady herself. The snow tumbled down in the lavender light, and heat emanated from her skin. Her face so hot, she imagined it sizzled every time a flake hit her skin. And the pain in her throat, it was like a blade. *What should I do? What should I do? What should I do?*

That feeling of detachment came over her, as though she were hydroplaning across the surface of herself. She had the distinct craving for a cigarette. She hadn't smoked since her college days, when all her friends were going through one crisis of the soul after another. With Silas, there had been no crisis, no need to smoke.

Elsa thought about their last morning together, the smell of coffee and pancake syrup, the three of them sitting around the breakfast table. She could still see it, Hester being tossed into the air, Finn banging away on his high chair tray. He threw his fork, she went to retrieve it, the floor sticky with smeared syrup.

"I'm going to need a couple of eggs with these," Silas said.

"What's that?" She was wiping the floor.

"I need the protein," he said. "Something about working outside, I can't make it through the morning on sugar alone."

She'd stood peevish, confused. "You want me to make you some eggs?"

"I want some eggs!" Hester cried.

"I thought you wanted pancakes, I made you pancakes."

"Eggs, eggs, I want eggs!"

Finn banged away on his high chair tray.

"I'll do it." Silas got up. "The girl needs her protein." He got out another frying pan, he made the eggs.

Loading up her arms with more firewood, Elsa went back into the house. Kicked off her boots but kept on her coat, and by the glow of her headlamp, she knelt before the woodstove and opened the door.

Across the iron lip the ashes piled cold above the rim. Chunks of dormant embers, gray-scaled and charred like fingers pale as bone. She couldn't build a fire until she shoveled out the ash, and she couldn't shovel out the ash until she emptied the ash can, the ash can full, and she had to bring it down to compost outside.

Two in the morning and she pulled on her boots and wrapped her arms around the ash can, the soot and the dust filling her nose.

Outside in the dark she punched her feet through the snow to trudge out across their field. Leaning forward, she tipped the ash can, shook out the grit, thrusting, throwing so the dusty plumes streaked across the gloaming in deathlike tails.

16

Wearing insulated overalls and his old Stormy Kromer cap, Ethan put the snow thrower into first gear and rolled it up the aluminum ramp into the flatbed of his pickup. Bright sunshine bounced off the new snow piled thick on the ground and he slapped the back closed and climbed up into the cab. He sat, reluctant to start the engine. Inside his chest where his ribs wrapped around his organs, he felt the vibratory hum of the last hour and a half, the sensation not pain, exactly, but uncomfortable, like yearning. He didn't even realize his eyes were closed until Luvera tapped on his window.

"When will you be back?" she said.

He pushed the button to glide down the glass. "An hour, maybe more."

"Are you wearing that elastic wrap the doctor gave you?"

"I am."

"I don't like this." She locked her arms across her chest. "I don't think it's a good idea. Doc said six weeks. You're doing too much."

"You have to admit it looks pretty good." He'd done their driveway with the blade of his truck at first light, snow-blowed all the paths to the outbuildings before getting to the chores, out of necessity, she had to see that. Still, she wasn't budging from the side of the truck, her brow plowed with thoroughfares of disapproval.

"Can't somebody else go over to Elsa's?" she said. "Did you call around?"

Last weekend when they brought the priest over a second time for last rites, he saw Silas. He wished he hadn't. It would have been better not to have that picture in his mind. The boy had withered, his muscle mass gone, the skin melted in pools soft and pale as winter butter.

He said to Luvera, "She has to be able to get out."

Shifting into high gear, Ethan accelerated onto the county road, the first time since the accident that he'd driven by himself. He could go all the way to town, the roads clear, the landscape smoothed and polished, the sky a broad and plain quality of blue it only got after a snowstorm in winter. He turned onto their dirt road and shifted into a lower gear. Up ahead he saw the swale of snow that marked the entrance to their driveway.

It was nine years ago that he and Silas had cleared that drive-way together, the year Silas graduated from college. He remembered the look of pure jubilation on his face. "I got it all marked out," Silas had said, sitting right there in the pickup next to him, nearly bouncing out of his seat. "Just follow me. You'll see, it's the perfect distance from the road." They left the truck parked on the side of the road and walked in. Sure enough, his nephew had hammered stakes into the ground with red string that he wound from peg to peg, a kind of trail wide enough for a vehicle to pass through. When they got all the way back to the clearing, there at the top of the hill was the outline for the house, the wood stakes with twine twisted and strung among the wild blueberry shrubs that covered the hill.

It takes a certain kind of person to do what Silas did, to look at a hill and see a home, and it takes a certain kind of woman who can look at that same hill and agree with you. For all her inexperience with country living, Elsa had it in her to try anything, and she'd put up with quite a lot. The two of them together had transformed this place, and that was why she was good for him. Maybe Elsa didn't know how to milk a goat or run a snowblower, but she did know how to champion a dream.

It took an hour to blade her driveway. He sat comfortably up in the cab, shifting the gears to scoop and lift and dump. When he was done, he parked at the bottom of the hill in full view of the house. As he climbed out of the cab, the ghost of his injury pulled on him like a passenger he carried—the fear of the pain that might come back.

"Uncle Ethan!" Hester waved to him from under the cover of a makeshift porch, its walls made of hammered plywood, topped with a corrugated plastic roof. "We got snow! How much did you get?"

"Same as you. Eighteen inches." He unhooked the back of the truck bed, pulled down the aluminum ramp.

"My mom said I can help if it's all right with you!"

"Then you'd better come down here."

The whole time Hester followed him, walking three steps behind like a little duck while he tussled with the snowblower throwing chutes of snow. They took it slow, first cleaning up the driveway and then blowing a path up to the house. Through the woods they made a path up the hill to the generator shed and around the solar array. Elsa had already trudged up there to push the snow from the panels, the grids iridescent in the sun. When he was done, the quiet rang in his ears and the snow crystals thrown out by the blower lingered and sparkled in the air.

"Now we've got to bring these water jugs up to your mama." He pulled off his gloves, flexing his hand to get the feeling back. "Can you help load these into the sled? They're pretty heavy." He pulled one down from the back of his truck. "Maybe it's too heavy for you."

"No, I got it." She negotiated more than her share, and they loaded the sled and pulled it along the newly plowed path up the hill to the house.

"You keeping up with your studies all right?" he asked her.

"Yes. I'm doing online school. My mom lets me use her computer."

"You're lucky. When I was a kid, I had to walk to school."

"Was it hard?"

"Uphill both ways. In a strong wind."

Hester got quiet.

"Me and my brother, Robby, we only had the one pair of shoes between us."

Her mouth dropped open.

"Robby got to wear the shoes and I had to carry him on my back the whole way so he wouldn't ruin the shoes." He parked the sled in front of the porch, bent to pick up one of the water jugs.

"Is that true?"

He straightened. Her face inscrutable in the winter sun. "No. I was just fooling with you."

"Why do people do that?" she said. "Tell things to kids that aren't true?"

The planes of snow out in the field were so bright, he had to look away. "I don't know," he said. "It's just what people do."

"Were you testing me?"

"No. No, it wasn't like that." He picked up one of the jugs, she picked up another. "It was just a story my grandpa told me when I was little, only I didn't figure out the joke until I was much older." They got to the front door. He looked down at her. "You're a much smarter kid than I was. And that is true."

The front door opened before they knocked. Elsa stood with Finn hooked to her hip. She shielded her eyes from the snow bright and said, "Nothing's changed," before Ethan had even asked. "He's the same." But she was not. Her cheeks pink and febrile, her hair rough and uncombed. Finn tugged at her shirt, food crusted in the wrinkles of fabric, a sour smell emanating from her skin. "Thank you for bringing over the water," she said. "Just leave the jugs there. I'll bring them inside before they freeze."

He set the jug down. "If you and the kids want to come over and bathe—"

"Sunday," she said, and twisted her face toward the sun. "We'll come on Sunday, while you're at church, if that's okay. I'll wash the sheets." Finn reached out and grabbed a fistful of her hair. Elsa turned away, untangled his hands, and set him down. Even in her sickness she had a way with him, gentle but firm, never rough. Hester slipped past and went in.

"That's fine," he said. "But you don't have to wait until we're gone. It doesn't bother us none." His hand moved beside him as if pulling a yo-yo by its string; he reached for what he wanted to say, the words stalled, spinning around. "Anyhow," he said. "We need to talk, you and me. We need to revisit this."

"Revisit what?"

"This." He gestured at the makeshift porch, the house. He had to be firm this time. He had to let her know that he would brook no argument. "You and the kids can't stay here all winter by yourself."

"Ethan, we already talked about this." Behind her in the doorway Finn squawked. She turned back around and picked him up, bounced him against her hip. "I am not moving into town. I can't handle a move right now, and we have everything we need right here."

"I understand. We wouldn't want you to move. Just come and stay with us at the farmhouse."

"I appreciate the offer—"

"You wouldn't have to pack much. You can have your own room."

She smiled and moved Finn to her other hip. She didn't invite him in. He stood feeling foolish on the porch.

"We're fine," she said. "We're staying. This is where we want to be. This is where Silas needs us to be."

He walked back down to his truck alone.

17

Elsa Arnasson stood alone at the bottom of the hill and looked out at the trees backlit by the sun. Day fourteen, and Silas was still breathing on his own. She was doing better, she told herself, a little weak, maybe; she was losing weight and tired, always tired. Ethan had plowed yesterday, so she could get down to the woodpile with no trouble at all. It had gotten colder, and it snowed some almost every day, loading down the trees, the branches white, a silhouette of fish bones strung along a gum line of sky.

Pulling wood splits out from under the tarp, she made a pile at her feet. There was still plenty of firewood, more than she thought, and so much left unsplit. The sun pinked in the trees and the branches groaned and creaked. The snow weighed them down, all the branches drooped across the paths in multiple archways of white, the trees leaning against other trees, and sometimes they broke or snapped under the weight, a weight that seemed to Elsa to represent her life: she was those trees, those heavy branches loaded with white.

A long arm of sun reached through the trees to gild a patch of woods. Elsa turned, as if called, putting a hand on the woodpile to steady herself.

From the trees came a whisper, a movement of snow, falling from a branch. It slid off and landed with a thump. The branch winged up. It bumped into the branch above it and knocked that snow off. More branches shook free, in turn, a cascade which sent the branch above it free and more snow thumping and more branches swinging until the occurrence grew deeper into the wood, and that entire patch of forest came alive with sunlit powdery bursts.

When it was over, the trees stood upright and serene, the branches freed of snow. The snow for its part on the ground, still pure and white. But at rest, no longer a burden.

From up at the house came the muffled shouts of her children. She heard them as she had heard the trees, the sun, the snow, as if they had been talking to her, communicating in their own solitary language.

Loading the splits one at a time into her arms, Elsa shivered from the sweat drying under her coat. Above her, the wind rattled in the plastic sheeting wrapped around the second story of the house. Even when there was no wind, it crackled as if breathing, taking in and expelling air. She opened her front door and went in.

"Mama! Finn is crying for you and we ran out of water!"

"I know," she whispered hoarsely. "It's okay, Hester. I'm here now."

Elsa dropped the splits by the woodstove and leaned into the chair. The walls of her throat had swollen closed, pressed together, so she couldn't get sound to come out. When had that happened? Bits of sawdust and bark fell from her as she peeled off her gloves. Going to the doctor would mean leaving Silas alone, and driving the hour into town, and sitting with her kids in a waiting room among the sick. Her son sat on the floor now with his face puffed and wet; Hester stood on a chair in the kitchen, all the cupboard doors thrown open, empty cup in hand.

"He keeps making the sign for 'water, water.' He was crying and I didn't know what to do."

Elsa gave her daughter a thumbs-up. She dipped a bowl into the pot of warm water on the woodstove and washed her hands before picking Finn up, then dipped him a cup of water. They sat, she and her children, they sipped warm water and listened to the fire.

"How come you were gone so long?" Hester wanted to know.

Elsa looked to her and touched her throat.

"You lost your talking?"

She nodded yes.

The little boy watched their faces with the nib of the sippy cup in his mouth, his eyes roving back and forth. The girl watched the fire as it snapped in the woodstove, and Elsa looked out the window at all the trees still piled with snow, how they leaned and drooped under all that weight, how they moaned and creaked and sometimes broke. Hester waited for her mother, and Finn reached out and patted her face, but she stayed gone in her mind for a long time.

Silas wasn't an art student, but his family knew the family who owned the land used for the Hoenettle Sculpture Park. Once a year in July they held hot pours for the community, demonstrations where they melted metals with blowtorches that sparked at dusk. Elsa at nineteen went with a group of coworkers from the restaurant where she worked in the warehouse district downtown. Of all the places she could have gone, she ended up in Minneapolis because she heard they had a thriving arts community, with coffee shops where people drank cappuccinos out of great big bowls.

Silas volunteered at the park during the summer, drove the equipment used to hang the sculptures. The pieces were huge and required cranes or bulldozers for installation. One piece, titled "Reclamation," was the attic of a house. That was the art project— the entire top part of a house as if it had been sliced off and planted in the ground. The roof rose out of the grass and the entire structure listed to one side, like it was being swallowed, but to Elsa, at the time, that had been a good thing. The stability of a home in the earth, permanence, what she never had.

The first night there was a bonfire and a band playing on a raised platform stage alongside a field of growing corn. Faces bathed in orange light watched as the hot metal was poured into molds, and it was so warm, she thought she could smell the kernels cooking in their silken skins, ripe enough to burst open right on the stalks. This feeling echoed inside of her, an intensity building that wanted release, wanted expression, but the only way she knew how to say it was through art, and that was a language she only spoke because of Winnie.

They had buried her in the mountains where she had finally found peace. Elsa flew out from Rhode Island and met her father, who flew out from China, where he'd been on a business trip. They scattered the ashes in a dry dusty wind among the burnt lodgepole pines that stood like sentinels around them.

On the way home, Elsa watched through an oval window spritzed with rain as they deiced the plane. A pink foam oozed out from a brush they stroked across the wing, the same pink as the turbans Winnie wore after she lost her red hair. When they sprayed out the water to rinse it off, inexplicably the foam turned bright apple green. It coated the wings in a thick, syrupy sheen and melted the ice. It was May but snowing in the mountains. The rain turned to flurries as the plane sat waiting for half an hour on the runway, before they finally canceled the flight.

It was a small airport, and Elsa walked through, dragging her carry-on, and kept right on walking. Didn't book a new flight or go to a hotel, didn't even call her dad. Instead, she rented a car and drove around in what she thought of as her mother's mountains, climbed up and twisted down, hairpin turns, scenic overlooks, first in the Uintas and then the Tetons, east through Wyoming, north through Montana, then across the windswept plains of the Dakotas, where gnats dotted her windshield like snow.

Elsa drove to the middle of the continent because it was neither east nor west and that made it feel like her own. She decided on the city of Minneapolis for no reason other than she had chosen it herself. She'd never done anything just because she wanted. She'd always had a game plan, a vision, a path. She had lists with goals and tutors and timelines. She had a family that placed conditions on their love—expectations, agendas, standards that had to be met.

That summer when she met Silas, he was more than just a boy-friend, a lover, a best friend; he was a grounding force and a living example of what she'd never had: the freedom to be herself.

Elsa woke to Hester shaking her foot. She had fallen asleep on the couch after getting Finn down for his nap. She rose and they bundled up together and went outside to bring up the rest of the wood. They loaded the splits into a plastic sled. Hester pulled it using a rope tied to the front while her mother pushed from behind and together they hauled the sled up the hill. The sun slapped down at the tree trunks, leaving handprints of gold, and snow scales like fairies flickered through the woods.

Halfway up the hill Hester stopped. Her face lifted toward the unfinished house, her skin starkly lit and smooth as the curving planes of snow. The wind changed. A cloud slid over the sun and blotted out the light; a gray shadow fell across her face.

"Hester? Are you all right?" Elsa whispered, bent over the sled.

Hester looked around at the tops of all the trees, at the pine and spruce tips arrowed against the sky. Something changed in the light again, the clouds uncrossed from each other and a sword of sun came pointing down at the girl. Elsa saw her daughter dazed and aglow inside this shaft of light. Hester didn't move or turn away, she seemed unaware of it. The light winked out. Elsa shivered. Hester went back to pulling the sled.

Later when they were unloading the splits, Hester stopped again, this time standing on the porch with her arms hung by her sides and her face tinted green from the light filtered through the plastic roof.

"I think . . ."

Elsa turned and waited for her daughter.

"I think that Papa is already dead."

They stood separate in the quiet. A gentle snow tumbled down in the gray air, the space between the flakes wide. Elsa reached out to touch her daughter's coat.

"We're going through a hard time," she whispered, the only sound she could make.

"Mama, when you die, does it hurt?"

"It might hurt to leave the people you love."

"Do we have to leave?"

"I don't know. Some people believe we go to heaven, others believe in ghosts. There's also the belief that when our soul leaves this body, it goes into another body."

"What do you think?"

"I like to think that dying is a peaceful thing, like walking into another room, or putting on a different hat. But no one knows."

"Papa knows."

"Yes. Papa knows."

The hot pour at the sculpture park lasted three nights that weekend in July. Elsa came alone that Sunday and stayed late with the band, drinking beer in the field by the burned-out oak. The tree had been struck by lightning years ago but survived, the entire left side of its trunk ripped open and scorched, its secondary limb shorn, but still it rose immense and satisfying at the edge of the field. Its surviving branches with leaves unruly cast a large and rare bit of shade. At night this spot was cooler than all the others, and it was here the crowd lingered and smoked and talked about art and meaning and the necessity of good bands.

When she saw him, standing in a circle of men and older boys, he did the unthinkable. He looked at her and smiled, an unrestricted smile, clean-spirited and openhearted, full of glee. She felt herself come alive at once like a tree budding in spring.

At the night's end he whispered in her ear, "I have something to show you." Her cheek tingled from the brush of his voice. "Follow me."

He led her across the park, a field of prairie grass and wildflowers, cut and divided into a maze of walking paths. She held his hand, and he took her off the path through tall grass that whiskered against her bare legs. Chemical fumes scented the air from a nearby sculpture, a collection of canvas heating tubes suspended in a net, hung twenty feet up in a kind of giant hammock strung between poles. "Industrial Resurrection" it was called, and she had tried to come up with a better name, something with the word "elephant" in it because the canvas tubes were like elephant trunks and the smell and the heat produced wild, undomesticated urges inside of her.

"It's in here," he said. "But I don't want you to get wigged out."

He had brought her to the very edge of the park, to a long, dark structure she hadn't noticed before. The sign in the grass said it was called "Summer Evening," and she thought, how appropriate.

"Why would I get wigged out?"

"I dunno," he said. "We're kind of off from the others and you only just met me. What if I'm a weirdo?"

"Are you?'

"Maybe." He smiled. "It's hard to know sometimes, you know? Whether it's the world that's crazy or just you."

"Yeah," she agreed, swatting at the bugs.

He led her around to the back of the building. It was painted the same color as the sky after the sun set and the dome turned magnetic and deeply violet. The sun that night had gone down hours ago. A slow moon floated in the east like a bulb; in the west a haze of light hung over the city. He took her hand, and his was warm and expressive, not limp and lifeless like so many other hands. Already she had such strong feelings for this boy, and yet they had only just met. At the opening of the structure he stopped and turned back. "You ready?" he asked.

"I guess."

"Don't be scared."

She laughed as they entered through a small door, ducking to fit inside. In front of them was a black wall, and Silas turned sharply to his right, confident, still holding her hand, the smell dusty and enigmatic, his hand pulling hers as they turned again and then again, caught in a terrible maze of tight, dark walls.

"You doing all right?" He was only visible by the whites of his sleeves, glowing in the dark just in front of her.

She squeezed his hand.

They came out, at last and finally, into a room filled with rays of starlight that seemed to come from another planet, as if they had stepped out onto a meteor in orbit. The blue box they stood in seemed to float, all the walls around them sealed except for the partitions built into the far side. There it was nothing but slats, spaced and angled with precision, a design that allowed entrance of the eastern light of a summer moon. The air outside filled with the whirrs of crickets and small winged bugs while inside the moon spilled its magnum opus, its fingers wraithlike in the small colorless box. Etched lines of calligraphy spelled out across the floor, and Elsa thought she could read this language and know the infinite, the essential, the unknown. It felt to her as though she were touching the Universe.

The wind blew, the shadows shifted, and like a funhouse the box tipped; she reached out; he was there, warm and solid and strong. He stood like a tree with deep roots, and his hand entwined with hers. His lips when she closed her eyes were soft and alive and more demonstrative than she had ever dared to hope a pair of lips could be.

Later, years later when they were out walking together on their back forty, after Hester was born but before Finn, he had stopped walking and looked out through the woods. She stood next to him like she had that first time at the sculpture park, and it still felt good and easy and right.

He had turned to her and said, "If you listen to the trees, they tell you things."

She'd laughed. "Oh really? Like what?"

She hadn't expected him to have a real answer. But he did. He'd looked out across their land at all the fallen trees, behemoths of the forest that had come down in a storm or strong wind, and she never forgot what he said.

"When it's your time to go, don't fall on your young."

Getting up from her bed, Elsa checked that the children were asleep, and closed their door. She crossed through the house in the dark, the glow of snow outside casting a gray light through the windows. After putting on her coat and lacing up her boots, she picked up her gloves and fussed with where to put them. She'd need them later.

In the kitchen she found some old towels and a bucket and brought those into his bedroom. She sat on the wooden chest at the end of the bed, found his foot under the blanket, and held it. Silas, the man she had married for better or for worse, in sickness or in health. Well, she had the one, now she had the other. The smell of his body, the sweat and the meat of him.

"How is this possible?" she'd asked the nurse yesterday.

And the look on her face, sympathetic, but not alarmed. "I've seen stranger things than a man alive in his condition. Sometimes, it's hard to let go."

He was holding on for them, Elsa knew. Holding on to all the things he left undone, the house he was building and the well that wasn't dug. Her father put his faith in money and Luvera believed in God's will, but Silas, he found his solace in the trees.

The trees that morning had been loaded with snow, and then, the snow fell. She didn't understand nature, its movements or what directed it, and so it had seemed at first that the snow had decided to fall, like a suicidal pact among snowflakes: *One, two, three, jump!* Then she wondered, had it been the tree? Did the tree tell the branch to move, give it a shrug? But no, the tree didn't move, and there had been no wind.

After watching closely throughout the day, she discovered it was neither the snow nor the tree but the sun. It was the sun, warming the snow so it slid off the branch. It softened it just enough to loose its frozen grip. A tiny bit of warmth from far away, removed but watching, and the rest would follow. That was when she knew: she had to be the sun for her Silas.

Elsa squeezed his foot. "All right," she whispered, and stood with her supplies. She went to the outlet and pulled the plug for the food pump. She folded back the blanket from his body, his chest shrunken and skin bluish white, slack around the bones. Her eyes teared up, both from the sight and the smell of him; she detached each line of plastic tubing from the port of each bag, letting them drain in the bucket, leaving the gavage in his nose, the PICC in his arm, the catheter bag strapped to his thigh. She coiled the tubes on his chest so that she could reattach them later. And she watched him, but nothing changed.

At the foot of the bed she gripped his bony ankles and pulled, but his skin loose and baggy caught in the sheets and his weight surprised her, his body thick and limp. She braced herself, yanked and grunted until he came off the bed and thumped over the edge, his plastic neck brace bouncing on the wood trunk. Elsa fell backward into the dresser, hard, knocking over picture frames that clattered around her shoulders and head.

"Mama?" a small voice whispered from the other room.

Elsa moved her hair out of her face. "It's all right, Hester. Go back to sleep!" Her voice squeaked, adrenaline like grease to her throat. She sat on the floor with her husband's feet tangled in her hair, his body half cocked on the wooden chest.

"Was that Papa? I heard a noise in his room."

"No, honey, it was just me! Go back to sleep!"

"But what was it?"

"It was me! I bumped into the dresser and I knocked some things down. Stay in bed!"

"What things?"

"Picture frames."

It was quiet for a moment while her daughter worked this out.

"Are you hurt?"

"No, Hester, I'm all right. Thank you. Go back to sleep now!"

"Okay, Mama."

She waited in her coat, sweating, quaking with a strange kind of hilarity. The quiet resettled but a manic energy twisted through her mind. Standing, she buckled his harness, pulling the straps tight. *Wouldn't want to drop you again now, would we?* She strained against the strap and dragged him from the room, breathing deep through her nose and trying not to make noise—*she sounded like a horse!* It felt less like she was doing something and more like she was being carried by the fierceness of a momentum, what she could only follow, what had been set loose all those weeks ago inside the stillness of that blue, blue day.

The gloves on the kitchen table where she had left them. The baby monitor in her pocket. The fever in her head. The front door she swung open wide.

Outside, the moon cast lines of purple shadow through the trees and she marched away from the house pulling his body across the snow. He slid more easily outside, shushing along the top crust of snow. She hardly felt the weight. After all these weeks, all these days, something inside of her had dropped away, or maybe she'd been the one to do the dropping—the shame, the worry and guilt—she could no longer hold all these things, they had to go. It had been twenty-six days since the accident, fourteen days since they took him off the machine. She was nineteen when they met, twenty-two when they married. They knew each other for ten years and, curiously, the temperature outside was only ten degrees.

In the middle of the field she dropped the strap. He lay there nearly naked on the snow. The baby monitor hummed in her pocket and a distant dog barked. The low globe of a frozen moon hung like a lantern behind the trees.

Elsa hovered over him, watching. Her breath exhaled in white streams. The trees near and far popped as the sap froze and cracked the wood, the sound a restless knocking, an invisible fist rapping against doors with no one there. She shivered and moved her feet. The moon lifted its light. The dog stopped barking. The snow sparkled dry.

He shivered on the ground. Or was that a trick of the dark? Elsa crouched, put a hand to his heart. A tremor, almost imperceptible, vibrated his chest. "It's all right, love," she said. "We will be fine." And she was crying.

The harness scraped across the snow, its silver buckle glinting. His arm twitched, his legs jerked, and then his body came alive. It shook in a spasm and his eyes sprung open their icy glare, tubes flinging in spastic shadows, his body unhinged from the stillness he was so long bound to, all those days, all those nights, and she cried out and held him and covered his body with her own.

Something inside him clicked. A turning off, as if by a switch. He went still. Beneath her his chest groaned with the slow creak of a tree branch as it fell, achingly, deflating beneath her. All movement stopped. His pupils dilated like dark ice melting in warm water.

You are free, she thought, holding her breath. She pressed his hands to his chest. Silas was free.

Above them all was still save the plastic sheeting around their house, a giant white lung, breathing.

SPRING

18

Ethan Arnasson sat hunched at the kitchen table over the tractor parts lined up on a rag draped over his leg. An old Tupperware container held the dirty parts soaking in solvent, and the
tractor head rested on sheets of newspaper. He rubbed at a six-inch
bolt, digging out the grime while outside the rain pattered along
the windows.

"Is she planning to sell? Or get a job? She has to be running out
of money." Luvera sat at the table with the butter churn, a glass
jar with a crank handle and wooden paddles, the same kind his
mother once used. She draped a kitchen towel over her lap and
squeezed the churn between her knees. "Though I suppose she
wouldn't say anything to you about money even if she was, and
who knows what's going on in that head of hers." She looked up.
"How short did she cut it? All that hair. I hope she at least donated
it to one of those places that makes wigs for cancer patients."

He choked on a laugh.

"What? She had a lot of hair. Pearl Jones didn't have half the
amount of hair and she donated." She cranked the handle, her
back stiff as a board, her voice at the same pitch as the wet smack-
ing of the paddle, *flap flap flap,* and it wasn't right to keep children isolated like that, and had he ever seen any schoolbooks or
homeschool programs? Did she even have a program? As if Elsa
invited him inside all the time when really it had only been that
one occasion.

He wished he hadn't mentioned it now, should have realized

he'd be stirring up the hornets' nest. Ethan could predict the habits and patterns of his wife, knew what would annoy her and the tone she would take before she even spoke a word, and yet were these annoyances of hers to ever disappear, he would be indefatigably lost. He depended on them, relied on their energizing blaze the same way he relied on the sun to come up each day. Were Luvera to not complain, he'd inquire as to her health.

"It's just unrealistic to think they can stay living there," said his wife, going on like the rain. "Maybe she got through one winter but only with help. How many times did you go over there? It was a lot, I know that."

He knew her concern for Elsa and the kids came from a place inside her so lonely, she had to dress it up again and again with her good intentions and worries. All they had now was this old farmhouse, and he'd never felt the emptiness of it so much as he did that winter. The quiet, cold days a banquet of sorrow they each sat at alone, digesting one memory after another.

After the funeral they kept Hester and Finn at their place for two weeks, would have gladly kept them all winter had Elsa not called once she felt better to say that she wanted them home. Ethan couldn't argue that. Every week he went over there to bring her water; he left the jugs at the bottom of the hill where she left her empties. Sometimes he would see her, out there shoveling snow, swinging the ax. In his estimation Elsa was doing what she could to do things the way Silas would have wanted them done, and he didn't doubt her ability to homeschool the children if that's what she had it in mind to do.

Still, he was struck by how much she had changed. With her new, short hair, the bones of her face were more pronounced, sharper, it seemed, and so, too, was her tongue. "Easier to take care of," she'd said during his visit. "With this length, I don't have to wash it as much."

"I suppose."

"But you don't like it."

"I didn't say that."

"You don't have to."

He regretted not saying something when they put Silas on that medication. It must have prolonged his death, the way he hung on, it was unnatural, and that couldn't have been easy for her. Still, he thought she would see reason once he passed. He thought her staying at the house was about Silas. But the more he went over there and saw her hauling around water and slamming that ax, the more he thought it was about something else.

"I don't think she's suited to life out here, I really don't," Luvera was saying. "If you're going to live out in the country, you've got to learn how to do things yourself or go without. And you know that's not how she was raised. It's not just you who's been helping her out. She has men from the logging crew coming over, splitting her firewood, fixing her generator."

"What's this?"

"Tommy Kroplin, from the logging crew. Netta said he's been going over there every other weekend."

"Going over to Elsa's?"

"That's what she said."

"So, you're hearing this secondhand."

"Well, she doesn't invite me over for coffee."

It was Good Friday when Ethan had come with the water and Elsa invited him in. He sat at her table and she brought out a plate of pastries, which he couldn't eat, he had no appetite, but he sat with her and drank the coffee. "We're doing all right," she said when he asked. "We got through winter, so that's something, right?" He nodded and fingered the handle of his mug. "So, what's next?" he'd said. "Where will you go?" She sat up straighter in her seat. "Oh, we're not going anywhere," she said. "We're staying right here. This is our home."

He set a clean bolt onto the newspaper.

"I understand that it's hard to get things done with children underfoot," Luvera was saying. "But she could bring them over here. I would be more than happy to watch them, but she doesn't even ask. Hester used to love helping out with the animals in the barn."

She cranked the handle—*flap flap flap*—and how they had been feeding the draft horses all winter long, and if Elsa wanted to sell any of the equipment they had just going to waste in the barn—*flap flap flap*—they could raise some money to finish the house. Her thighs and hips spilling out over the wooden seat. Good childbearing hips. "Yet another waste," he imagined her saying—*flap flap flap*.

Sometimes her voice got inside his head and he couldn't get it out. When his mother beat the cream into butter all those years ago, it didn't seem to him quite so loud. All those hundreds of times on all those ordinary mornings, what came so easily then, the peaceful, perfunctory motions of an ordinary day. He and his brother having coffee, their uncles coming around, the cream and the sugar and the way they all teased Mother. Just everyday mornings, routine, but the dearness of those times came back to him with a fierceness like hunger.

"You got any cream for that coffee?"

"What?"

"Cream? For the coffee?"

"Of course we have cream. I'm sitting here with the cream from what you milked yesterday."

"That's good."

"What's good?"

"The cream. For the coffee?"

She stopped her cranking and thudded the churner down on the table. "Does Elsa bring you cream for your coffee? When you go over there?" She stood, opened the fridge so the condiments in the door shelf rattled. "Some kind of fancy cream she gets delivered from Paris, France?" She yanked open the silverware drawer so the cutlery jumped. "You've always taken your coffee black, Mr. Arnasson. We've been married forty years and always black." She set the cream down, held on to the spoon.

"Mrs. Arnasson?"

She turned over the spoon in her hands.

"Do you have something to say?" he said.

"I want you to talk to me."

"About what?"

"I don't know. What do you and Elsa talk about when you go over there? Do you talk about the accident? Because you haven't, you know, not once. At least not to me." She sat down and slid the spoon across the table like an offering.

The rain that fell on the window glass wiggled down in shadow drops that crawled across the table like a disease. He wanted to tell her about the accident, but he didn't know how to say the boy's name. It took him years after his brother died before he could say "Robby" without feeling the stain, how he'd let his brother down, it spread through him in a silent bleed. He didn't know how to talk about the past without stirring up the pain, but he wanted the boy's name to live on in their house. He noticed that Elsa wasn't afraid to say his name.

"Did you know she's always wanted a sister?"

"Who, Elsa?"

He nodded. "She's an only child."

"Well. Everyone always thinks the grass is greener."

"She's had a very different life than you and me."

"I'll say. Private schools and horseback riding with winter breaks in mountain chalets."

"You know how to ride a horse, Mrs. Arnasson."

"Only because I had to. We didn't have ATVs or four-wheelers. Your family was the one with all the fancy toys."

"That was Robby," he chuckled, remembering. "He always talked our uncles into getting the newest-fangled contraption, his enthusiasm so infectious nobody could say no to him." He turned the bolt over in his hand. "You know, right before it happened, I thought I saw him."

"Who?"

"Robby. In that moment just before the tree cracked, something about Silas standing over there was so much like him."

"You thought Silas was Robby?"

"Looked just like him. When he was younger, the way he moved, it near about stopped my heart." He set the part down. "I wish he could have known her. I wish Robby could have met the woman Silas married, seen the family they made. He would have been so proud."

Luvera scraped her chair back hard across the floor. She went over to the back door and pulled on her jacket. The dog trotted over, wagging its tail.

"I'll just go over there myself," she said, pulling on her boots. "I'll bring the water this time. You stay here with your coffee and your cream." She opened the refrigerator, jiggled all the condiments in the door shelf.

"What about lunch?"

"Make your own lunch," she said. "We have to get this squared away, all that equipment just sitting in our barn, the draft horses and what they eat, all the vet bills." She grabbed a jar of milk, a carton of eggs.

"Did I do something wrong?"

"I don't know, Ethan, did you?"

It was as if he were inside a fishbowl, the glass wall between them distortive. He didn't know what it was she thought so urgent and important. She backed out of the driveway with the windshield wipers flipping. His wife, driving away. Disappointed, Maggie dropped to the floor. The rain pinged heavy against the window glass.

Ethan slid over his coffee. He took up the spoon and gave it a good stir; then he poured in a thin ribbon of cream and watched it swirl, making a pinwheel, a time machine that took him back, unwinding all that he'd done.

Robby when he talked to you always smiled like he couldn't help it, no matter what he was saying, he made people laugh. When he raced motorcycles out on the ice—and it didn't matter whose bike he rode—he leaned way down on the curves so low, the snow burnished his pants, and he always came in first. He always won. That was Robby.

Ethan watched from the sidelines, the responsible one, the older brother; he played it safe. It never occurred to him that Robby wouldn't bounce back, that he wouldn't be okay.

Since before kindergarten Robby carried an inhaler, and by fifth grade he'd advanced to a nebulizer with its plastic medicine cup. The neb became a part of Robby, like his skinny arms and legs. In grade school they raced dirt bikes together and studded the knobby tires by hand so they could go faster in the snow. As they got older and the lakes froze, they fit motorcycles with metal spikes to race out across the ice. When the air turned cold and filled with woodsmoke from chimney fires, that irritated Robby's lungs, but he never wanted to get left behind. During the fall they'd be outside playing football, and he'd have to run back and forth into the house for his neb. Ethan never thought about that, how hard it was for his little brother to keep up, to be a part of things. He never suggested, for example, that they stay inside, maybe play board games for a change. Robby never complained. He went into the house, where he'd have his episodes, and the wheezing when it got bad would scare their mother half to death, and she'd call for an ambulance, and off Robby would go, wailing sirens all the way.

One day Ethan came in from doing the chores to find all the

52

windows open and the doors flung wide, the entire house eerie quiet. Their parents were at an auction several towns over.

He was seventeen, Robby twelve.

"Hello?" Ethan called out. "Anybody home?"

Only the curtains fluttered.

Rounding the corner, he found Robby on the floor, legs sprawled out in front of him, face blue and eyes bulged. Robby held one hand pressed to his diaphragm, the other propping him up. His mouth hung open and his eyes when he lifted them held pure fear. No fooling around. Ethan scanned the house with its flipped books and strewn papers, Robby's backpack emptied and turned inside out; he put two and two together and ran from room to room until he found it, the nebulizer, but by then it was too late, and Ethan had to call the ambulance himself.

The ride into town was not the glory ride he'd always envisioned it to be. Robby slumped on the gurney with all his attention focused inward, the light gone from his eyes. The medics fit him with an oxygen mask and hooked him up to a machine that could monitor his vitals, and they talked to him in low, steady voices, trying to keep him calm. All the way there it was like sitting on the edge of a pin. He was afraid to inhale, to take up too much of the air.

But Robby made it, he came back, his parents and everybody at the hospital so relieved. And that was the thing. They were constantly made to feel grateful for Robby's ongoing existence whereas Ethan was just the one always there.

19

Luvera Arnasson barreled up the hill of the long dirt drive. The rain in the process of eroding the snow, the ground slushy and slick, and she gunned the engine, her tires spinning hard in the mud. Sliding the last few feet around the corner, she fishtailed left and jammed the wheel right. She barely got up the last few feet to the large bare lot where she could turn around, but she knew how to handle the Jeep.

Rain spit on her windshield. The wipers whined.

The house sat up there in the hill like a ghost ship wedged ashore, the plastic sheeting torn sails that hung in strips. *For the love of Pete,* she thought, and all the steam went out of her. The last time she saw the house was Christmas, three months ago. She called them to check in, but Elsa rarely answered the phone. When she did, she didn't even bother to hide the disappointment in her voice. Luvera gathered up everything into her arms, pulled up the hood on her raincoat, and hurried outside.

The rain pounded until she escaped under cover of the temporary porch. "Hello!" She knocked on the door. "It's Aunt Luvey! I've come with the milk!" She pulled down her hood to check again that the family car was parked at the bottom of the hill. Garbage bags stacked higgledy-piggledy made a wall to her right, and to her left a pile of wood splits were dumped haphazardly on the floor. Someone could trip over those splits, she thought, kicking them aside, and didn't Elsa know where the dump was? She knocked and called again. Maybe they couldn't hear her, she thought, she could hardly hear herself with the rain clattering against the plastic roof.

Luvera checked the door. It was unlocked. She pushed in.

"Elsa?" she called softly in case the baby was sleeping. "It's me, Luvera." The door to Finn's room stood open. She heard no other sound but the rain pinging on the chimney pipe, and all the lights were off. The house dark and cold, deserted in the middle of the day—it was almost noon, lunchtime, and where else could they be in all this rain?

Moving carefully, she stepped over toys and ducked under the clean clothes that hung around the woodstove. The dining room table was crammed with art supplies, stacks of mail, a bucket of rocks. From the kitchen came the light scamper of rodents, the clink of dishes stacked in the sink. *Good heavens,* she thought, *how disgusting.* Luvera set the eggs and milk on the counter, the house so cold it was like a refrigerator.

She wrapped her jacket tighter around her. Outside the wind blew, the ceiling beams creaked, and from above came the patter of rainfall. There on the wall was the face of Silas. He was everywhere, hung on the walls and cupboards, drawn in pencil, in crayon. His face, among the other drawings done by the children, what Elsa must have done, the colors strange and psychedelic, hasty, unfinished, but the face. Elsa had captured him. It was something Luvera could feel: his smile and the light inside him his very countenance in every single one. The drawings were alive on the page; it was more than just resemblance; it was the light of him.

Luvera brought a hand to her throat.

It wasn't that she was jealous; she knew that did not become a woman of her age. No, it went far deeper than that. What lurked in the far recesses of her heart because she wouldn't articulate it, wouldn't awaken what could only twist its infliction inside of her, the guilt she felt for making Silas suffer, insisting that he could get better when really, it was his time to go. Silas was never hers to begin with, and she knew that. She'd always hoped he would marry, start a family of his own. But then he had chosen *her,* and Elsa with her upbringing had required from him so much care! Nothing about who she was made her suitable for life out here, but it was more than that, and Luvera would never say it, would never even confess it to a priest, but in the darkest, quietest places of her heart, she reckoned with the unfairness that some people should be given so much, and then look around to what others had, and take away even that. Because she couldn't stop herself from thinking how Silas would never have agreed to take on such a big logging job at the end of the harvest season had he not been trying to please his wife, had he not been in such a hurry to finish the house. It was too much! Anyone could see, but he did it anyway, for her, even though he must have been exhausted, because she couldn't wait.

Luvera wiped her face and turned away, fumbling in her pockets for a tissue. Her big-hearted, tree-hugging golden boy and his wife, so tall and stunning. The day they got married, not even in a church but outside in an open field with pollen and seed spores floating around, making everyone itch and sneeze. Elsa wore a dress of smooth white satin with little pearl buttons all down her back. And Silas had come to them after the ceremony, embraced first Ethan and then her, taking her hands in his own and smiling wide as the whole sky. "Just give her a chance," he'd said. "I know you'll come to love her just as I have. She could use a positive role model in her life."

That stuck in her head, it had surprised her, him saying that, because she would never think of herself as a positive role model, although she had always wanted a daughter.

Elsa was nineteen when her mother passed, Silas ten when he lost his dad. Luvera supposed that was the common bond between them, losing a parent so young. She looked again at the pictures of his face, and that was one thing she always felt from him, that he appreciated her. It was quite the opposite of the way she felt around his wife. The first time they met, Elsa's eyes had dipped down to the slippers Luvera wore in the middle of the day, and Luvera saw it, the judgment on her face. Still, he had asked her, *Just give her a chance.*

A strange kind of warmth passed through her. The rain outside accelerated, pounding against the window glass. They needed a fire going in the woodstove, a pot of soup bubbling on the stove. She should wash the dishes and the windows so that the sun—when it came back—could shine through the gloom. The warm feeling grew, and she was suddenly glad that Elsa and the children weren't home and hoped they would stay gone a few hours at least. Shrugging off her jacket, Luvera rolled up her sleeves, and thought, *Where to begin?*

20

Elsa Arnasson stood outside in the rain in the woods behind the house and raised her ax. She brought it down and cracked the log in half, sidestepped, swung, cracked the log into quarters and peeled away the splits. Rain drenched her hair, her face; it gusted sideways through trees and splattered mud on her creosote-stained jeans. She wiped water from her face, tossing the splits, and pulled down another log; then cracked and halved and quartered and split. The ax head thudded as the steel blade cleaved and her boots turned on leathered mats of slickened leaves.

Behind her through the trees the back of the house sat flush with the ground, where Hester and Finn sat in the unfinished second story, dry for the most part, protected by the Tyvek wrapped around the studs. Elsa had packed them a lunch and snacks, gave them each a soda made with cane sugar because she needed some time alone. She wasn't in a good place. Thick patches of snow clung to the shadowed ground but the rain had pummeled and cleared the paths. Silas had made these paths, driving around in the ATV; he'd sawed and stacked these logs years ago when they first started clearing their land. The spring season in many ways the harder season because of the wet that came with the cold, and they had gone through the pile of logs split by the men, but she wasn't worried, not anymore.

Water dripped from her hair, her lips; she pulled down another log and kicked aside the splits. All winter she had hauled water and heated water, built fires, chopped wood. She stood the logs up and attacked them one by one, swung her ax, threw it down, heaved and sweated and swore. She had swung the blade between her knees and over her head and across one shoulder like a fighter; she had swung and slipped and missed and fallen; stood the logs up and hit them again and then again; she kicked and cursed and yelled until her fingers froze and her face went numb and her eyelashes froze to her skin. The air so cold it ripped through her lungs and turned her breath to ice, while the snow slid away from the tarp, dry as sand. Every day she went down to the woodpile and put into those logs what she wanted to get out of herself.

It was grief that taught her how to use an ax.

Her body had lost its softness, the cords of her muscles now tight and hard as the wood she beat upon. Her hair kept getting in the way, so she had chopped it, tied its bulk into braids and snipped through. Every day she pushed and shoveled snow—from the footpaths, from the solar array. She cleared and dumped and emptied and washed, these practical motions what she pressed herself through like a sieve, the sloppy juices of life drained away, the dry, hard bits left behind. She went to bed when her kids did and fell into dreams that repeated her days: haul water, shovel snow, split wood. It was these motions that saved her, gave weight to her reality, grounded her thoughts, focused her days.

What she had learned: Grief isn't just about the person you lost; it's about losing the person who you were when you were with them, and who you go on to become.

She told no one what she did that night and never would. Some things only made sense in the moment they were done. She'd been the eye of her own hurricane that night, so certain and calm, her directive given, after all, by Silas and the trees.

Like a ghost track in her head, she replayed his last days, what she did, what she said, and how so much of it she wished she had done better, or not at all. If she could have told Luvera no. If she hadn't changed her mind. If she could have held on one more day. The fever, it did things to her mind.

She remembered the struggle of pulling him back inside, hauling him up into the bed. She'd had superhuman strength that night, repositioning him, reattaching all the tubes. She sat with him and waited until dawn, nodding in and out of sleep.

In the morning she called Luvera and said, "It's done," as if his death had been another chore. Luvera took it only to mean that he had finally passed and nothing more. The nurse asked no questions—she saw the state Elsa was in and sent her to the doctor for antibiotics. Family and friends gathered at the service and with her children Elsa stood like a still life cast in stone. Luvera cried, Ethan wept, and Hester wailed her heartache to the moon. Elsa envied their grief; how pure it was, about one thing and not so much else.

In those first days, Silas came to her in dreams that felt more like visitations because of their visceral quality. He was whole again, and he smiled, always he smiled. He wore a white shirt with sunlight spilling through the sleeves, glowing lanternlike in the gloom. Each time he would lift his hands and pull open his shirt so the buttons popped and the fabric parted. There, where his chest should be, was instead the bark of a tree trunk. And he continued to smile, as if this were a good thing.

Elsa didn't know what the dream meant, or why he came to her again and again. Sometimes, she thought she felt him with her when she lay in bed, late at night in the waking moments between dreams. She'd turn on her side and feel the depress of the mattress move down behind her, the weight of his body nudging in and the scent of sawdust and orange peels warmed from the sun. How she wanted to turn to him and touch him, the contours of his face, the bristle of skin and his small bottom teeth. But when she moved, he was never there.

She felt these things, strange things that she did not know how else to explain.

There was the night she stood in the doorway of the children's bedroom, listening to the sound of them sleep. This just weeks after the funeral, when she'd finally gotten better and asked Ethan and Luvera to send the children home. It was as though she'd gone through a tunnel and had come out the other end, only to enter another tunnel, one that went deeper in. The world looked different to her now, and she worried about being able to take care of them. Someone tapped her on the shoulder. She spun around. But no one was there.

Winter clothing hung over the woodstove, snow pants, jackets, scarves, but the tap had been on her other shoulder. It was logical to assume that she had brushed up against the clothing, and in the end that's what she told herself, but the tap had been on her opposite shoulder. Like a school prank, where someone touches you on one side, and you turn around only to find no one there, because they are on the other side. That had been a favorite of Silas. He thought it so funny.

And then there was the Mylar balloon Finn got from the hospital, a dopey blue cupcake filled with helium that floated on a string. She was in the kitchen one night when she felt someone standing near, a faint brush of movement, of air. She spun around. That cupcake sat right there at eye level, right where a face would be. She squeaked and grabbed it by its string, led it back into the bedroom, where she stuffed it under Finn's bed. Helium balloons do that, she told herself, after a certain number of days, they come down off the ceiling and float around like that, right where a human head would be.

But a few minutes later, she watched from the kitchen as the balloon dipped under the header of the doorway, drifted out into the living room, and crossed slowly but surely over to her.

Was he still here? What did it mean, that he was still here? She saw him everywhere in the things he made, the wooden rafters and ceiling beams, all the lumber he milled by hand. The memories of who they were lingered like woodsmoke in the air.

Loggers came in January for the timber on the county land. Heavy equipment screeched and roared and rumbled through the frozen woods. They logged the land adjacent to hers, and they did this every winter, logging certain sections of state-owned property, but never had the machines come so close. Never had she been able to glimpse them moving like mechanized predators through the trees. They rolled over the ruined ground on steel tracks, long-necked cranes with great big claws that clamped around the base of trees and severed their trunks—they pulled the trees right off their stumps while they were still vertical, great leafless canopies, removed from the sky. It felt like an attack, the sight of it apocalyptic in its ruin, the grind and screech and roar of a raid. All the land ravaged, the stumps left raw and exposed, the cut branches piled in thick tangled webs aboveground, while beneath she imagined all those bereft and reaching roots. All winter the logging trucks carried away the trees, stacked and stripped in caged flatbeds that rattled and shook.

The view from her window remained unchanged, but she felt more vulnerable, exposed, with so many trees gone.

And then there was Tommy.

He had come in February to fix the oil leak in the backup generator because it was the only one that started in the extreme cold. He'd asked her if there was anything she needed, and she said yes. Tommy in the generator shed where Silas had always been, his fingers covered in engine grime; he'd used the tools that had once belonged to her husband, he'd worn Carhartts and a flannel shirt, the fact of him and the heat of him in that small dark room.

Behind her through the woods a wind gathered, an invisible force that whipped through the trees. It thrashed in the branches and shook loose a shower of rain that had caught in the leaves. There came from back in the woods the crack and break of a falling tree. With a thud it hit the ground. She jumped and turned around.

Elsa didn't see where the tree had fallen, but there across the woods was her clothesline, broken. It was cut, again, and when had that happened? Her eyes darted wild, alert, but nothing moved from behind the trees. Rain in straight pins came sideways through the trees and she hadn't noticed if the clothesline was down before because she'd been distracted by the rain.

Slowly she hefted her ax and stepped off the path. Sodden clothes lay twisted in the dirt. They would have to be washed again, and when had the line been cut, and who had done it? Up behind her sternum that darkness rolled, and the wind quickened, and the tree branches creaked overhead.

Late last night when she came out from the bathroom wrapped only in a towel, a thud had come from outside her window. Out there in the field, she thought she saw Silas, or the shape of him—a man, whisked back into shadow. A bear, she told herself, coming out of hibernation. Everywhere the woods around her were waking up, giving birth, life stirring in the mud. It made sense she would feel their presence, it made sense that she would feel watched.

But, it was easiest to imagine that it was him. How he held on, how she felt him even now, an astral shadow watching over the land.

Her actions on that night opened up something inside of her. A portal, an inner door to a dimension she had not known existed. A place inside her that seemed to go beyond, a place where layer upon layer of unspeakable acts existed, not just hers alone, but others as well, a secret lair of hidden motions, furtive acts, committed by all of humankind. In the recessed pools of her imagination the act distorted, what she had done, it became bolder, more depraved, and isolated from everything that came before. She saw him in dreams whose images haunted her days, Silas, sitting up in their field, Silas, emaciated and gray. And what he said, what he always said, *Whatever you need, my dear. Whatever you want.*

She rolled out another log, this one big around as a tire. The damp wood clenched her blade and she wrenched it free, pulled out the splitting wedge, flipped her ax head, and sent it in.

The ring of metal against metal, glint of steel, hard enough to defy reason, defy sense, but her mind told her stories and she believed them. These thoughts played over and over with a pull she couldn't resist, thoughts that ran like a faucet she couldn't shut off. And the crows at dawn had a terrible screech, but only because grief was a predatory thing and she had always thought him better than her in so many ways.

The sky opened; more rain fell. Sweat gathered in the gully of her backside, under her arms, and around her face. The steel wedge pierced the log until it sat flush with its top, riddled in cracks. Her swinging slowed and stopped. Letting the ax hang by her side, Elsa circled the log like a lion stalking its prey. She read the wood, looking for her mark, the one place where it was weak, where it would bend to her will; she flipped her ax head back around and shored up her grip, lifted and slammed, lifted and slammed.

The wood popped, the blade pierced, the log split and moaned, reluctant to give way until the steel wedge dropped through and the log stretched—a snarl of rich stringy oak, tearing but not breaking—and she threw the ax, fell to her knees, and reached in with both hands pulling, wrenching apart the two halves, the jaws of the beast, the wild creaking bones of her heart.

21

Hester sat under the roof surrounded by the plastic sheeting of the unfinished second story. Finn toddled back and forth in front of her, carrying one leaf at a time from one end of the enclosure to the other, talking to himself. The rain rattled loud on the plastic covering tacked to the beams, and the wind blew the strips that had come undone, the strips whipping like curled tongues with the rain spitting between. She could only sometimes hear the thud of her mother's ax.

"Yummy," Finn said, carrying a leaf. "Yummy."

"No, Finn. A leaf is not a yummy."

She huddled in her pink coat with its hood trimmed in faux fur, while the wind reached through the opening in the plastic. Their lunch was in a bag next to her on the floor, but she wasn't interested. Finn squatted and laid down his leaf on a pile he'd made. Bouncing as though pleased, he turned away to look for more.

Something in the corner caught her eye. Under a crowd of leaves brown and curled as burnt chips, the flesh-colored weave of a bandage poked out. The memory of her father tugged on her stomach, and she crawled over and dug through the leaves, pulling it out.

"Yummy," Finn said again from behind.

"No, Finn, this is not a yummy." It was the wrist brace her father wore when digging the trenches for the wires. It had sat up there all winter buried under the leaves in the corner of the unfinished house. His brace held the shape of his arm, and touching it brought him alive again in her mind.

She hugged it to her chest and closed her eyes.

All winter he had been fading from her mind, the exact picture of his face coming apart like puzzle pieces mixed in her head. She didn't know why she couldn't put it back together again. He used to come to her in dreams so near she could feel the warmth from his skin and see the light in his eyes. "Hester Pester," he would say, "I'm here." And she would wake with his love certain inside of her. She had never noticed before, how relaxing love was. But the dreams had faded and she hadn't felt his spirit in a long time. At night when she closed her eyes, she asked him to please come back, to please just tell her one more time that he was here so she could memorize his face, feel the tickle of his beard. But he didn't come, and she wondered why and what she had done wrong.

Hester removed her coat and rolled up her sleeve. The brace damp and so cold it shocked her skin, its smell of leaves and sand and something else, something sour, but touching it brought back memories. She could hear him laughing, the way he teased her for saying "eatmeal" instead of oatmeal, how he tossed her up into the air.

Papa had been her person, the one she could talk to, the one who always understood. It wasn't that her mother didn't understand, she did, but she was often distracted by Finn and didn't always have time. Papa would stop and listen. He told her the truth about things even if it was hard. Like when his mama died and she asked him if he was sad, and he said, "My heart aches."

At the time, Hester hadn't understood what that word meant, "ache," but she understood it now because it filled her like the hollow part of a hole. Her mother said that anything was possible, and Aunt Luvera said that miracles happened when the pure hearts of little children prayed. Hester had believed. She prayed in her own private way. But it wasn't possible for her papa to get better and it never was. She didn't understand why they had all lied.

"Yummy," Finn said. He shoved his grimy fist in front of her.

"No, Finn, not now." She turned away. "I don't want a yummy."

She clutched her arm to her chest and tightened the straps on the brace. Closing her eyes, she hugged her arm wrapped in the brace, but even with her eyes closed she heard Finn plop down beside her, babbling and kicking at the leaves.

"Go away," she said. "I don't want to play."

"Yummy." He uncurled his hand, shoved it in her face. A gray raisin covered in grime sat in the cup of his palm. He must have gotten into the bag with the food.

"Finn, don't eat that. It's dirty."

"Yummy." He opened his mouth just as she glimpsed the wiggling legs of a fat wood tick.

"No, Finn, no!" She screamed and lunged, but he closed his fist. She grabbed his hand and tried to pry his fingers apart, yelling, screeching, "Not a yummy! That is not a yummy!"

Finn held his fist tight to his chest and wailed.

Hester called through the wind and the rain, "Mama! Finn is trying to eat a wood tick!"

But the wind snatched away her words and came back with a new intensity; it clattered against the walls, the plastic strips snapping and waving all around. Then, quite suddenly, it stopped. Thick patches of steam rose from the snow, and the mist took shapes that twisted and crouched, moving like animals low across the earth.

Her brother looked out, quieted by the moving mist. His chest heaved and his cheeks pinked, the hair around his forehead moistened into dark peaks.

"Finn. Give me. The wood tick."

A raindrop landed on his nose. He looked up. The plastic sheet lifted off the rafters like a great crackling bubble and then settled back down. Hail the size of deer pellets struck against the strips, chunks of ice rolling across the boards, and the sound of it rose to a clatter. Then, as before, it stopped abruptly, all of it, the hail, the wind, the icy clatter.

Finn hiccuped and looked about. The plastic walls brightened and filled with sunlight as though someone had turned the dial of a great dimmer switch. As if they were wrapped inside a giant lemon drop.

Finn uncurled his hand. The wood tick had swollen so fat with blood, its skin stretched to a grayish green, and black legs poked out on either side of its body like coarse hairs. Without pausing or breathing or taking her eyes one speck off her brother, Hester reached for the bag with their lunch. She felt around for the red boxes and removed an actual raisin.

"Yummy, Finn." She spoke softly, as if he were a wild animal that might spook. "This. Is. A yummy." She plucked away the wood tick and replaced it with the fruit. Sweat popped out on her own brow. "Go ahead, Finn. You can eat that now. Go ahead," she said. "That is a yummy."

22

The day after the storm Elsa made herself wait. She did not go over to the farmhouse because she'd been too shaken—didn't trust herself to know what to say. But the day after that, sunlight flitted through the windows and they had their first blue sky since Easter. She drove up the short driveway and parked next to the barn with the milk house attached and the house there to her right.

She opened the back car door and Finn got out by himself, toddling across the ground. Patches of snow still spread out across the fields like a cobbler topping over dark, jammy dirt, but the driveway and yard were clear, tufts of green already sprouting. Another truck sat parked next to Ethan's relic, the new hired hand, presumably, someone Ethan had found to replace all the work that her husband had once done.

A group of pullets wandered in from around the milk house. Hester and Finn squealed and chased the young birds into a sunny patch next to the goat pens. They were away from the house, and that gave Elsa the freedom to say what she needed to say. This was good, she thought, marching up to the front door because the garage was closed. She knocked and waited, looked around again at the curtained windows of the house. But no one answered the door.

Back out into the sun where Hester and Finn chased the birds—the older hens jerking their necks with feathers fluffed, and Elsa called out to them a few words of warning and then ducked inside the milk house.

"Hello? Ethan? Luvera? Is anyone here?" She couldn't remember the name of the new hired hand. Ethan had told her about him when she invited him over, and she felt embarrassed now by her little display, the scones she'd baked, the flowers she'd bought, the fire glowing cheerily in the woodstove. She'd wanted to show him that they were doing okay—she'd done it!—she'd gotten them through winter. But apparently, she hadn't done enough. Apparently, her house needed cleaning and her woodpile needed straightening.

Elsa'd been splitting wood in the rain behind the house when Luvera had come over, unbeknownst to her. She'd been in a mood—needed to be alone. After splitting logs for three hours in the rain, she'd come back to the house to find that someone had stacked the wood splits she'd left heaped on the porch. They were arranged in the same way that Silas had always done it, neat and tidy squares of four. Her chest had bunched into an icy fist as she stood there shivering with the kids stomping behind her on the porch, all of them tired and hungry and dripping wet. She'd been afraid to go in.

The plastic tubing above her head flowed with milk and she walked down the main aisle of the barn painted gray and washed clean with nary a scrap of straw or chaff of dust. She spied Ethan, slipping off the black rubber teatcups that drew out the milk. He stooped to post-dip the cow's teats into an iodine solution, which would stain his hands yellow were it not for his rubber gloves.

"Ethan? Hey!" She waved self-consciously.

Ethan straightened, peeled off his gloves.

"I'm sorry to interrupt you," she said, again raising her voice over the noise of the pumps. "Luvera isn't at the house. Is she here? I need to talk to her."

He looked out across the rows of stalls. "What time is it?"

Elsa didn't know because she had nowhere to be, no time card to punch, no one expecting her other than her children and their end-less needs. The hum of the vacuum pumps seemed to vibrate louder the longer she stood there, and she had to shout. "Is she due back soon? I can wait for her. Did you know that the chickens are out, running all over the yard?"

Ethan raised a hand, indicating she ought to stop yelling. He led her into the back office of the barn, an area that doubled as a tack room and where he kept an iPad, a printer, and several shelves of binders. He closed the door and the room fell into quiet.

"It's good to let them out after a storm," he said of the birds, "otherwise they start to peck at each other from nerves."

"The same thing must be true for people," she said. "Hester and Finn have been fighting all morning, but now they're outside running around, happy as can be."

He regarded her for a moment, then sat behind the desk. He opened a binder, licked a finger, turned a page. "You get any hail out at your place?"

"Hail? No. Wait. Yes."

"Which is it?"

"Yes," she said. "During the storm, I think we did. Yes, we got hail. I remember now."

He regarded her again in a way that reminded her of Silas, how he could always tell when something was on her mind, but rather than asking her what it was, he waited for her to come out with it. She was glad he focused on the pages in his binder.

"I just need to talk to Luvera," she said. "I need to ask her not to come over to my house when I'm not there and mess around with my things."

"Is that what she did?"

"Yes."

"That doesn't sound like her."

There wasn't a chair on her side of the desk and so she was standing. Her body started to rock from side to side, the same swaying motion she often used to soothe Finn. "I'm sure she had good intentions." She crossed her arms as if holding herself together. "But I'm not okay with it. I thought someone had broken into my house."

"To clean?"

So, he did know. She bit down on the inside of her cheek. "Just, please ask her to call first and talk to me before coming over." She had a flash of guilt about all the times last winter when the phone rang and she'd yanked out the cord. She had to get better at answering the phone. "Could you just please tell her that for me, please?"

"Anything else?"

"No, that's all. That's what I came over here to say."

He licked a finger, turned a page. "I expect you can tell her that yourself. When you see her next."

Fingers of sunlight came through the window, illuminating Ethan but leaving her in shadow. She'd just made another mistake. She ached from the effort of holding herself together in what she hoped was an acceptable pose, a presentable manner, her skin sensitive to even the touch of her own clothes, as if she were sunburned.

Elsa wondered how she ever did this, how she ever went out into the world.

"Look, I don't mean to pit you against your wife."

"Of course not."

"I'm sorry if that's what it sounded like."

"No reason to be sorry. I don't expect you can do any harm on that front."

"Nor would I want to."

"We can agree on that." He closed the binder, opened another one. "Did you hear about the recent forecast? Another storm system is heading from the west, due to arrive tonight."

"Another, a what?" She uncrossed her arms. "More rain?"

"Or snow, depending. You never know what you're going to get this time of year." He turned pages in his binder. "Watch the radar. Another system coming up from the south will hit this weekend. These spring storms can be hard on the trees." He looked up at her. "Did you lose any trees during the last storm?"

"No. I don't know." There had been that tree she heard fall somewhere in the woods. She couldn't meet his eyes, he was so much like a father to her, always tired but his voice unfailingly kind. "I'll have to walk around," she said. "Nothing fell by the house."

"Well, that's good." He closed the second binder. "They can be a real beast to clean up." He scribbled something on a piece of paper he then tucked into the front pocket of his shirt, and he stood to put the binder back in its place on the shelf.

When he finally did speak to the problem at hand, he was at the shelf and not looking at her, his bushy hair winging out in gray tufts from the side of his head. "People like to know what they can do to help," he said, his voice low, soft. "Luvera likes to stay busy and she loves those kids. If you don't want her coming over to your place, then tell her what you do want. Just tell her what you need. She'll be more than happy to oblige."

Elsa drove into town instead of going home. She hadn't meant to upset Ethan. The thought that she had, that he might think less of her now, disturbed her even more than her frustration with Luvera. She wasn't seeing things clearly, wasn't in her right mind. She wanted to show them that she was fine, that she would carry on; instead she'd made another mistake.

She thought about her house, his bedroom door, how it had been shut all winter, and she wondered, did Luvera go in there? Did Luvera see the stains on the mattress, his unwashed clothes? She couldn't wash his clothes, his smell still alive in them, she didn't want to fold them up and put them away inside dresser drawers that he would never open again.

Sometimes at night she wore his shirts, curled herself around them, and imagined he held her in his arms. She inhaled the sawdust and pine resin and engine grease and diesel fuel. The scent of his personal musk in the folds of worn flannel soft as skin.

Tommy had smelled just like him. He had moved quiet and steady, his presence like a tree in the wood. When the temperatures stayed below zero for weeks and only the backup generator would start, the oil leak got so bad, she'd needed his help. A day in February under a sooty sky, the temperature thirty below. Tommy had come over and they loaded the kerosene heater onto the sled and hauled it up the hill. Their breath mingled in the pearly air and the exposed patches of her skin burned in the subzero cold.

They had brought the heater into the shed, the door so narrow he turned sideways to fit through. He had knelt and fingered a match and lit the wick soaked in the kerosene, brought up the heat in a fiery crown. It threw orange light around the dim room and he adjusted it with a silver knob, his gloves off, fingers bare, and the skin around his eyes also bare—everywhere else covered with wool or fleece or hair.

After the kids had gone to bed, she came back up there to bring him a thermos of coffee. The snow bounced moonlight and the air so cold her boots squeaked like Styrofoam with every step. She wore long johns under her jeans and two shirts under her sweater and a winter coat and hat. She found him crouched on the cement floor, tools spread out on a greasy cloth. He stood when she came in, while she turned to make sure the door was shut. She felt him, there. When she turned back, he stood above her, hardly any space between them. In the pooled flickering of his gaze she saw all they had lost, a shared intimacy, their yearning a shared weight. No words, the engines quiet, the door shut. In the warm hiss of the kerosene heater that threw orange shadows across the room, she fell toward him. Just for a moment she wanted comfort, a place to rest. She wanted connection, to feel his strength and hear the heartbeat in his chest.

She lay with her head pressed in the open vee of his canvas jacket. He cupped a hand around the back of her neck, and they were the only two people in the world. His heartbeat thudded under his flannel shirt and his fingers brushed against her hair and stroked the bare skin at the base of her neck. His touch, the pads of his fingers, exigent.

Before that time, they'd only ever hugged—on the day of her wedding and the night of the funeral—a quick pat or squeeze from woolen arms.

But his touch that night erupted a fire over her skin and the pain of it attracted her, lured her in. She lifted her face and he pressed her with his lips—he was right there, and she did not like the taste of him, the stench of his mouth, but his fingers came alive with their need. He held her face, his beard scraped her cheek, and she felt the press of his callused fingertips; she stumbled backward against the wall and the darkness uncoiled from within—a desperate hot rising thing—and she pulled at his clothes, wanting more of his skin. They clung to each other clumsy and rough, they wore so many clothes; she had to kick off her boots, peel down her jeans; her one bare leg as he lifted her up, pressing her back against the pegboard, maneuvering; she twisted sideways against a shelf, shoved out the tools near her head. A quick succession of groans and thrusts, the clatter of falling things, the release, a kind of hope.

He set her down gingerly; she tugged at her clothes. In the harsh return to that dark, cramped space he moved to the other side of the room.

It would never happen again. In her mind the act a consummation of their loss. They never spoke of it, then or since. Silence ranged long and awkward between them, but she lived with it by

thinking of all he had done and how at least she had given him
something in return.

Elsa lifted Finn into the red plastic shopping cart and Hester
climbed inside to sit next to him. She rolled them into the store,
past bright displays of flowers and chicks, and bought them each a
box of popcorn to keep them occupied. Everything clean and dry
and new, gardening tools, potting soil—with the snow melting she
was expected to come out of her cave. It took everything she had
just to maintain, to keep things the same. But it was spring, time
to renew!

She loaded her cart with nontoxic cleaners, sponges, a mop. She
felt like one of those roasting birds with a pop-up timer—*ding!*
Grieving done. Time to come out into the world!

It hadn't even occurred to her to wash the windows. Her mom
had never washed the windows—Winnie hired cleaning ladies. Elsa
fantasized about cleaning ladies, imagined them dragging their
carts full of rattling supplies across her field, chatting all the way,
"Oh honey, don't you worry, we've seen worse." And she would start
up the generator and they would run their vacuums and nozzles and
hoses and make all of it, the whole mess, just go away.

Elsa had no idea where she was supposed to bring the garbage.
They didn't have curbside pickup, they didn't even have a curb.
Silas always took it someplace, but she'd never asked where. All
winter she'd brought the bags outside where they froze, piling up
under the eaves of her temporary porch, but it was spring, and
they were starting to thaw. Tommy took a few of the bags for her
the last time he was there—he could do that, he said, tossing them
into the back of his truck. He drove away with her trash, and she
had no idea where he went or even how much a person had to pay
for something like that.

They were getting low on money. She had to make sure she saved enough to get the well system put in, but this was the money they lived on. She wanted to buy new bath towels, kitchen mats. But there were hospital bills and the property tax bill that came back in December still sitting unopened on the table in a growing pile of bills like the growing piles of stuff she had put off dealing with in and around her house.

A store employee stood in the aisle stocking a shelf. She wore khaki cargo pants with maroon sneakers and confidently unpacked items from a box, scanned them with her store gun. Elsa needed to get a job. It had been five years since she'd worked anywhere but on their land, and she couldn't imagine what marketable skills she had to offer. Always thought she would go back to school and get her degree, thought she would know what to do when the time came, but the time was now, and she didn't know.

At the end of the aisle, her awareness of the store fell away, and she was sucked back into that long dark tunnel where she stood frozen, isolated, alone in her head. She had lost her person, the one individual she could always count on to take her side. She felt unbalanced without him, half undone, like the seed trees left by the loggers, how those trees stood alone out in the clearing, where for most of a life, it grew a shared canopy with another tree. She'd only known Silas for ten years, but they had been the best ten years, and she had done the most growing.

She just didn't know who she was now.

As if in answer a voice broke into her head with a proclamation that rang like a bell.

"This is Elsa and she is a princess."

Elsa turned, and the reality unfolded in the aisle across from her: a young mother and her daughter, standing in front of a cardboard Disney display. They weren't speaking to her, they were discussing the characters from the movie *Frozen,* a cluster of life-size cutouts, and the cartoon character that just happened to share her name, shared even the color of her hair. The mother looked familiar, the daughter did not. A hand went self-consciously to her neck.

"Oh hey," Tommy's wife said, because Elsa was staring, she couldn't look away. "I like the new hair." She flashed a quick but harried smile.

"I'm Elsa, too." She said this to the daughter. The girl looked to be around Hester's age; she wore a pink top and a glassy-eyed stare.

Tommy's wife laughed. "Sorry," she said. "We're all tired. Back-to-back birthday parties and I still have to get Astrid to her soccer practice at the school."

"I didn't know you also had a daughter."

"Yep. One of each and another on the way." She put a hand on her stomach and only then did Elsa see she was pregnant. It wasn't entirely obvious; she was perhaps five months.

"Congratulations." The girl had bits of yellow cake around her mouth. "Do you know, girl or boy?"

"Girl."

She nodded, the scene so surreal—her kids in the shopping cart like caged animals trapped. Hester poked pieces of popcorn to them through the bars of the cart and the little boy took them into his pudgy hands, but the girl did not. She held herself still in front of her mother and stared.

"Sisters," Elsa said. "That's really great." She'd never had a sister, never played soccer, never ate plain yellow cake. *This is Elsa and she is a princess.* She felt how she held herself apart from this family, and the thought popped into her head that they should get their daughters together for a playdate; there had to be some way, Elsa was sure, to make the situation with Tommy okay—but she just couldn't remember Tommy's wife's name. Sweat creased and pooled in the backs of her knees.

"Well, it's good to see you." Tommy's wife wore jeans today, the kind with white stitching. "We should get going."

"Thank you," Elsa said, "for everything you've done." Her voice desperate, as though she were shouting from high up in a tower. "You have such a beautiful family, you've done so much, I can't say thank you enough." Her nostrils flared and the bones of her face ached.

Tommy's wife started to say something but then stopped, tilted her face.

"All the times Tommy came over this winter," Elsa said, "all the things he's done. I never learned how to use a chain saw, I don't know anything about how to fix the generators—we run them to charge our batteries, for electricity." She said this to the kids. "So, it was a huge help, having him fix the engine like that. Especially when it got so cold."

Tommy's wife held Astrid's shoulders in front of her and gave them a squeeze. "That's my Tommy," she said. Her words had a charry edge. "He would give the shirt off his back to help someone in need. That's just who he is."

Tommy's wife hadn't known, Elsa realized. "Yes. That's really great. Thank you again, thank you so much." Elsa moved her cart and lowered her head—*she hadn't known Tommy was coming over!*—their conversation a mistake, they would never be friends, and why had she thought they ever could?

Clouds from the west stippled the sky as Elsa drove home. Tommy's wife who knew how to run a snowblower, a chain saw. She probably plowed her own driveway, or at least knew how. She grew up hunting with her brothers, if she had brothers, and drove around in mud-spattered ATVs.

This is Elsa and she is a princess. Elsa spent her childhood practicing Schubert, giving recitals, studying art. She ate desserts designed by pastry chefs, flambéed sugar tarts. When they first moved out to the land, she'd relished all the outdoor chores, but she didn't do the hard ones, or what she found distasteful; she only did what she thought interesting or fun—the romanticized version of countrified life. She picked wildflowers, scratched dirt.

The wind tugged at her jacket and rustled the plastic shopping bags as they hurried up to the house. When the first of the raindrops hit against the window glass, it wasn't yet dark.

"A snake in the grass." That's what Silas had said, the reason he and Tommy grew apart. "I can't trust him. He always wants what other people have." Elsa unloaded her shopping bags and put everything away. She thought about that night in the generator shed with Tommy, the greedy press of his fingers against her skin. He'd been ready, as if waiting for that moment all along. *A snake in the grass.* She heated water on the woodstove, shifted dishes in the sink. She didn't know how to take care of what she had. "A tree never wants to take anything away from another tree." She'd thought Tommy was coming over because he wanted to help, because of his connection to Silas.

She'd thought life in the country would be good for her. Thought it was about following recipes, picking flowers.

She'd mistaken her loneliness for independence.

23

Hester sat at the kitchen table, cheek in hand. Rain pattered against the window and clattered on the plastic roof of their temporary porch. Finn in the living room played with his trains, their mother with her back to them at the kitchen sink. Spring, and all her school friends were on break. On the computer were a pair of frogs in lime green. They used their tongues to pull sight words across her screen—*make, could, go.* The brave tree hadn't made it through the winter. *One, had, by.* When they drove by it on the way to the store, she saw it out there in the clearing without any snow, and it tipped slightly to one side.

"Mama, what's wrong with the brave tree?" she'd said.

And her mom looked out her window. "It doesn't look too good, does it?"

Hester wanted to stop the car and get out and do something to help it, but she didn't know what. Her mom lifted a hand and waved and said maybe it was because they were getting all this rain and it took root in soggy ground.

On the laptop her online teacher appeared. The lessons were pre-recorded, so Hester couldn't talk to her, and the teacher couldn't see Hester, but she acted like she could. "Now you try!" she said. Hester put her hand under her chin and read out loud: "Make, could, go." Rain blew in gusts against the window glass and fluttered the plastic roof of their porch. "One, had, by." When they drove by the tree on the way back home, it had looked even worse coming from the other direction. "These, so, come." The cartoon frogs came back and hopped around and sang another song.

At the store in town, she had seen Ben and Owen. They were huddled at the end of the movie aisle and when Ben saw her, her heart did this silly thing—it jumped like a happy frog. She made her way over to talk to them, but Ben said something to his brother, who was looking through the movies and not at her, Owen didn't even see her, and Ben must have said, "Let's go," because they both turned and went away. Her heart in an elevator box dropped to the floor. Ben hadn't even waved goodbye. It was obvious he didn't want to talk to her. She felt foolish for being so happy to see them—they weren't her friends anymore, she hadn't seen them all winter. Her life, sinking into soggy ground.

"Bobo," Finn said, and smacked his train. "Bo-bo." That was his word for broken. *And the o says oh, oh, oh, oh-oatmeal.*

On her screen a talking mouse was walking across a turning globe. The mouse wore a red-and-white-striped T-shirt and it went places—paddled in boats and slurped noodles and scuba-dived. They never went anywhere. Brianna went to Disney World. Hester had called and invited her to go roller skating at World of Wheels but Brianna said no. She was packing, she said, going on a family trip for spring break.

Finn was crying now and beating his train against the wood floor.

"Mama, Finn broke his train."

"Hooray!" The mouse hopped off the globe. "Now you try!"

Hester didn't know what she was supposed to try.

"Oh, Hester, can you help him please?" Her mother in the kitchen. "My hands are covered in soapy water."

It wasn't just that Ben didn't want to talk to her, it was that he didn't want Owen to see her, like he was protecting his brother, like losing your father was some kind of contagious disease.

She got out of her chair and came over to Finn and sat with him on the floor. The wheels on one of his wooden coach cars were stuck, not turning around. She didn't want him to break his favorite toy. Taking the coach car into her bedroom, Hester got out a paper clip from her desk drawer, stretched it out to make a tool, and dug around in the axle with the pointy end. On her desk: butterfly wings and rocks and a tiny mouse skull she found in an owl pellet because owls swallow their prey whole but can't digest the bones. Once, during circle time at school, she brought in her mouse skull in a cardboard jewelry box her mother lined with soft cotton, and everybody wanted to touch it. Hester popped out a lump of pine needles that had gotten stuck behind the wheels.

"Here you go, Bugaboo."

Finn gripped the coach car in his pudgy hand. When he put it down on the floor, and the wheels turned, he looked up at her as if she had just put the sun back into the sky. She patted his head and went back out to the kitchen table to finish her lesson.

"Thank you, Hester," her mother said. "If you want to concentrate, you can go in your room. I got Finn now."

"No, that's okay." She slid into her chair. "I like to be out here."

She hit the resume button. The green frogs started singing again on her screen and the rain pattered and Finn pulled along his train. Hester knew the real reason why the brave tree was struggling. It wasn't just because the ground was wet, or because it had no friends.

It was because it had lost its family.

24

The wind came from the west, stripping the trees along the sides of the highway, and taking down a few power lines, but nothing had hit the barn or the house. Ethan drove into town early Saturday, the roads shined from the rain and littered with branches and debris, but the road crews were out early, sawing up the fallen trees. Fresh sawdust mounded like anthills on the shoulders of the road, the raw edges of tree trunks protruding from ditches. Ethan parked his truck at Hal's Feed Bin, their motto in white lettering on the door, IF WE CAN'T FEED IT, YOU DON'T NEED IT.

The banter from the men and women who stood behind the long counter of registers broke the silence he'd been driving in. That and all the damage he'd seen from the storm gave him the feeling that he'd just pulled through something. He negotiated around the endcap displays and down the narrow aisles with the red and white diamond pattern on the creaking, bowed floor.

"Live bait, coming through!" Judy Golden, a friend of theirs from church who'd worked there over twenty years, scooted past holding out a plastic baggie filled with crickets. She caught his eye and smiled. "Zip-a-dee-doo-dah!"

She said this whenever business was bustling.

"Arnasson," a voice behind him said. "That you, loafing in the aisles?"

"Coleman," he said. "You caught me." He hadn't seen Paul Coleman since the funeral, a poultry farmer who lived out in Hoyt. Decades ago, when Paul had his back surgery, Ethan took over the hundred poults Paul was raising for Thanksgiving dinners. During his first week, five of the males broke their legs. Their knees just snapped, giving out, and Ethan would find them lying there trampled upon and pecked apart by the other birds. He called Paul in great distress. "What am I doing wrong?" And Paul told him not to worry. "They're bred that way," he said, "so they can fatten up faster." Someone had worked out all the math to prove you landed ahead, even with all the broken knees. That was the year Silas became vegetarian.

Paul grinned now and hooked his hands on his hips. "How'd that storm treat you? Lose any trees?"

"Yuh, quite a few," Ethan nodded. "And every single one of them fell down on my fence line."

"Ain't that the way of it," Paul chuckled, shook his head. "We got that same problem out at our place, only I get the grandkids to help. They haul away the branches while I run the chain saw. Saves me a buttload of time." The two men were the same height, Ethan with less bulk to him almost by half, lean and rigid as a shovel in his town boots and dark jeans, Paul next to him round and pale, his prodigious belly drooped over powder-blue jeans. They stood at the end of the aisle between the birdseed and cages of live birds, the spring chicks peeping behind him in the large black bins and the peaty scent of food pellets and sawdust filling his nose.

"How are you and Luvera making out?" Paul said. "You two doing all right?"

Ethan gave a nod, and he could hear Luvera's voice inside his head, as if she stood invisibly beside him, *That man talks about grandkids as if they were standard-issue, right along with the gray hair.* He hadn't told her about Elsa's visit to the farm. Thought it interesting how after everything they'd done for her, a winter of plowing both his driveway and hers, and all the food his wife made and sent over, and how he'd made sure they had water, that Elsa would drive over to the farmhouse to complain. The first time she'd come over with the kids in months, and she'd been upset. She'd been *not happy,* he saw that. He didn't offer to haul away the garbage piled under her porch, and he didn't go over there that morning to see if they'd lost any trees.

What'd been bothering him about Elsa—it wasn't just her appearance that had changed, it was something inside of her. She'd become harder, mean, like an animal gone feral, having to fend for itself. She'd made her decision to stay, but he still didn't understand why.

"Well, say hi to her for me," Paul said, giving up on their conversation. "I think I just remembered what I came in here for."

Ethan watched him shuffle away down the aisle.

"We got us a songbird." Judy appeared beside him. "A real singer. Did you see him yet?" She indicated the tower of birdcages he stood next to, and she must have thought he was looking at them. Inside were all different kinds of birds from large to small, the mourning doves on the bottom, the smaller birds on top.

"Who's my pretty bird," she said in a cutesy, high voice. "Can you sing for me? Can my pretty bird sing, bee-bee-bee?"

A yellow bird dropped down to a swing and shook its twilled feathers.

"Oh come on, you can do better than that," she cooed. "Come on, pretty bird. Who's my pretty bird? Bee-bee-bee-bee."

The bird hopped sideways on the perch to face her. His yellow breast puffed up and he let loose a series of rolling notes that sounded about as complicated as advanced algebra. Judy looked at him, pleased.

"Not bad," he said. "Does he know any Crosby, Stills and Nash?"

Judy laughed. "We've had singers before, but not like this one. You should hear him when he gets going."

Ethan found himself inspecting the cage. "This what he comes in?"

"Oh no, you got to buy his accommodations separately." She lifted a hand and pointed to the front register. "Do they know you're here? We've got your order all ready."

He brought the truck around to the open loading dock next to the store, and the young men who worked there hefted down his bags of grain. Their yellow gloves flashed in his rearview mirror and a memory came back to him sharp and exact: Silas as a boy, the first time they took him to Hal's to see the young spring chicks—bundles of soft yellow fluff. Silas couldn't have been more than eight; he leaned in over the black bins where the chicks waddled around at the bottom under the heating lamps, peeping and tromping over sawdust curls. They were so young, all of them, Luvera before she had lost the baby, before he had lost his brother, they were all in the store together, he and Robby and Robby's son, and Ethan didn't know then what a privilege it was, to be together like that. Someone—Judy probably—lifted out a chick for the boy to hold. The memory of it so crisp and exact, he could tell the time of day from the way the light slanted across the boy's pure dear cheek.

"You're all set!" they called to him from the loading dock. Ethan put his truck into drive and pulled away.

Luvera hadn't been herself lately. She stayed up late into the night poking around on the computer, and then in the morning reported to him all kinds of information about the terrible state of the world—the toxins in plastic, additives in foods. She worried about Ebola and terrorist attacks. Conspiracy theories, sex offenders, and the altering of our DNA. She called her sister and sometimes they talked. Mostly she worried about Elsa and the kids.

Ethan was stopped at a crosswalk. An old woman with a walker had come out of the Spur station across the street. She stepped down off the curb, her purchase in a plastic grocery bag that dangled from her walker, and he could hear the double click of its metal legs every time they hit pavement, *click-click,* step, *click-click,* step. He waited with the other cars while she crossed the street, *click-click,* step, *click-click,* step, her progress so slow, it was painful to watch.

It was Luvera's mother who had sent the first statue, a porcelain blue jay that arrived on her birthday in a Styrofoam case with a cardboard sleeve. Few things took Luvey's breath away like new-born babies and the sound of a church choir, but the moment she'd unwrapped that bird, her eyes shined and she'd gasped, "Oh, what's this? What is this here?" It had a wooden stand with a gold-plated engraving in cursive script, "Blue Jay in Flight." The wings hand-painted, it came with a little certificate of authentication, along with a catalog so you could order more.

Ethan ordered her a cardinal for Christmas and then an oriole. She got a finch from her sister and slowly, the birds multiplied in their living room. They were a deviation for her, the one area of her life where she forfeited practicality for beauty's sake. It was they who became the defining décor upon which all other decisions were made. She sewed slipcovers for the sofa, matched new drapes. There came doilies and glass domes. Ethan obliged, ordering more birds, ordering domes.

And then came the year she started sending them back. It happened after they lost Katie, the baby Luvera carried for five months and then miscarried. He ordered her chickadees because he thought they might cheer her up, but she didn't want the chick-adees. "They're the only bird I see out here all winter," she'd said. "Why would I want fake ones?" So, he sent them back.

He ordered a cedar waxwing instead. It arrived chipped. The replacement came as a pair, two birds joined together, and even though it wasn't what he ordered, he thought it a nice gesture from the company to give them the extra bird at no extra charge. But Luvera didn't want the two-bird arrangement. Ethan sent the dou-ble waxwings back in their custom Styrofoam box, requesting the single in exchange. They waited two weeks, then two months. He wondered what happened to the bird, so one day he called up the company and was told they no longer made the single cedar wax-wing, it was discontinued, out of stock, and they had already cred-ited his account. Luvera threw up her hands and said forget the whole thing, she'd never meant to collect birds anyway.

"You're back," Judy said when she found him standing by the birdcage.

"How do you do this," he said. "Does it need to be let out? For exercise?"

"The bird? Oh sure. You want to do that maybe once or twice a week. Cover your mirrors and let them fly around the house."

"They house-trained?"

"I've never seen one that was," Judy said. "Put down some news-papers and get the good food." She pointed to a wooden bin filled with shiny seeds. "For some reason, the cheap stuff stains the up-holstery. I don't know why. But if you get the good stuff, they make less mess, and if they drop on your furniture—you know, you can't put newspaper over everything—it comes right up with a sponge and soapy water."

"That right?"

"Don't ask me why."

"I think I'll take her."

"Well, she's a he. It's only the boys that sing."

"That right?"

"Every once in a while, we get a girl who sings, but it's rare. This boy here, now he's a real singer."

"Better get me some of the good feed. And whatever else I need."

"Okey dokey."

She looked up the price on a handwritten piece of paper taped around a post near the cage and weighed out a few scoops of the seed. The bird was eighty-nine dollars, and she ran him through what all he needed and hit him with the grand total. "Still want to do it?" she said.

The little bird hopped up onto a wand that stuck out on one end of the enclosure and gave a loud and assertive cheep, as if speaking up for the old man.

"I guess that means yes," said Ethan.

Judy laughed. "Well, zip-a-dee-doo-dah!"

25

Luvera stood at her kitchen sink with her hands in the sudsy water and eyed the oatmeal bowl sitting next to her on the counter. It was Ethan's bowl from early that morning, the gray paste of the cooked cereal still filling up the crockery. It needed to be scooped and scraped before she could put it in the dishwasher, but every time she looked at it, she felt the chill of glaciers set adrift inside her body.

Ethan never left food in his bowl or on his plate; it wasn't how he was raised. Always he bowed his head, grateful for every crumb, and if there was a bit of crust he might give it to the dog, but usually he scraped his plate clean, especially during planting season, coming in hot and dusty from the field. Always he was ravenous, always he wanted more. Last Sunday when they were putting in the wheat, she got up early to make him his favorite: biscuits and gravy. He only ate half before he stood to go out.

"What's the matter?" she said. "You didn't like it?"

"It was fine. I'm just not hungry."

"I made it the same way I always do."

"It was very good," he said. "I have a stomach thing."

A stomach thing she could understand, but a stomach thing only lasted a few days, and this had been going on for quite a while. She tried to think for how long.

Five days had passed since she went over to Elsa's house and cleaned the windows, washed the dishes. When Elsa finally called, it was to say that Ethan no longer had to bring them water. She was going to get the well put in, soon, she'd said. "I can fill the jugs my-self." Luvera had so many questions. Was Finn learning new words? Was Hester going back to school? She'd ordered new rain boots for the kids—Hester's in bright green with little frogs, Finn's a nice robin's-egg blue. She wanted them to visit, to hear the kids talk. But Elsa said she had to go and hung up without inviting her over.

Behind her Maggie thumped her tail. She sat by the door that connected to the garage from the kitchen. The grackles under the bird feeder lifted away, and Ethan's truck blundered into view. Luvera peered and squinted through the window. He was getting skinny, she thought. At night the knobs of his spine poked through the bedsheet, and it sure took him a long time to get the feed, lon-ger than usual. Did he forget what he went into town for? Take a wrong turn on the way back home? She rinsed and dried her hands.

She didn't want to think about what she would have done had the tables been turned and it was her husband instead of Silas caught up under that tree. Every time Ethan bent by the spigot under the eaves of the barn to fill those blue water jugs up, she sent him with something: eggs, butter, fresh jugs of milk. Protection, all of it, insulation to keep the same horrible tragedy that hap-pened to that woman from ever happening to her because things just happened—lightning fell from the sky, homes burned to the ground, tornadoes took out entire towns; people were raped and robbed and pillaged. Being a Christian was the only leg up she had against the sin and chaos that overboiled in this world.

He came around to the passenger side of the truck and from the front seat removed a giant, white rectangular *thing*. *What in the world,* she thought. Throwing the dish towel over her shoulder, she hustled into the living room and opened the front door. They never used the front door. The only people who came in that way were the priest and sometimes Elsa.

"Why are you coming in this way?" she asked. "Why didn't you park in the garage?"

"I've got the feed to unload." He stepped in awkwardly with the *thing*, about half as big as he was and held out from his body. He turned around, as if unsure of where to put it. "Here." He handed her a paper sack. "Hold this."

"Mr. Arnasson, I've got a bone to pick with you."

"Now, Mrs. Arnasson, just give me a minute here." He set the large rectangular tower down gingerly on the rug.

"You feeling all right?"

"I'm feeling fine. A bit sunny, even."

"A bit sunny?" Luvera glanced at the contraption on the floor. "Ethan, why didn't you finish your breakfast this morning?"

He hung up his jacket, pegged his hat.

"You hardly touched it at all, and last night, you hardly ate your dinner. Is there something going on that you're not telling me?"

"You mean like an affair?"

"Ethan, this isn't funny."

"Man's got to get his daily vittles from someplace."

She swatted him with her dish towel and he hooted, a sound she hadn't heard in years. From inside the white thing came a shuffle. The hair on the back of her neck bristled.

"Ethan, what was that?"

"You'll see."

"Is something alive in there?"

"You'll see."

"Ethan, what did you do? This is not a zoo. I have enough to take care of as it is." She followed him into the dining room. He walked stiffly, holding out the *thing* with a curious set to his face, one of concentration, maybe excitement even. He set it down on the table and more harrumphing came from inside the white vinyl covering. As he unzippered the sides, Luvera set down the paper sack, while Ethan squinted and rolled the cover back.

"It's a bird," he said.

A bundle of yellow hopped forward.

"It's a bird!" she gasped, and a hand flew to her throat.

"That's what I said."

"What's it doing here?"

"Well, he's a songbird." Ethan whistled and directed with his hands. The canary at the bottom of the cage hopped around. "Just give him a minute. Let him get adjusted. You should have heard him earlier in the store." He whistled again with his cheeks going in and out.

Luvera hooked both hands to her hips, preparing to ask him what in the world she needed a canary for and who would feed it and clean up after it, but before she could strike the proper tone, the bird let out a series of high musical notes that seemed about to burst sunshine into the room. She inhaled, surprised. For a minute neither of them spoke. Then the bird hopped up and did it again.

"It can really sing," she whispered.

"Oh, wait till you hear him," Ethan said. "That's nothing." He folded up the covering. "You should have heard him before, going on in the store."

"Hal's Feed Bin?"

"Yuh."

"That where you got him?"

"That's where."

"You mean, you bought him?"

"I tried to get them to give him to me, but they said no." From the brown paper sack, he removed the bag filled with the birdseed and a bright pink and green bell toy. He set them on the table in a kind of display. He looked to his wife. "It opens here," he told her, fingering the cage. "Let's see."

He popped the latch, and the little bird hopped out. His yellow toes curled around Ethan's finger, and she could tell by the way Ethan stiffened that he was not expecting that, but he held his hand out and very slowly straightened.

"He likes you," she said, maybe a little jealous.

"Oh, he likes everybody," he said. "Here." He moved his hand very slowly sideways away from the cage, the bird still riding along on his finger.

"Oh, I don't think this is a good idea." She held out a finger. The bird hopped on. It hardly weighed a thing, the warm clutch of its feet, the soft tremble of a heartbeat. She nearly forgot to breathe.

"There now, Mrs. Arnasson. Say hello to your new bird."

"Hello."

The bird looked at her, opened its beak, and let out a high-pitched trill.

"Well hello to you, too," Luvera said. "Well hello. Welcome to our home. Yes, you're home now. Here you are."

"Welcome home, little buddy."

The bird tilted its head.

Luvera whispered, "Should we put it back inside now?"

"I reckon we should."

"Wouldn't want it to fly away now, would we?" She moved slowly, putting her hand into the cage. He hopped off onto his perch and ruffled up his feathers. "There you go, honey. Back inside where it's safe."

They both watched the bird with a kind of helpless astonishment. Luvera stood with one hand pressed to her heart, while Ethan stood next to her. He put an arm around his wife, and they stood like that together for a while, stiff at first, and then she tipped her head back into his chest, and they were together in a way that they hadn't been in a while.

"I've always liked the name Charlie," she said.

"Okey dokey," he said. "Charlie it is."

26

Hester was already outside waiting for her mom. She wore her old pink garden gloves for flipping over rotten logs, and her papa's wrist brace, tucked under the sleeve of her jacket. Loaded in the wagon were her ant farm with its blue-moon space gel, several buckets with plastic lids, and two shovels for scooping dirt. The rain had washed away all the snow, so today was the day. They were finally going to get ants.

A big shiny car drove up and turned around, gravel popping under its tires. It sat in the driveway at the bottom of the hill, and after a moment, a lady got out. She wore clothes like the people who came to her papa's funeral, black pants that flapped around her ankles and pointy, gravel-scraping shoes.

"Hello," the lady said. "Is your mother home?"

"Yes," Hester said. "Who are you?"

The lady went around and opened the back hatch of her car, took out a round glass dish with a white towel she adjusted over the top.

"You don't remember me? I saw you a few weeks ago at the store." The woman shut the hatch, but her engine was still on, and two little heads craned around in the back. "I'm Cherice," the lady said. "I knew your father when he was in high school. He worked with my husband Tommy on the logging crew."

"Oh," Hester said. "We're going to get ants."

"That's very interesting." She didn't sound interested. She wobbled up the dirt path in her pointy shoes. She had yellow hair like her mom's, but it was smooth and curled, and parts of her face glittered with sparkly powder.

"Can your kids come out of the car to play?" She remembered the girl now; she went to her school. The boy squashed his nostrils up against the window glass.

"Not today. We're not here to play."

"What's he called?"

"You mean his name? That's little Tommy and his sister Astrid. You played with him when we were at the hospital last fall, don't you remember?"

Hester got the feeling that she had done something wrong by not remembering, and her pants felt sticky and too tight. She wished her mom would hurry up and come out. When they got up to the porch with the garbage bags piled up, they smelled really pewy because they were thawing now, and Hester felt embarrassed. Tommy's mom adjusted the white towel on her plate and knocked on the door. Hester wanted to push past her and lock the door so Tommy's mom couldn't interrupt them, but then the lady turned to her and lifted up the towel.

"It's an apple pie," she said. "Do you like apples?"

"Yes."

"Good, because I made it for you."

"My brother likes apples, too."

Her mother opened the door. She stood blinking in her flannel shirt and stained jeans. Her hair was not shiny and smooth, it was fuzzy and tied in a short stub at the back of her neck. "Hello," she said. "What have we here?" She looked really pretty when she smiled.

"Little Tommy's mama made me a pie," Hester said.

"Oh. What a nice surprise." Her mom opened the door and they went in. "We were just going out for a walk or I'd invite you to stay and have pie."

"Oh no, I can't stay," Tommy's mom said. "My kids are waiting in the car." They stood in their jackets in the living room in the dark because her mother had turned off all the lights. "I just wanted to bring you this," Tommy's mom said. She moved back the towel, showed her mother the pie. "Oh, wow," her mother said, and Finn in his boots jumped around. "Yummy, yummy, yummy," he said. He spun in circles and plowed into the couch.

"Can we talk for a sec? In private?" Tommy's mom said. "It will only take a minute."

"What's this about?"

"You know what it's about."

The woman stood there in her pointy shoes.

"Hester, why don't you and Finn go outside." Her mother plucked Finn off the couch and set him down by the door. "You can get started and I'll join you."

"No," Hester said. "I don't want to go without you."

"It's okay, Hester. I'll be right there."

"When?"

"When I'm done talking to Tommy's mom."

"Are you going to eat all the pie?"

"No, honey," Tommy's mom said. "We are not going to eat the pie. I promise."

"Yummy," Finn said. "Mum, mum, mum." They were standing by the door and Finn was jumping and pulling on their mother's arm. Hester felt a buzzing in the bones of her face.

"I don't want to go without you! You promised you wouldn't get distracted, you said!"

Her mother's nostrils flared and the rims of her nose turned pink like she might cry. "Hester, take Finn and go outside. Now."

"But you promised!"

"I am not asking, I am telling. Out, now."

The wagon had four tires and a handle that you pulled and four steel-mesh walls all the way around. It was big enough for Finn to lie down in, and Hester could sit in there with her legs stretched out. The gates had little pins that you turned to make the sides fall down; that was how they emptied the sticks out, a nifty system, her mom said. Hester pulled the wagon far back into the woods. They walked for a long time before she felt ready to stop. It didn't matter. Her mom would just have to find them.

Nothing moved. Leaves thin and bleached as ancient paper spread everywhere under the trees. No bugs, no cold or snow or wind, and so she kept walking because the woods wanted her to, and everything looked the same.

After a while Hester parked the wagon off the path and crouched to flip over logs. She poked and inspected. White centipedes squirmed in the dirt, and she scooped them into pots for Finn, who sat in the wagon with his red shovel and spooned them back out. Her mother didn't come, and when Hester stood up, the path was gone. She couldn't see it at all, it just disappeared in the woods with the trees that looked the same, just miles and miles of long tall poles and flat leaves.

It didn't matter, Hester thought, rolling over more logs. It smelled of mushrooms and wet sand. She didn't care if they were lost and neither did Finn. He sat in the wagon she had parked at the top of a rise that sloped down through the trees. The wagon— for no reason that she could see—took off rolling all on its own— like it had someplace to go, like it wanted to go there without her—and Hester when she caught a glimpse of it moving through the woods dropped the ants. Finn, still inside, held on with his body leaning forward, his face focused, cheeks flushed.

"Finn!" she shouted, and ran at top speed. The wagon rattled and banged and whizzed over bumps and branches and stumps. When the handle got knocked, it fell, and the wagon flipped over and the gates flew off and everything inside got spilled out, including her brother.

Hester slid down the hill, falling hard on her knees. She scooped her brother into her arms. Blood poured down his face bright ketchup red, it pooled and bubbled and spilled out between his teeth. Around her in the leaves the sides of the wagon lay bent with the wheels still spinning. She felt hot and dizzy and fuzzy in her head. Finn on her lap cried, and she held him and tasted copper pennies in her mouth.

A dog barked. A big dog, it stood several feet away in the space between the trees with its feet shivering from the force of its barking in the leaves. It watched them, the ugliest, dirtiest, meanest-looking dog she'd ever seen; its head shaped like a rock, ears laid back, fur smeared in different colors like it couldn't make up its mind about what kind of dog it wanted to be so it was all of them—black, tan, brown, with fleshy patches of pink. It slung its head between the jut of its haunches and crimped its black lips to reveal sharp, oily teeth.

Finn stopped crying then; he watched the dog. It lowered its head and picked up the skull of a deer that had lain all winter under snow. The skull had brown matted fur, one eye webbed in mold, antlers twisting up crooked and deformed. The dog held it with black lips curled.

Leaves rustled and shifted. The dog skulked around them through the woods. Hester held her brother and they tracked the dog with their eyes, both of them watching as it roved in an arc. It set the skull on the ground, lifted a leg, squirted out pee.

"Fish! You come back here! Come here now."

A man came out from the trees. He was a giant, the biggest man she had ever seen, bigger even than her papa, big as an outhouse. Across his wide chest a crossbow was slung, and a knapsack hung on his back, his face round as a pie plate with black hair that spronged out. It bounced past his shoulders as he stalked out in his boots, crackling over branches and leaves.

The dog Fish set the skull on the ground and growled. They could hear the chuff of its breath, the dry rasp of its paws ticking in the brush.

"Don't you growl at me," the man said. "Don't you bite these kids."

Finn's chest lurched and shook. His ears glowed red as stove coils and his cheeks speckled in a heat rash down to his neck. The dog was to their right, and Hester held Finn to her left. She tried not to look at Fish, but he growled at them whenever he set down the skull. She held her brother tight and didn't move. A feeling like bees stinging crept up the back of her legs. They were bent in a way that hurt, making her uncomfortable and hot. She wished Fish would go away. Who would name a dog Fish? A dog was a dog and not a fish.

He snarled through slimy lips.

"What are you kids doing?" The man knelt by their broken wagon. He wore a puffy jacket over pants that were the same color as the trees, gray and white and brown and tan mottled together so he matched the woods.

"That's it now, Fish, you come here." The dog came over and the man put a hand out and held the dog by its harness. "Where's your mama? She know you're out here?" He was talking to her, Hester realized. It felt like she was waking up from a dream into another dream, and she didn't know which part of it was real.

"He got hurt." She didn't know she was crying until she opened her mouth and tasted the salt. She wiped her face with her sleeve. "I don't want him to die." Her chest hurt. It ached when she talked but she clamped everything down and tried not to make any sound or movement in the leaves.

"It's okay," he said. "Don't be afraid."

"I'm not afraid. I just don't want your dog to bite my brother."

"He won't bite. Not if I tell him not to." The man reached out to touch his dog's head, his hands big as slices of bread. Little balls of beige crumbs sat trapped in the tangle of his black beard, and when he took off his knapsack and came close, he smelled strangely of wet turtle.

"I have a first aid kit," he said. "I always bring one with me when I hunt in these woods. You just never know." He spoke calm, not like he was worried or upset. It was a normal thing, to see blood in the woods. "What's your name?" He had bandages and a pair of scissors and little blue-and-white packets of wipes in his kit. He also had a chocolate bar. Finn was interested in that.

"Finn." Hester answered for him, Finn's eyes wide as the top of filled buckets.

"Hello, Finn. My name's Al." He unfolded a moist towelette, held it to her brother's face. "Some people call me Big Al, but you don't have to. Don't matter to me." When Al wiped her brother's chin, Finn pulled back and burrowed into her coat, but Hester held him and squeezed her brother tight around his chest.

"It's all right," she said to Finn. "If you die, it won't hurt at all. It will be like taking off your hat."

"That's right. Shouldn't hurt a bit," Al said. "The body protects you when you get hurt, it throws you into shock so's you don't feel a thing."

Hester watched Al clean off the blood on her brother's face. When he asked Finn to look up, his mouth opened and blood dribbled out mixed with his spit. Behind them the dog moved again through the leaves.

"Oh, I see," Al said. "Looks like a split lip." Al daubed at her brother's mouth. "Don't look bad, though. Just a little cut. You'll be all right."

Finn clutched all his fingers around Hester's arm and kept his head pressed to her chest and that made her feel solid and strong. She felt him breathing against her, felt his heartbeat and the heat coming from his head. He trusted her, and she had to protect him. He needed her; they were bonded in a new way now.

"What's your name?" Al said. "My name's Al." He said this to

Hester as if she hadn't just heard him tell it to her brother. "Do you live here in these woods?" The wet wipes Al used were sitting in a pile on the ground covered in her brother's blood. The dog named Fish slowly crept behind Al, sniffed at the wipes, and took one in his mouth.

"I have a place just south of here out on Yarrow Road," Al said. "I like to hunt in these woods, turkeys, sometimes grouse. I used to hunt deer but can't no more. Does your daddy take you hunting?"

The dog held the bloody towelette between its paws and pulled at it, shredding the cloth with its teeth. The dog was eating her brother's blood.

"Bobo," Finn said. Al turned the broken wagon over and picked up the loose gates flung out on the ground. He kicked at the leaves looking for the pins but only found one.

"Looks like the front axle got bent." He wiggled the handle around. "How far are youse from home?"

"We don't have a papa anymore," Hester said. "We're going through a hard time."

From far away up on the hill behind the ridge came the echo of a voice or maybe an animal that had chittered in the trees.

"I'm sorry to hear that." Al's breath wheezed as he packed up his first aid kit, and there was something different about his eyes. One of them wandered off by itself, in a different direction from the other, and that made him seem confused or lonely, or maybe mad. He fitted everything back into his pack and slung it over his head and adjusted the crossbow on the other side of his chest. All the papers from the bandages he just left there littered on the ground.

"I can give youse a ride," Al said. "My car is just on the road."

Hester took the hand of her brother and they stood. Across from them at the bottom of the hill a flat stretch of trees ended where a car was parked on the side of a dirt road. A dark blue sedan low to the ground with dead grass and matted leaves around its tires.

"Come on," he said. He held out the chocolate bar. A whole

Hershey bar in brown-paper wrapping, and he gave it to her little brother.

A wind crawled toward them through the leaves, ruffling only the top layer. An ominous buzzing sound came from across the road, a dark sound like the hum of bees, an entire swarm of them, Hester thought, hiding behind the car in the woods. A hot prickle rose along her spine. She had a feeling then, like something bad had happened back there. A voice floated down from behind them on the hill—her mom, calling them home—and it came to her then how wrong it was to take candy from a stranger, how wrong to go with him in his car.

"We have to go!" She grabbed Finn's hand. "Run!"

And together they scrambled up the hill through the woods.

Later, after she told her mother about how Finn got hurt and about the big man in the woods and his dog named Fish, and her mother carried Finn into the house and he stopped crying because he wanted the candy—Hester made him drop it when they started to run—she saw the wagon. It sat parked at the bottom of the hill next to their car although they had left it in the woods. Her mother had carried Finn all the way home. It was dinnertime, and they were both inside.

Hester padded slowly down the dirt walkway. Something colorful was inside the wagon. Only two of its sides were on, and the handle stood up. Inside the flatbed were stacked the other two gates, one of the buckets, and the ant farm, which had cracked. A small stuffed animal sat on top of it all. A bunny with excited blue eyes painted on its fleshy face, it wore a hot-pink dress with a white ruffled apron, new but not soft, the fabric scratchy, stiff, and cheaply made.

The air felt deliberate and cool on her face. It was so quiet, she heard the whine of a car out on the road, its engine winding up far and away. Smoke from their chimney clumped out and blew apart across their field.

She thought of Al's rattling breath and turtle smell and weird eye and the feel of her brother's hand, warm and trusting in hers. She gripped the handle of the wagon and pulled. It came with a hitching scrape, and the bunny shivered on top. She dragged it into the woods behind the woodpile and stuffed it with leaves and branches and piney boughs so that she didn't have to look at it again.

As she walked back up to the house, the woodsmoke rolled out across the unfinished second story and the plastic crackled and swelled. Something else lying out in their field caught her eye. Hester paused. It was the glass pie plate brought over by Tommy's mom. It lay inverted in the matted grass with beige lumps and chunks of apple scattered out across the ground.

27

Elsa lay awake on Hester's bottom bunk and listened to another storm. Blue lightning glimmered along the bedroom walls and muffled thunder rolled around them in the dark. She counted the beats between the lightning strikes, the storm moving closer, the thunder shaking the house.

She remembered the storm they had during the spring when Finn was twelve weeks old. The rain poured down around the little house, and they were wrapped in a cocoon of white noise, the perfect insulation for predawn lovemaking. Next to her in bed Silas poked her in the ribs, but she pulled her knees tight to her chest. He stroked her neck, wrapped one leg around her hip.

"Not now," she groaned, "I'm tired. Let me sleep."

"But there's a storm," he whispered in her ear, "kids won't hear a thing." And it was true, but she held back. Always she held back. Even before the baby came, even when she wasn't pregnant, he had to draw it out of her, slowly, painstakingly. Having sex was different from making love; he wanted to know her, the real self she kept locked away in some room. It took years before she could open to him, not because she didn't want to, but because of something inside of her, something hard and stuck and unyielding as stone. Over the years, she had started to emerge, this new version of herself, how he saw her, kinder and nobler and who she wanted to become.

She didn't know how to get close to people. Her conversation with Tommy's wife had gone its own way like a live hose gushing water. "How can you not know where the dump is?" she'd said. Words sprayed every which way. Elsa couldn't follow, couldn't control it, didn't have any idea what to say. There must have been some way to explain it—how much Tommy reminded her of Silas, how being near him made her feel calm, secure, more like herself. Instead she'd said, "Nothing happened," which wasn't true, and that had only made Cherice mad. "Of course nothing happened," she'd snapped.

And worse, she'd let her kids down. She hadn't kept her promise to Hester, and they'd gotten lost in the woods. They met a hunter who gave Finn candy and offered them a ride in his car. Who was this man and where did he live? After Cherice left, Elsa stood outside calling their names, the foul odors of garbage wafting from her porch.

All week she'd been trying to get rid of the garbage. She'd plugged in her laptop, waited for the dial-up, and learned about a recycling center in the west end of town. She wrote down the address, loaded up her car with the garbage crammed in the back with the kids, and drove the thirty miles in; when she found the recycling center, it had been shut down—closed!—the notice posted on the outside of the fence. It gave the address of another transfer station—that's what they were called—but it was located in a neighboring town, only open on certain days, not on that day, and she'd had to drive the hour back home with all her garbage rattling in the car.

A heavy thud came from out on the porch, followed by a clatter, and a clink. She sat up, got out of bed.

In the lambent flares of heat lightning a pair of yellow eyes flickered and glowed. A dog, large and with its head shaped like an anvil, slunk across her porch. Attracted by the smell, no doubt, now that her garbage had thawed. It tore open her bags, nosed into cans.

She threw on a sweater, grabbed a flashlight, and opened the door. "Go!" she yelled at the dog, her voice quiet and low. "Get away!" She stepped forward, stomped her foot.

The dog didn't move, its body lean and dark from the drizzle.

"Go!" she yelled with a hiss. "Get! Get out of here!"

The dog lifted a leg, shot out urine onto her porch, then picked up a can and slunk out to her field. Lightning forked behind the trees and lit up the yard. The dog humped out to the middle of her field. Thunder snapped and growled.

All night long the dog came and went from her porch, rustling through her garbage and setting loose rolling cans. In her mind its movements strange and haunting like the shapes in her nightmares, as if her dark door had let it in, opened up a kind of Pandora's box so now all manner of horrors were drawn to her, the depraved and grotesque, the alone and distressed, moving in from the outer edges as all night it thundered and poured.

In the morning she found her field littered with garbage and strewn with debris. Bottles, cans, shreds of paper in the dead, matted grass. Sticks and branches of every size with swags of pine-needled boughs. A large balsam fir had fallen by the garden, and the shorn limb of a maple lay across her field like a giant clawed hand. On the porch, garbage bags lay knocked over at her feet, their sides bulging and split with entrails of soggy tissues and fruit peels across the boards.

She dressed Finn in a sweatshirt with a hood, pulled on her work gloves, and got out the rake. She would take care of this today. She would find one of those transfer stations and throw her trash over the fence if she had to. She raked and stooped and filled new bags. She brought them down to the car and found her driveway blocked. Three balsam firs, their trunks no bigger around than soup cans, all fallen across the driveway with their wet spiny boughs. She tried to lift one, but it was long and heavy and wouldn't budge. She fisted a hand to her waist and brushed away bugs, the air steamy and filled with gnats and whirling things.

Elsa hunted in the woodpile for her ax.

She wanted to forget. Forget everything that had happened, everything she had done, everything she had failed to do and couldn't say. She was so sick of being the person who didn't know, the person who got it wrong. She was so tired of making mistakes. She wanted to leave—which was how she'd always solved things whenever it got hard. Leaving solved everything, fixed every problem, made everything go away.

But it only started the cycle up all over again.

She raised and lowered her ax. The blade bit into the wood, and bits of yellowed pulp chipped out, spongy and damp. Her boots crackled over the evergreen boughs that had fallen across the dirt drive, and the smell of sap and freshly shorn trees scented the air. Finn toddled about dropping sticks into puddles. He crouched and peered, while mosquitoes landed and bit. Welts swelled up in red patches on his skin, and wood frogs clattered and clacked in the bogs.

She didn't want to leave. She wanted to learn how to stay. To understand deep and abiding friendship—to be a friend like that. To be liked by Ethan and Luvera. To be certain about what to do and who she was and where she belonged.

"Mama! I had a bad dream!" Hester stood outside the house in her pajamas, hair mussed, pajama bottoms riding up around her calves.

"Go back inside, Hester. Get dressed."

Noticing all the damage from the storm, Hester fell quiet. She padded down the hill in her bare feet and stopped short of the mud where their driveway began. "What happened?"

"Another storm." Elsa slammed the ax.

"Mama, can I ask you a question?"

Again she slammed.

"Mama, is hell real?"

The heartwood bound the two halves of the tree like a cord, and she slammed the blade again and again.

"Mama, is hell real?"

The tree snapped.

"Mama?"

"He's fine, okay?" she yelled from the driveway. "I'm sure your papa is not in hell. He's doing better than we are, I swear to God. Now please, just take your brother and go back inside." She tossed the ax, gripped the trunk, and dragged it away into the woods. She fought with the branches that poked out from the sides of the tree, snapping them off, throwing them down, waving and slapping at the bugs.

"Sometimes trees go bad just like people," Silas had said, explaining the finer points of sustainable forestry management. She heard his voice inside her head as if he were there beside her. What he once said about trees, "If the heartwood starts to rot, you have to take them down before the rot takes over and the lumber goes bad."

"And what do you do with rotten people," she'd asked. "Do you take them down, too?"

He'd laughed, and she'd been pleased that she'd made him laugh. She wished now she'd paid attention to what he said.

Hester took her brother and disappeared into the house. Hester who should be back in school, but Elsa needed her help, there was too much to do. There was his bedroom and all his clothes and the mattress where he had lain; there were bills and property taxes she hadn't paid; the unfinished second story, not to mention how they needed running water. She'd been looking for a job these past two weeks, but they all required some kind of a degree, or the places were too far away. "You could sell those skylights," Tommy had said, seeing them stacked there in the trailer. "Being in perfect condition like that." Tommy who left apple cores in her generator shed where Silas had once left orange peels.

She attacked the next tree. Her back slickened with sweat and a hunger gnawed at her stomach and folded in her gut. A halo of gnats and black flies spun around her head like electrons circling a nucleus. She lifted and swung, lifted and swung.

"How can you not know where the dump is?" She kept hearing Tommy's wife; she grew up here and knew where everything was. *How can you not know? How can you not know?* And Elsa didn't know how to do that—how to say what was on her mind, how to admit she made a mistake, how to speak up when she didn't understand. She didn't know how to do that! She'd never learned. She was always too busy trying hard to get it right, always afraid of being rejected for getting it wrong.

"People like to know what they can do to help," Ethan had said. But she didn't know, and she had gotten it so wrong with him and Luvera, how much they'd done for her all winter, hauling jugs of water around, Luvera sending over dinner. *This is Elsa and she is a princess.* They hadn't talked in weeks.

A large truck with a dented Wisconsin license plate pulled up, black tires rumbling over the gravel with its steel grille several feet off the ground. It stopped halfway up the driveway in front of the first fallen tree. Elsa, a hundred yards away, stood tall with her ax, beating on another balsam fir. She didn't even acknowledge him until he opened the door and stood out on the pea gravel, wearing his work boots, his flannel shirt.

"Hey," he called out to her. "You okay? Any trees down by the house?" Tommy, standing by his truck. Its engine purred and the mosquitoes thrummed and sweat fell in ribbons down her back. He came to check on her, to see how she had fared after the storm.

"We're fine," she said, raising one arm. She didn't look at him. "All good." She didn't know what Tommy had said to his wife or what his wife had said to him. It was none of her business. She went back to her tree, hacked at the wood, but she felt him there, moving around by his truck.

From the flatbed he got out his chain saw, pulled on the rip cord. The engine revved in grinding bursts as he squeezed the gas and bent over the first fallen tree. His blade sank into the trunk like a knife through butter; he sidestepped, cut the other end in half, then in half again; he tossed the pieces out of the driveway. Less than thirty seconds it took him to do what she'd done in half an hour. And she was spent.

He let the saw idle and kicked the branches away, moving them off the driveway. Walls of sadness welled up inside of her and she felt bathed in sweat. She wanted to scream, to hide her head, to be held in a pair of arms that smelled like Silas. Grief moved through her like a mountain range and it carried with it so much debris. She pressed her arms across her eyes, dropping her ax. She couldn't trust herself; she wanted to die; she didn't trust anyone.

"Hey." Tommy stood beside her in the driveway. She could smell the gasoline from his saw and the sharp, acidic resin of fresh-cut balsam fir. "You all right?" He kicked at the boughs with his feet.

"Get away from me." The waves were crashing now. "You need to go away!" She was sobbing, the sorrow heaved upon her cliffs. "Please, I'm just, I'm not in a good place right now."

"It's all right," he said. "You don't have to be in any kind of a place." He'd turned off his saw, the wood frogs gone quiet. Suddenly his fingers landed on the back of her neck and she jumped and pushed him away.

"Stop that! You can't do that, Tommy. You need to stay away!" She was screeching—what was happening to her? Was she going hysterical? Was this what people meant when they talked about someone going hysterical?

She turned her back on him, removed a glove, and wiped the snot that slicked from her face. Bugs everywhere. They stuck to her sweat and circled her head and itched her skin—she wiped her face and swatted—the bugs everywhere, creepy crawly disgusting things. "I hate this place," she said. "Oh my god I fucking hate this place!"

Tommy's boots crackled on the boughs. He stepped away.

"I remember the first time Silas showed me this place," he said after a minute. "It was early spring, and there wasn't a fleck of snow, no leaves on the trees. It was dirt and mud all around, the ugliest time of the year. He thought it was so great."

A single wood frog croaked its lone voice in a jangled note through the air. When Tommy looked at her, his expression like maybe he'd stepped in dog doo.

"I can come back later," he said.

"No. No, you should not come back. You have to stop coming." The waves had cleared; she was in a dangerous place. "Your wife came over. Did she tell you? She made me pie." The words certain. She could say anything. "She's scared, Tommy. She's pregnant and scared."

"Why would she be scared?" He lifted his saw, stepped back. "What did you say to her? What did you tell my wife?"

"Nothing. I didn't tell her anything because there's nothing to tell."

"Damn right," he said. "I was doing you a favor."

"Yes. Thank you for the favor. But I don't want you to come over here anymore."

"What do you mean?" He stood holding his saw. "I thought you wanted this."

"What did you think I wanted, Tommy? Why are you here? Why do you keep coming back?"

He stood in the driveway, his mouth twitching.

"I'm sorry," she said. "But you have to stop coming."

"Fine," he said. "Fuck you, too." He tossed his saw into the flatbed and climbed into his truck. He backed away in one hard line to the end of the driveway, yanked the wheel and squealed his tires and gunned it out onto the road.

SUMMER

28

June dried up the water in the ditches and filled the earth everywhere with flowers. Small white blooms creeping from the duff—star-shaped and heart-shaped and leggy daisies that propagated in the fields; bright yellow petals floating in the gullies, purple flags dotting the bogs. Ethan made the drive a few times a year during summer once the planting was done. He got in his truck late in the afternoon and drove the twenty miles into Sterling. He didn't mess with the radio, the drive solemn, quiet, and Luvera stopped coming after those first few years. He didn't mind going alone.

"There he is," Bean said, wiping down the bar. "I been wondering when we'd see your ugly mug. It's about that time of year."

"Yuh," said Ethan. "Here I am."

Bean had a clean face with small eyes and short hair, but it suited her. She wasn't the kind of woman to rely on decorations; those she saved for her place.

He ordered two tap beers and placed both hands out on the bar. They didn't use to have the TV mounted in the corner. It hung the size of a car door up there on the wall. Around him the tables filled with elbows and knees going far back into the oblong room, a shack if ever they took everything out of it. Bean had it crammed with mariner memorabilia—photos of old tankers and ore boats, anchors and buoys with thick rope strung along the walls.

He pulled in his beer and lifted the mug. *Here's to you, brother.* A thin mustache of foam sat for half a second on his upper lip, the ale bitter, the bubbles sweet. It warranted another sip.

Back in the day he used to come here with his uncles after working a shift; their logging work was seasonal, and the crews worked around the clock during winter, even when it snowed. They operated the tracked feller bunchers, while the masticators hummed through the night, the bright pole lights shining Goliath from above.

Robby always preferred working outside. "What's better for my lungs than fresh, clean air?" He'd go out to the fence and call in the cattle: "Here boss, here boss," and they would come home. Ethan would go out there calling, "Here boss, here boss," and they'd stay out there in the field. But they knew Robby, and he could tell them apart. "That's Agnes," he'd say. "That's a calf of Nellie." He'd walk right out there in the middle of them, check to see how a pregnancy was coming along, how an injury was healing. They weren't just a sea of black and white to him. They were individuals with personality.

His brother was like that with people, too. He'd go out to the bar after a workday and listen to their stories; it gave him something, like fuel in his tank. Kept him going during those times when his breathing came ragged and he had to sip life through a straw. It never made any sense to him, Robby's asthma, it didn't square up. Something so elemental as an inhale, the basic rite of breathing essential to all living things, and yet his brother couldn't do it? His little brother who could do everything else better and easier than him, Robby who raced motorcycles out on the ice. Robby couldn't breathe? It made no sense.

Ethan brought the glass to his lips and let the pool of warmth inside him grow. Sometimes he only stayed for an hour, other times he ordered a burger. Once, he closed the place down, a particularly hard time, the year they lost the baby and he hadn't wanted to go home. His sorrow amorphous, faceless, floating large as an undertow, and it had dragged his wife so far down, he wondered would she resurface again. Say what you wanted about her—and he knew people did, the old hens in Luvey's prayer group clucking all the day long, not because they felt sorry for her, miscarrying another child, but because they felt superior—God hadn't yet smote them, at least not with the kind of luck this family had had. But she bore it, his wife. Always she stood back up and carried on.

Bean stood with a towel, drying out a bar glass, her face tipped toward the TV. He knew he ought to say something neighborly; in his mind he investigated his options.

"They make it look so easy," Bean said, watching the screen. Athletes from all over the world, competing in the Olympic trials for the summer games. They leapt over hurdles with their legs flung straight.

"They do," he agreed. He stared at the screen and thought about Elsa. He'd heard through the Luvera Arnasson grapevine that she got the well put in, and he thought, *Good for her.* But it would have been nice to hear that from her firsthand. It would have been nice if she'd brought the kids around, at least once in a while. He didn't understand what they had done that was so wrong. He set his beer down on the bar.

Of course, maybe his mistake was thinking her behavior had anything to do with them.

Once, a long time ago, he thought that grief was about feeling sad. But it wasn't the sadness that gripped you, that wouldn't let go. It was the regret. He suspected this about Elsa. She was haunted, he thought, by something she did, or maybe something she did not do that she wished she had done, and she'd been in the clutches of this for quite some time. He recognized the slight tremor in the depths of her eyes as the same look that stared back at him from his own. She couldn't get over it, whatever it was, and he wanted to remind her that at the time she did the best she could, whatever it was, he wanted to tell her that it was all right. She'd been a good wife. She needed to forgive herself for whatever it was and be kinder to herself so that she could be kinder to them.

If you beat yourself up all day long in your head, you become a mean son of a bitch. He knew because some hurdles tripped you up, every time.

Robby's last day was like that. It started like any other, the year they were building the addition to the barn. Robby slabbed out the boards on his band-saw mill—it shrilled up and down all afternoon long and he stacked up the boards on a sawhorse. It was early in the season, the daisies had just bloomed, the treetops glossy and full.

"We still on for tonight?" he called out to him from behind the saw in a break between boards. Robby's work pants and shirt covered in wood chips and sawdust. "Burger and beer at Bean's?"

Ethan remembered that moment because he hesitated. There was a hitch even though he'd already worked it out, a slight pull and the feeling that maybe he shouldn't cancel, maybe he should just say, "Sure, let's go." But the rational part of his brain—and the stubborn part—insisted he had a better plan.

He explained to Robby that his brother-in-law was coming into town the next day and that he was expected to take him out so that Luvera and her sister could talk.

"I thought we might wait for him," he said. "Go out tomorrow night instead of tonight. Would that be all right?"

"Sure," Robby said. "The more the merrier. We'll do it tomorrow."

He tried sometimes in his mind to reconstruct Robby in that moment, looking for a sign of letdown or disappointment, but it was no good. The moment had not been preserved for safekeeping. He didn't know at the time that it would be their last day together. Always Robby wanted to be going out when Ethan preferred staying in. He consolidated the number of trips into town, whereas Robby wanted more excuses to be out in the world, as if he knew he would die young and had a shorter amount of time to get it all in.

Had he gone along with the original plan, he'd have given his brother a ride as he often did, the two of them jostling along in the pickup on the back county roads. If he'd had that beer with his brother, Robby wouldn't have worked late, wouldn't have inhaled those extra particles of dust; he wouldn't have gone into town alone and been driving home late at night when his lungs hyperin-flated; he wouldn't have swerved when reaching for his nebulizer, his lungs wouldn't have ballooned up to occupy the entire thoracic cavity with the grayish-whitish patches of mucus that populated his airways like plugs and sent him driving off the road.

"Is this seat taken?" A young man in a denim jacket with a dark beard stood next to what must be his date. She clutched a rhinestone-studded handbag, her bangs neatly combed and sprayed so they just grazed the tops of her brows. Her mouth stretched into an effortless smile, and she widened her eyes, excited to be out, a young couple, just starting their life.

"No," Ethan said, "go right ahead." He tugged down the last of his beer and laid a twenty on the bar. He left the second glass where it stood, full to the brim.

29

For several long minutes Elsa let the water cover her body. It poured from the tap, its stream muscled in the low light. Water, coming from her spout. She still couldn't get over it. Water, the sound and power from its origins deep within the earth. She had a renewed respect for all the resources she'd taken for granted most of her life, and a deep appreciation for even the simplest of creature comforts. Closing her eyes, she lay back in the tub.

Her fight with Tommy last month had made her realize how angry she was. At Luvera for asking her to put Silas on those drugs. At herself for changing her mind and saying yes. At Silas for getting caught under that tree. At the tree for falling, the sky for raining, the wind for blowing. All of it. She'd used that anger and had gotten quite a lot done. She sold the skylights, paid the property taxes, got the well system installed, and all the late hospital bills were on a payment plan. She was even sleeping in her own bed, on a new mattress that she put on a credit card—even though Silas never approved of credit cards—but she had a job interview tomorrow and knew the owners, Bob Westman's daughters. They owned a place out on Highway 53, just fifteen minutes away, a café and greenhouse where they grew vegetables and plants. They needed someone part-time to help make and serve food. She could do that.

Sitting up, she took her mug of tea from the corner shelf.

"People like to know what they can do to help," Ethan had said. And she needed Luvera's help watching the kids while she worked.

When she thought about how much Ethan and Luvera had already done, and Hester who was doing all she could to help take care of Finn, and how many times people brought over food, and the men from the logging crew who had sawed up all that wood—they were, all of them, just trying so hard.

She wasn't the only one in pain, the only one grieving. They had all lost Silas.

The steam from her tea feathered up from her cup, milky in the candlelight. She thought about Tommy's face during their fight— he'd looked stricken. Maybe he didn't know why he kept coming over, maybe he did it for more than one reason. Maybe they were all trying to be better now that Silas was gone. She leaned forward, set her tea on the shelf.

She couldn't go back. All those years playing that game—*What would I be doing now?* And she couldn't go back to her old life, not because she wasn't free to, or because she didn't have the money. She couldn't go back because she was no longer that person.

When she turned off the tap, steam rose from her skin. It curled in white wisps and twisted through the humid air. Water from the spout dripped into the tub and she shivered and sat back. Across from her on the counter the candles threw out blankets of gold that fluttered along the walls, the only sounds the hum of the baby monitor and the last few drops of water dripping into the tub.

Sometimes, when things went still, she thought about that night, how it took a lot longer than she thought it would. How his veins turned purple when she sat with him until morning and her breath fogged out because the house had gotten so cold.

He was so unlike any boy she had ever known, him with his salads and unsweetened iced tea. He covered her eyes with his hands, *I'm going to show you the most beautiful place on earth.* The scent of him—orange peels in the sun. *Surprise!* He took his hands away and showed her this field. But he had been the surprise, the biggest and best of her life.

A hot welling rose in her throat and she closed her eyes as the tears came—how they always came, and would they never cease to come? And in this buzzy, midnight state of mind, she called to him, a plea, a whisper on her lips from a lonely place that he had once unlocked, *Silas,* she called to him, her voice a mere slip.

As though in answer through the thin skin of her eyelids swung the dark pendulum of a shadow.

Elsa opened her eyes and sat up. All along the counter the candle flames hopped. They flickered and danced, the firelight lapping crazily at the air as if a figure had just passed invisibly through. Another movement caught her eye: the tea tag hung over the side of her cup, violently swinging back and forth. *What had done that? Had she done that?*

Hugging her knees to her chest, she held herself perfectly still. There was no breeze, the door closed, the air unstirred. Goose bumps prickled her flesh, and water dripped into the tub. The flames reposed.

It came from up above on the unfinished second story of the house, a slow, tentative footfall, *clomp, clomp*—someone or something up there, moving around. *Clomp, clomp, clomp,* it came closer. The ceiling beams creaked and moaned.

She felt it, someone or something leaning in, waiting. Every pore on her skin opened up with the sharp acidity of pure fear and she called out to him in the private cell of her mind, *Silas?*

All at once the candle flames moved.

Bolting, shedding water, she flicked on the lights, grabbed a towel, and blew out all the waving flames. She heard her own voice when it spoke: "Who is it? Who's there?"

She hurried to the front door and checked that it was locked. She grabbed a flashlight, scanned the windows, but the light only bounced back. Checking the front door again—it was locked— she stood shivering in her towel, her hair dripping wet. She wanted the ax.

In the children's room Hester and Finn slept, their faces serene. Elsa scrolled her flashlight across their ceiling and then under their beds; it glinted across spiderwebs and the beaded stuffed-animal eyes. Shutting their bedroom door, she listened again.

The back of the house sat flush with the grass—anyone who wanted to could go up there and walk around. Could it be Tommy? Had he come back? She hadn't seen him since their fight. In the oily gloss of the windows she caught the gleam of her own reflection, the ghosted sheen of a young woman standing alone in a towel. She was surprised by how small she looked, how alone. And then with a start she realized that the house with its glass windows was the only source of light for miles around, and that anything or anyone outside that wanted to could see in.

She flipped off the lights, threw on a sweater, and went to lie down on the bottom bunk of Hester's bed.

Childish, stupid, she should just sleep in her own bed. But she couldn't make herself go in there, the bedroom they'd shared. She had felt something, heard footsteps on the roof.

She had called his name in her mind and then the candles had moved.

Elsa used to hear him up there during the day, when putting Finn down for his nap, or fixing dinner. Her husband's footsteps on the ceiling, putting up the two-by-fours for their walls. There had been no pattern to his footfalls, sometimes fast, sometimes slow, loud, or soft, or hardly there at all.

She listened to the house. Wind moaned in the chimney vents, and the ceiling beams shifted and popped. From the bathroom the faucet dripped into the tub, and she should get up and drain the water, turn the baby monitor off. But she couldn't.

She could picture him up there, Silas, watching over the land, this place that he so loved.

The scent of candle smoke and warm fruit lingered in the air.

Had Silas moved those candles for her? Had he been trying to make her smile? Always in their life together he did every kind and loving thing, to make her happy, bring her joy. But what gratitude had she shown? What reassurance given? What comfort, what love?

She had been so hard on him when what he was building had been for them. Why couldn't she have been more patient? Held on a bit longer, believed? Their life together a first story without the second, a part one without the part two.

That was the real disservice, she realized, not just how horribly she handled his final days, or how many mistakes she'd made since, but how hard she made him work to keep her happy when he was alive. She hadn't shown it, not enough, how happy she had been.

30

They arrived at the end of lunch. A lady in a flowered apron came out of the kitchen like she was happy to see them. "I'm Doris," she said. "But my friends call me Dee because I buzz like a bee!" Hester liked the way she put her hands on her hips and laughed with her whole body. The Veggie Den looked like a house and the café was in the front room filled with tables and chairs, connected by a hallway painted green and dotted with cows to the back room called the Den. There, long wooden tables sat flush with benches, cozy couches, and mismatched chairs. Shelves filled with puzzles and games sat in a long row under the open windows.

Hester got her brother a train puzzle and sat at one of the tables while her mother interviewed for her job. It was a wood puzzle, the kind with little red knobs where you had to fit the shapes in. Live potted plants sat on each of the tables; theirs had a pink flower, and all the windows were outlined in little blue lights. Hester thought she might like coming here, it seemed like a good place.

At the table across from them a big man fished out items from a large cardboard box. He had a girl with him and a dog wearing a harness with red patches on it, and they all sat together, the man and the girl at the table and the dog underneath it.

Hester recognized the dog—big, ugly, with blotched and speck-led spots. The man had the big mess of black hair, but it was tied back and tucked in today. Hester sat up on her knees.

"Finn," she said. "I think that's the man from the woods. Big Al and his dog."

Her brother lifted his head. "Daw," he said, and patted his leg with his hand, the sign for dog. Al had a craft project on his table with wooden beads and cement blocks the size of bricks with bendy wires sticking up that looked much better than a wooden puzzle. He talked to his daughter but she didn't talk back. She shook her head and moaned or rocked, crossing her arms in front of her chest. Hester thought the girl was maybe a few years older, maybe in third or fourth grade. She had eyes that glowed like the little blue lights and her hair tumbled down rich and black as the soil in the pots.

Inside Hester a warm feeling rose. At school Brianna had been her best friend, but Hester wasn't at school anymore. Plus, Brianna had left all their grasshoppers trapped in the sandy bowl on the playground to die. Hester still didn't understand why her friend would do that.

A yellow bead rolled off Al's table and fell onto the floor. It was on the other side of the table, away from the dog. Without disturbing her brother or her mother, Hester slipped out of her seat, picked up the bead, and brought it to the girl.

"Is this your bead?"

The girl didn't answer. She looked away.

Big Al spoke up. "Go ahead, Anya. Say hello."

Anya still didn't say anything.

Al shook her elbow. "You can do it, Anya. Just say hello."

"It's all right," Hester said. "She doesn't have to say anything."

"No, she has to learn." Al capped a hand over Hester's hand. "It's all right, see, Anya? It's okay, she's a nice girl." The dog under the table growled. Al kept patting her hand. His body smelled of wet turtle and laundromat. "Anya just gots sensory issues," he said. "She don't like being touched. Does it bother you if I touch your hand?"

"I don't really want you to."

The man lifted his hand, cool air rushed in. "I'm sorry. I just needed to show her it was all right. I hope I didn't upset you. My name is Al, this is my daughter, Anya."

"I know," Hester said. "I remember you from the woods."

He stopped and looked at her, his one eye looking off. "Did youse get the wagon? I brought it over."

"Yes, we got it. Thank you," she said.

It was different seeing each other when they weren't in the woods. Al wore a checkered shirt that was buttoned down, and when he bent to take out another cement block from his box, she saw sweat stains under his arms and in a saddle shape on his back. His breath rattled and his one eye wandered off, but he set down the cement block in front of her.

"You can do a sculpture if you want to," Al said. "We got plenty of beads, all different colors."

Finn had toddled over and stood next to her. The dog under the table growled and shriveled its lips.

"I don't want your dog to hurt my brother," Hester said, taking Finn's hand.

"Fish, you hush." Al got out two baggies filled with beads and Fish laid down his head.

"Daw," Finn said.

"He's working right now," Al said of his dog. "Best not to disturb him."

"He's a worker dog?"

"He comes with me everywhere I go. Found him in the woods one day half starved and I fed him and now he's my best friend. We take care of each other."

Whenever someone came into the room Fish lifted his head and tracked them with his clotted eyes. They dripped thick fluid that leaked from the corners and stained the sides of his face with black tears. When the person he was watching finally sat down, Fish put his head back onto his paws.

Hester felt sorry for Al, that Fish was his best friend. She sat down at the table next to Anya, and Finn climbed in beside her. Al brought out another cement block studded with bendy wires, and she didn't know which eye to look into when he talked, but he had a sadness in him, and Hester understood that now.

Her own sadness lived inside of her like a secret color. She believed there were those people who could see this color and those who could not. She had never noticed it until after her father died, never even knew that such a color existed, but now that she did know, she looked for people who saw it and understood. Dividing the world in terms of people who did and did not know, what she looked for—without knowing why or even that she did it—was a new set of friends who understood this without her having to explain. She was attracted to sad people. The reasons for their sadness may be complicated and what she could only guess at, but it made her feel closer, somehow, to her papa.

"What are you making today?" Hester addressed the girl, but her father answered.

"Anya likes to thread beads. She also makes jewelry." Al showed her a necklace he wore tucked under his shirt. It was a single blue bead on a piece of string, and the dog growled when she leaned in too close to look. She sat slowly back.

"She made another one with different colors." Al reached over to show off the bracelet on Anya's arm, but the girl pulled away.

"See what I mean?" he said. "I can't never even hold her hand."

The plastic-coated wires twisting up from the blocks were all different colors and bent into different shapes. One end of the wire stuck into the cement, the other end left open. The thought of sliding a bead down along the wire was irresistible. Finn pounced on a bead with his chubby little hand and pushed it down.

"Good job, Finn," Hester said.

"You can pick whichever beads you want," Al said. "Rotate the colors, do different patterns. We got more." He took out another baggie of beads. "You can make your own sculpture and take it home." Sweaty ribbons shone on his forehead and trickled around his ears.

Hester picked up one of the beads and slid it down a wire, making a silly sound to entertain her brother. Finn copied her, he did the same thing only he did it wrong, so the sound was funnier, and Anya laughed. A new expression of liveliness came into her face then. She picked up a bead and slid it down, making a quick, funny snort. Her eyes flicked up and they both smiled. It was just the small squiggle of a smile, but it pleased Hester, that Anya had smiled, and in this way, they made a connection, and the little group came together.

31

I see you've made a new friend." Elsa put an arm around her daughter, and a hand to the top of Finn's head. From underneath the table a large dog growled.

"Mama!" Hester sat on her knees, wound up, alert. "Look what I made! We're doing art. This is my sculpture! Al said that I can take it home."

The man who was apparently Al reminded her of a bear, large and round with unruly black hair in a ponytail that bushed out from the back of his head. It must be his dog under the table, she thought, the dog brindled and wrapped in a harness. She regarded the sculptures, cement bricks with wires sticking out at odd angles, which the children filled with wooden beads. "That's very nice." She tried to make eye contact with Hester's friend. "Did you make that one yourself? I like the combination of colors."

The girl, who must have been Al's daughter, didn't react to the attention, only shoved her pudgy hand into a ziplock baggie and pulled out more beads. Her dress was obviously secondhand, tied with a bow drooped down her back. Elsa had an uneasy feeling about them, but she was doing it again, judging people based on what they wore.

"I'm Elsa Arnasson," she said, holding out her hand. "Hester and Finn's mom."

Al wiped his hand on his pants. "Al Androski." He shook her hand with a soft, spongy grip. Next to him on the floor the dog lifted its head, bared its teeth, and growled.

"Cut that out," Al said to the dog. "It's all right."

Elsa reshouldered her bag. It was heavy, filled with games and toys she'd packed for the kids that they didn't need.

"Did you get the job, Mama?" Hester said, not looking at her, busy with her craft.

"I did, yes." Her little plume of happiness drooped as everyone at the table kept their attention on their craft. "I need you and Finn to finish up now, please. We're going to the main office at the greenhouse to complete my paperwork." She looked to her son. "They have dogs in the greenhouse. Doggies, Finn. Do you want to come see the doggies?"

"No, Mama." Hester spoke for him. "We want to stay here and make bead sculptures with Anya and Al."

"They can stay with us," Al said. "We don't mind, do we, Anya? She's happy to have friends." He didn't look at Elsa when he spoke; his eyes darted away. Whenever she moved too close to the table, the dog growled and lifted its head, a mottled head shaped like an anvil, and suddenly she realized where she'd seen this dog before.

"I'm sorry." She turned to Al. "Where did you say you lived?"

"I'm right on Yarrow Road. About a mile out from your place. I hunt in those woods. That's where I met your kids."

Goose bumps stood out on her skin. She looked at Hester and Finn, but neither of them looked at her, both of them industrious, pulling and sorting beads.

"It's a nice piece of land youse got," Al said. "Always wondered who was building back there." He reached out and patted his dog. "We come here every Tuesday, so Anya can do her crafts. They say the hand-eye coordination is good for her reading. It's part of her homeschooling."

"I'm homeschooled, too!" Hester stood up on her knees, the dog Fish growled.

"Now you be quiet," Al said to the dog. "It's okay."

"Can Anya come over to our house, Mama?" Hester lowered

her voice for the dog. "We have a big table for doing art. My mom teaches art. Do you like art, Anya?"

"Oh, we like art," Al answered for his daughter. "We have lots of finger paints and markers, don't we, Anya?"

"Please? Can she come over and do art with me?"

Elsa took another step back, clutching her shoulder bag. A feeling of vertigo crept over her then: the gunshots, the footsteps on her roof, the feeling she'd had all year of being watched. Was it Al, watching them? Was it Al and his dog, coming onto their land?

"I see you've already met one of our regulars." Dee appeared, grinning with hands on hips. "Hi Al. How's it going? I didn't see you come in. Must've snuck right past me."

"We brought our own snacks today," he said, "from that festival youse had last weekend."

"Oh, it's been so crazy here. We had a record turnout." She said to Elsa, "We hold a festival here every solstice. Artists set up their tents, and we have food and music and a live auction."

Elsa nodded. She hadn't slept well last night, her nerves raw and exposed like the wires stuck in the blocks. Even during her job interview with Dee—who was quite possibly the most down-to-earth person she had ever met—she'd felt apprehensive.

"We got us some of that kettle corn," Al said, reaching into his box. "It's real good if youse want some, I got it right here."

"Oh no." Dee flapped a hand. "Don't even get me started on that stuff. One kernel and I puff up like a blowfish."

"Are you allergic?" Elsa asked, trying to participate.

"Don't I wish. Ha ha, no. My problem is, once I start eating the stuff, I can't stop!" Her bosoms shook with a hearty laughter, and everyone joined in. Elsa forced a laugh and tried to join them; she wanted to have a light and pleasant conversation, but she couldn't stop thinking about how Al had offered her kids candy in the woods, and now he was giving them more food, the popcorn already out on the table. Why was he being so nice to them? What would have happened that day if they'd gone with him in his car?

"You ready for your tour of the greenhouse?" Dee said.

"Sure." Elsa pulled up the strap of her bag. She stood there feeling alone, separate, a pale, aching creature shedding her grief like a skin. Al was accepted here by Doris and the greenhouse community. He belonged, this strange man and his daughter and dog. "You can go, Mama," Hester said. No one else seemed worried or concerned. She was the one ill at ease. She was the one who judged. Al and his daughter were quite possibly the closest thing she had to neighbors and she didn't want to be unneighborly. "All right." She kissed the tops of Hester and Finn's heads. They were in a public place, she'd be right back. "I guess you can stay here with Al and your new friend. Don't go anywhere until I get back. I shouldn't be gone too long, right?"

"Nope." Dee leaned back in her kitchen Crocs. "Shouldn't be long at all."

There were five greenhouses, each one a hooped and transparent polyethylene structure that housed row upon row of neatly ordered plants. The plants sat on tables that were threaded with tubes that warmed the soil, each pot with a white tag that stuck up from the lower left-hand corner, listing name, species, and preference for shade. All the tags in all the same corners, all the planters the same, and Elsa felt comforted by this neat and orderly world, the scent of dirt and peat moss and the gentle banter of the ladies who called to one another across the rows.

Dee introduced her to the employees, all of them women who smiled or nodded as they moved off to do this or that, all of them purposeful; they had a sense of belonging here and knew what to do. Dee led her past the herbs and vegetables, showed her which ones she could use to restock the produce coolers in the kitchen and which plants were for the greenhouse customers to buy. Elsa forgot about her unease. In a small dusty office with a single window, they Xeroxed her driver's license and filed away her signed paperwork. Dee handed her a stiff apron sprinkled with flowers and a binder filled with all the Veggie Den recipes.

"You're officially an employee," Dee said. "You can start first thing on Friday. Six thirty for opening, and if you can stay late, we'll teach you how to close."

Elsa smiled and went to shake her hand, but Dee offered her a hug.

"Welcome to the sisterhood," she said.

Making her way back to the café, Elsa walked alongside the piles of mulch and stone swinging her arms. She got a job, her boss was a cool lady, and this seemed like a pleasant place to spend the day. Maybe she just needed to make her own friends, people who weren't connected to Silas. She looked out across the parking lot lined with all the trees.

The leaves were out now. She had felt them while up at the clothesline and wondered, *What's different?* It wasn't just the sound; it was a feeling of companionship in the air. They waved around as if they were encouraging her, and she felt oddly cheered. She'd never paid much attention to leaves before moving here. Her favorites were the heart-shaped aspen leaves that dangled all together in a breeze, chartreuse lockets that hung as though from floss.

It wasn't just that she wanted to stay for Silas, it was that she felt very strongly that the answers she needed could only be found here. She wanted to learn how to be a better person, and she held this belief in her private heart, this feeling that something out here was trying to get through to her, some ethos trying to teach her something that she needed to know. And maybe it was all in her head, maybe she was being silly—she still didn't know what was taking her clothesline down. But it was this hope that kept her striving, this belief pressed like a locket to her chest, that she might learn to be more like the man she loved by understanding the place he was from.

A breeze rolled through the canopy. It lifted the hair off the back of her neck and cooled her skin. A cry came to her on the wind, small but high, tunneling up from her dark door. Elsa pushed it down, pushed it back, but it climbed with tenacious fingers—demanding her attention—and the cry became a scream, not from within, but through the open windows of the café and she recognized the voice—Finn!

Racing across the parking lot, Elsa burst through the restaurant doors and into the back room with its couches and chairs where she found her children, both of them alone. Finn sat on top of a long wooden table with his feet bare, cheeks red, face wet. His breath visibly shaking his bewildered little body.

"What happened? Are you all right?" She scooped him up into her arms and reached for her daughter.

"Mama, I'm so sorry," Hester said. "He just started crying."

"Is he all right? Did something happen?"

"No."

"Did he get hurt? Did he fall?"

"No, he just got sad. He wanted you. Oh, what have I done!" She covered her face with her hands. Elsa sank to the bench, holding her son. The dog was gone. Al was gone. His daughter and all the sculptures with the beads—gone.

"Hester? What happened?"

Her daughter sniffed. Her shoulders rose then fell. "I think I upset Anya."

"Upset her how?"

"I don't know." Hester cried into her hands and Finn kept his face burrowed, his body trembling, both socks and shoes gone.

"Where's Al?"

"He left."

"He left you and Finn here alone? Why?"

"I didn't know."

"Didn't know what?"

"I don't know!" Her voice rose to a squeak.

Elsa confronted a table scattered with popcorn kernels and wrappers and empty soda pop cans, the puzzles they had gotten out now dumped on the floor, all of the pieces mixed. No evidence of Al and his dog, only what appeared to be his garbage. Hot bile rose in the back of her throat.

Al, who lived not one mile away, and what if he was out there watching through the windows, or prowling around the unfinished rooms of their house? She wished he didn't know where they lived. Wished the woods around their house didn't go on for miles and miles with predators and wild dogs and structures built before the time of permits, one-room cabins, dilapidated trailers on parcels of privately owned land. Where everyone owned guns.

"Is he all right?" An old woman teetered up to their table. Ivory slacks hung from her thin legs, hair fluffed around a pink and speckled scalp. "I heard your little one crying and I didn't see anyone over here with them."

"He's fine now," Elsa said. "Thank you."

"We could all hear it."

Elsa held on to her children. Glances came from across the room.

"I have to tell you." The woman leaned forward, put a hand on the table, her skin cracked and scaly like the claw of a chicken. She whispered conspiratorially, her mouth outsize with bright orange lipstick, the skin around her eyes pulled tight. "You shouldn't leave them," she said, her expression fevered, "not even for a second. Kids can disappear, you know. Even around here. It happens all the time."

32

The first part of their visit had been so pleasant. Luvera had been outside when they drove up unannounced—Elsa parked and the children came running—they'd been so happy to see her! Nearly knocked her over with their hugs, and then Maggie was there, wagging her tail and licking their faces.

Luvera brought them into the house, where they met Charlie for the first time, and he sang for them, and she taught them how to feed him some seeds. She brought up three dozen eggs from the basement and then planted herself in the kitchen chair to distribute her presents. From the large shopping bag, she pulled out their new rain boots but then kept going—giant hooped wands with scented bubbles for Hester, and for Finn, a yellow truck with a front loader attached. Oh, they had been so surprised, their eyes planets in the starry faces of their wonder.

"What do you say?" Elsa had prompted.

"Thank you very much!" Hester sat on the floor and tugged on her boots.

Her brother didn't say anything. He put the box filled with the truck on the floor, his face quiet and serious, as if too much noise or movement might make it disappear. Then he came around and stood in front of her chair.

"I love you," he said to her, utterly serious. His *l* sounded like a *y* and the words came out nearly whispered, but they all heard it. *I yove you.*

Oh, it had been the best afternoon she'd had since the accident last fall. But of course, seeing the children meant dealing with Elsa.

"That was really generous of you." They were in the milk house. Elsa was unscrewing the lids from her half-gallon mason jars and the children were outside. "I'm sure they'll get a lot of use out of those boots." Their voices and Maggie's barking drifted like a pleasant scent from outside. Giant bubbles floated past the windows.

"Well, I hope so. I had wanted to get them to you earlier when we were having all that rain." Luvera crossed the cement floor and flicked on the pump. "I hear you've been busy, that you got the well put in." The giant steel tank churned coldly in the center. "That must be nice for you." The room quiet and chilly in contrast to the bright outside.

"Yes. It is. Nice." Elsa crouched by the churn, turned on the nozzle. It let loose a cold stream of dairy. When her jar filled, she clamped the nozzle and brought the half-gallon container to the counter by the sink to wipe it down. Behind her the milk dripped from the nozzle and onto the cement floor like it always did, and Luvera slid a pie tin under it that she kept nearby to catch the drips. The next drop fell with a sharp *ping!*

Elsa spun around, flinging her arms out and knocking the glass jar from the counter. It shattered with a pop, bursting milk.

"Oh! Oh my gosh."

Luvera went to fetch the towels.

"I'm so sorry! What a mess!"

"It's all right, we've got plenty of rags. That's what they're here for." They knelt together and Elsa picked out the glass. Luvera used the old kitchen towels to sop up the milk and noticed a slight tremor in the young woman's hand.

"Everything all right?" She hadn't noticed it earlier; she'd been distracted by the kids. "You seem a little strung out." Elsa had dark circles under her eyes, her skin pale and wan, her fingers so thin. But then, everyone seemed thin to Luvera these days.

"What happened, Mama?" Hester and Finn cracked open the door, their faces peering in.

"Don't come in here," Luvera said. "There's broken glass. Keep Maggie outside and don't let her come in."

They shut the door, and the quiet returned.

"I start my new job on Friday. I'm a little nervous about that."

"A job?" Luvera stood with the rag. "Why, Elsa, good for you. That's wonderful." She wrung it out in the industrial sink and washed down the milk. "Where?"

"Out at the Veggie Den, that café next to the greenhouse? Four days a week to start."

"Oh, that place. Every time I drive by they're closed."

"It's breakfast and lunch only."

"Well, that explains it." She spread the rag out to dry. Why hadn't Elsa told her she was looking for a job? She could have helped, asked around, put in a good word. "What will you do when winter comes? That's when they *do* close, you know."

Elsa slid shards of glass into the trash and didn't answer. Probably she didn't know.

"Have you thought about putting Hester back in school? Might help, I don't know, make things a little easier for you."

"It's summer."

"Fall will be here before you know it."

"Silas and I always planned to homeschool." Elsa scraped more broken glass into the garbage. "We should know what gets put into our children's heads, he always said. We only enrolled her last year because we started building, and teaching a curriculum became impossible." She dropped the last of the glass into the garbage, and the sound of it splintered against what was already there.

"And you don't think things are impossible now?" She rinsed out the other rag, hung it over the sink. "What does Hester want? Have you asked her? Has she asked about school?"

Elsa got out the broom and swept the floor. "She keeps asking about hell. She wants to know if her dad dying means that she's going to hell because God didn't answer her prayers. I tell her no, of course that's not what it means. But she worries and is having bad dreams. She cries herself to sleep almost every night saying, 'Papa, Papa,' and I don't know what to tell her."

"Well I hope you told her he went to heaven."

"I know that's what you told her."

"You don't think that's where he went?"

"It doesn't matter what I think, Luvera, she wants him *here.*" Elsa stood with the dustpan loaded with debris. "But you don't want *me* here, do you? You think I should leave, give up on this place, sell the land and go back to where I came from."

It was so hurtful; it almost took her breath away. "No, honey. That's not what I want."

"Then what do you want? Why do I feel like no matter what I do, you're always going to disapprove? Like, you can't trust me to make a good decision about anything, even where my own children are concerned, and everything I do or want is just another mistake?" She knocked the dustpan against the garbage bin and put it away. The stainless-steel tank churned coldly in the center of the room. Elsa took her last jar and knelt. Luvera found a few mason jars left on a shelf. They weren't as big as the one that broke, but they would do. She set them on the floor next to Elsa.

"Thank you." Elsa filled another jar, then cranked the nozzle closed.

"You're welcome."

Elsa bowed her head. "And thank you for all the milk you sent over this winter. And for the butter and the eggs and all the meals you prepared." Milk dripped into the pie pan with a heavy *ping, ping, ping.* "I know I must seem ungrateful. Having you and Ethan here means everything to me, but you wouldn't know it, the way I've been acting. I've done nothing to repay you." *Ping, ping, ping.*

"Elsa, you're family. You don't have to repay us. You know that."

For a moment Elsa didn't move. She knelt by the churn, head bowed, back curved. The pinging on the pie plate stopped, the sound of the children's voices dried up, the stillness in the milk house absolute and solemn as prayer. When she spoke again her voice came whispered, tempered, private. "I've always thought anything was possible," she said. "That's always been my problem. I believe." Her eyes filled and her face contorted. "I thought my love was strong enough, but then last winter when he didn't die, things just got so hard."

It was as if she were being submerged; Luvera couldn't breathe, her body flooded with cold. She'd never meant to make things harder. She'd never wanted Silas to suffer. He was like a son.

Abruptly, Luvera threw open the door and rushed outside into the sunshine. "Hester!" she called. "Hester, where are you?" In front of her face she waved a hand as if clearing out bugs.

They came running in their shiny new boots. "Maggie ate a bubble!" Hester said. Finn made chomping sounds with his mouth. Maggie stood beside them swishing her tail in the golden sun. They seemed all right, Luvera thought, cupping a hand around Hester's head. She felt the warmth of the sun in the girl's hair as the light pooled through the trees, and it hit her: If Silas hadn't married Elsa, these children, these precious children, wouldn't be here.

"Do you want to see old Billy do his trick?" Luvera didn't know how to get Billy to do his trick; it was Ethan who always did that. But it hurt, like a pain in her chest, to think that this girl cried herself to sleep. "If your mom says it's all right, I'll give it a try."

Old Billy grazed in the field behind the long section of fencing beside the milk house, a full-grown male fainting goat with horns thick as tree branches. His fur hung in a shag rug of blacks and grays with the odd patch of brown, his body like one of those rag rollers in a car wash. But what distinguished him, what made him different from all the other goats they had, was his remarkable defense of freezing up and falling down petrified if so much as a sneeze surprised him. It was a great trick, one that neighbors and family had gone to lengths to see, and the kids loved it, their faces earnest and expectant in the midday sun.

"Our mom said yes!" Hester jumped up and down; Finn grinned and stomped in his boots. Elsa, out of the milk house now, loaded her glass jars into the car.

Luvera went alone to the far side of the barn. She slid her gold cross back and forth across its chain and tried to remember how Ethan did this. Did he use something to scare Billy with, or did he just yell? Ethan with his expressions, and Elsa had no idea how much he worried about her and these kids. It was the kids, she thought, he needed a house filled with kids. Pearl Jones at church had said it: "You don't really know what love is until you've had a child." And that had shamed her, because it was too late for them now, they'd never have their own family. Maybe she didn't understand how hard it had been for Elsa last winter. Maybe mothers felt the loss of a spouse differently. Did it hit Elsa harder, three times as much? Once for her herself and twice for the kids?

She smoothed down her blouse, tucked back her hair, and shot out across the dirt path that ran alongside the field.

"Booga booga booga!" She yelled and flapped her arms like a bird, her gold cross thumping her sternum. She swooped along the back of the barn, hustled past the milk house, past Hester and Finn, "Booga booga booga!" She flapped her arms and shouted as loud as she could.

The goat turned its head, lifted a hoof, and went back to tearing grass.

"Oh, for the love of Pete!" Luvera dropped her arms, face flushed and warm. "See that? He just doesn't find me scary."

"You scared me!" Hester was laughing, and Luvera realized she hadn't seen the girl laugh since the accident. "Can I try?" She was hopping up and down. "Please, Aunt Luvera? Can I be scary?"

Luvera looked to Elsa, and that was something they could agree on, the love they each had for these kids.

"Sure," Luvera said. "Go ahead and give it a try. But wait a few minutes. Let things calm down first before you come running out."

"Okay! Oh boy. I will!" Hester ran off, waving once before disappearing out of sight.

"I must look a fright." Luvera fixed her top, brushed off strands of hay. "I hope she won't be too disappointed if we can't get him to faint." She moved the clasp of her necklace around to the back of her neck.

"I don't think I've ever seen you run," Elsa said.

"Yuh," Luvera snorted. "It's been a while." They were standing behind the barn alongside the fence under the old oak tree. "You know, I might have said some things." There had once been a swing under this tree, a wooden plank Silas stood on as a boy—he didn't sit down, always climbing around. Of course, he risked it all, just like his father did, living a life that he loved. "I hope you know how much Ethan and I want to help you and the kids." The light from overhead poured down like liquid through the leaves, and when the wind shifted it dappled soft water marks across the space.

Elsa lifted her eyes, and they were warm and luminous. "I'm really glad you said that because I have to ask you something."

"Okay."

"It's all right if you have to say no. I would understand."

"What is it?"

"I was wondering . . ." The wind blew again in the tree. Water-marks dappled all around. "Would you be willing to watch Hester and Finn on the mornings that I work?"

"Well, of course."

"Really?"

"We'd love to have them here."

"My shift starts at six thirty, so I'd have to bring them over early."

"That's no problem, we're up early every morning anyway."

"Oh, that would be so great."

"I'm glad you asked."

"Booga booga booga!" Hester ran out from behind the barn, hair flying, arms flapping. She streaked down the path alongside the fence. The billy goat raised his head just as Ethan's pickup pulled into the driveway. "Booga booga booga!" She yelled in breathy, girlish spurts, then stopped and bent over, laughing, holding her stomach. "Oh my gosh!" She was caught in a spasm of giggles. The goat regarded her for a moment, looked around at them all, and went back to eating grass.

Ethan parked his truck.

"I can't do it!" Hester said. "I can't say booga-booga without laughing!"

Ethan shut the door of the cab, pocketed the keys, and shook out a handkerchief.

"We're trying to scare Billy!" Hester called to him. "But no one can do it!"

"That old man?" he teased. "Now why would you want to scare an old man like that?"

"Oh, please, Uncle Ethan! Please, can you do it?"

He looked so thin, his torso concave above his belted trousers. He blew his nose and glanced at the goat penned in behind the fence. "Well, I suppose it won't hurt him none." He tucked his hankie back in his pocket. "I'll give it a whirl."

Hester hopped up and down and clapped her hands and Finn spun in circles and sat on the ground. Luvera folded her arms across her chest. Ethan disappeared behind the barn. The sting of Elsa's words still clung to her. How could Elsa think even for a second that she didn't want them here? And of course she was happy to watch the kids, all she'd ever wanted was to be a bigger part of their lives. Why on earth would she have said no?

Hester stood between them, innocent of and oblivious to the

tension. After a few minutes the girl whispered, "Aunt Luvera, did he forget?"

"No, honey. Just wait."

It wasn't that Elsa disappointed her, it was that life disappointed her. Elsa wouldn't understand that, because things always came easy to her, and no, she didn't want them to leave, but living off the grid was extreme, even for someone suited to life in the country. Didn't Elsa realize the toll it was taking on Ethan, taking on them all?

An oily feeling rose to the top of her skin. *Did he forget?* Go wandering off someplace by himself? It had been a good five or ten minutes. Above them the leaves shifted and dappled watermarks across her arms. The goat continued to rip grass.

All at once from out of the silence:

"Brooooga brooooga brooooga!" Ethan came bursting out from the side of the barn, a bushy-haired skinny man in a button-down shirt, arms flapping, boots stomping, knees popping up over the weedy path like a giant high-stepping bird. He came thundering down the path, his torso so thin, but his voice, it boomed with a power that shook grass.

The goat jumped, its legs stiffened, and it fell over like a statue with a thud.

33

Summer evenings, after the sun had set and the children had fallen asleep, a blue aura spilled into the sky, a magnetic glow that ray by ray the night sipped away. Elsa stood outside on the porch smoking a cigarette, listening to the chittering of squirrels and the distant barking of a dog as the forest fell into a cage of shadowed bars.

She didn't go to bed with the children anymore, couldn't lie there and listen to the house creak and groan. "Fall will be here before you know it," Luvera had said. "What are you going to do when winter comes?"

After the kids went to sleep, she split firewood and stacked it to dry for winter. There weren't very many logs left under the tarp, and Tommy hadn't come around to help out since their fight. Elsa didn't know if they had enough wood to get them through winter, and she didn't know how to take down a tree.

Tommy's wife came into the café some mornings on her way to work, large and uncomfortable with child, her face swollen, puffed. Last week it was Elsa who made her iced decaf. Cherice jammed a straw through the plastic lid of her drink and said, "Thanks." Elsa said, "Have a good day," and that was all.

Elsa had thought living on the land was about being independent, but now she thought about what Silas said about the trees, how they were social creatures, interconnected; they didn't act as individuals fighting for survival; they acted as a family, physically connected to each other and the world, connected through a complex system of mycelium strands woven in an underground web. What they did for themselves, they did for each other.

"You're family," Luvera had said. "You know that."

But somehow, she hadn't known. The concept of family meant something different out here, or maybe she'd never understood it to begin with. It wasn't right, to be angry at Luvera when all she'd ever done was try to help. Elsa had to forgive her, forgive them both. If they did the wrong thing for Silas, it was at least for the right reasons. If she could believe that, then maybe she could trust herself to make good decisions again, trust the world to bring good things back into her life.

Tossing down her cigarette, Elsa tamped it in the dirt and went down to the woodpile with her ax.

Her arrangement with Luvera was working out so well, she had picked up more shifts, working every day but Tuesday, a deliberate avoidance of Al. She didn't want to believe he intended them harm, leaving her children alone that day; she didn't want to think of the incident as anything other than an unfortunate misunderstanding. But the thought of him and his mean dog disturbed her. She wished more than anything that he didn't know where they lived.

Rolling up the tarp, Elsa tossed out the logs. Darkness loomed around her gray as lint and she turned on her headlamp and reached for her ax.

She felt it at night, the draft of that dark place inside of her. The mistakes she'd made and the winter that nearly drove her out of her mind.

You won't have to go through that again, she told herself, *this winter will be different.*

Into a chalk maple, she swung her blade, the log dense and swollen with knots. She lifted her ax, hit it again, then again. The only wood left was the problem logs that she couldn't split last winter. All of them slashed with ax marks from her failed attempts.

But she knew how to deal with them now. It wasn't about strength or force of will; it was about showing up at the same place with a steady aim. It was about patience and staying with it until she heard that sound, a hollow, thumping crack that let her know it had surrendered, it had let go.

After that, in three or five more strokes, it would fall apart.

"They named her Gwendolyn!" Dee's voice sang out from the produce cooler. "Cherice had the baby and they're calling her Gwendie. Isn't that too cute?" All day she talked about the baby shower. It would be held at the Veggie Den on the first Tuesday in August, two weeks away. Bob Westman's wife and her daughters Dee and Robin were hosting. Elsa received an invitation, a hand-written piece of mail. Of course she had to go. But Tommy would be there, and she hadn't seen him since last May.

The sun boiled hotter and longer across the sky. It set in the haze of muggy evenings and caught itself behind thick waddings of cloud. She didn't leave the door open at night to allow the cool air through the screen but kept it closed, kept it locked. She brought up the ax from the woodpile and kept it in the house, just in case.

In town, Elsa picked up a baby gift and an electric fan and drove home. All month the humidity had been building up inside the small bedrooms of the unfinished house with no back windows for escape. She set up the fan on the highest speed to paddle air through the hot rooms, and the sound of it lulled both her children to sleep.

Shutting their door, she moved out into the kitchen, where the lights flickered and buzzed. She would have to start the generator and run it for a few hours because of the fan, which meant going up the hill in the dark. On the counter sat the invitation to the shower, the envelope addressed to her in a uniform, cursive hand.

And after August came September and then it would be fall.

She trudged up the hill through the woods with the ax, opened the door to the generator shed, turned on the motor, and waited outside for the engine to warm up. She brought the ax with her everywhere now. The woods at dusk had a granular quality, like the off-line static of an old television set, and the sound of the motor ricocheting off the trees sounded disconcertingly similar to human screams.

Looping around the shed, insulated in a cocoon of white noise, Elsa was lost in thought. *A snake in the grass.* She didn't know if Tommy would still be mad, and of course Dee didn't know about their history.

She *had* asked her about Al. "What's up with him and his dog?" And Dee had explained that Al lived off disability with his bad back and a glass eye and that Fish was an emotional support animal. "Of course, the dog doesn't have any training or paperwork, so we're not legally obligated to let him in here, but he doesn't bother anyone, and Al is family, so, that's what we do." Elsa understood. Al was family because he was from here and everyone knew him. But did they *really* know him? She didn't understand what had happened that day when she left him with her kids, or why he had offered them candy in the woods. Hester had been asking about his daughter, Anya; she wanted to invite her over. Elsa said no. She made excuses—there was too much to do, she was always tired after work. She hadn't seen Al since the incident and didn't want to. She avoided him on purpose, requested Tuesdays off, chose the cowardly way.

Footsteps rattled behind her in the leaves.

Elsa stopped, turned, and shined her light through the woods. Her flashlight illuminated nothing, the darkness diffusing the beam. All she saw were the hulking shadows of trees.

They must have been her own footsteps, she thought, walking on more slowly. She moved toward the shed, gripping the ax, and kept her eyes on the shadows. She couldn't stop herself from thinking how easy it would be for someone to park their truck, walk onto their land, and wait in hiding in the woods.

From behind her came the shuffle of footfalls. She stopped and spun around again with her light. *There!* Movement from behind the shadowed edge of a tree.

Someone or something was out there, watching through the trees. The clacking of the engine bounced off the hardwoods and everywhere she heard these sounds. She listened, holding her ax. Sometimes the footsteps came from her left, other times to her right. The engine rumbled and splintered through the woods.

Heart skipping beats, she ducked back into the shed and turned the dial to engage. Already, heat was building up inside the small room with the belt spinning and the motor chugging, so she propped open the door, hastily wedged in a stick under its bottom edge, and hurried back out.

She was down the hill by the house when it happened: Her entire body lit up with a strange, cold tingling. It was like the feeling she got inside her mouth after brushing her teeth and drinking water, only this was on the outside of her skin. All over her body, the sensation so intense, she stopped and stretched out her arms. Everywhere the hairs rose, lifting straight as wheat across her skin. Goose bumps prickled her neck, her arms and legs, her entire body alive with it, possessed of it, the tingling, buzzing hum as if a static electricity had filled the air, so unmistakable and yet she could see no earthly reason for it.

"Silas?" she called to him. "Is that you?"

The scent came to her in a hot rich wave—diesel fuel! The smell filled the air, nauseating and stirring as she ran back behind the house and up the hill, following the scent like a wild creature sniffing through the woods. Elsa ran, the smell of gasoline getting stronger as the sound of the engine crescendoed, her heart pounding, and a screeching laughter spiraled up and away through the trees.

The generator shed came into view.

Through its open door black smoke billowed.

Fighting her way through the smoke, one arm over her face, she went inside, instantly choking, the stench searing her nose and lungs. The motor was spinning, and there near the flywheel the return fuel line wriggled wildly like a headless snake, alive and spurting diesel.

Someone or something had cut the fuel line. *Why would some-one do that? Who would do such a thing?*

Layers of smoke rolled over the manifold cover. She grabbed a rag and went in, clenching the hot levers and holding them down while the engine kicked and bucked, burying her head in her arms to escape the fumes, coughing, choking, eyes burning as the motor juddered and fought to stay running. Tightening her grip, the hot levers burning through the rag, blistering skin, she held on. Finally, the engine came to a hard stop.

In the silence her fear reloaded.

Tossing the rag aside, grabbing her ax, Elsa leapt out into the night.

"Stay away from here!" she screamed, raising her ax. "Whoever you are, stay away! This is my home!" She jumped and turned, eyes wild and streaming from the smoke. There could be a fire, there could be a man, there could be someone at the house with her kids. She raced back down the hill, the lid to her Pandora's box flung open wide and all the darkest thoughts screaming in her head.

In the house she rushed into the bedroom to check on the kids. The edges of artwork taped to the walls fluttered in the breeze, and the fan blew cool air across their sleeping faces. Both of them peaceful, serene; their breath rose in quiet swells. Elsa wiped her face, lowered her ax, and shut their door.

In the kitchen she picked up the phone and half expected it to be dead, the line cut, but there was a dial tone. She called Ethan.

It rang and it rang and all kinds of thoughts raced through her head—had it been Tommy? Had it been Al? Who would do something like that to her generator? When Ethan answered she practically shouted, "He's here! He's in the woods and I don't know what to do." She was crying, coughing, and the phone crackled in her ear—she must have woken him although it was early, only half past nine. "I'm sorry to bother you"—her teeth chattered together as if she were cold—"but I don't know what else to do."

"Elsa? What's this now? Who's there?"

She cried out unintelligibly about the cut fuel line, then swallowed and redoubled her efforts to keep herself calm. "I don't know. Someone is out here in the woods." She went into the bathroom and turned on the light, shut the door and slid down with her back against the wall. "Should I call the police?" She huddled against her knees. "Can I bring the kids over there?"

"Tell me slowly," he said, his voice stronger now; he had moved into another room. "Start again. Is someone there with you?"

"No. No, I'm alone."

"Where are you now?"

"In the house."

"Okay. Is anybody hurt?"

"No. No one is hurt."

"The children are safe?"

"Yes. Yes, they're sleeping." She swallowed hard and lowered her voice. "I just checked on them. They didn't even wake up. Everyone is safe inside and the door is locked."

"Okay. Okay, that's good," he said. "Now tell me again what happened."

The stink of diesel fuel and smoke was thick on her clothes, and she tried to describe it, the cut line, the smoking manifold. She sniffed and tried to keep her voice from rising over the top. She was shaking, tears falling, and the phone kept slipping through her sweaty hands. They were black from engine grease, the skin of her fingers blistered. She got up and held them under cool water but standing made her nauseous and dizzy so she sank back down.

"Did you see someone?" he asked her. "Somebody in the woods?"

"No. Yes." She shivered, wiping her face with the back of her hand. "I don't know." Her voice cracked. "I thought I heard footsteps and someone laughing."

"Okay."

"This happened before."

"What happened before?"

She thought how to say it. "Acts of sabotage. I think someone's been watching the house. Someone keeps cutting my clothesline."

Ethan didn't say anything.

"Tonight he was out behind the generator shed in the woods. I *felt* someone. I heard his footsteps and I thought I heard him laughing."

Ethan remained quiet for several moments. She wiped her hand under her nose and tried to get her breath back so it was in her chest and not in her throat.

"Why don't you stay put and let me come over there and take a look," he said. "Those generators are pretty old. Silas got them secondhand."

"I know."

"Sometimes the fuel hose gets stiff and they break, or they can rub against the vibration of the motor and wear out that way."

The tears were falling, stupid, stupid tears, but she wouldn't let out any sound. She held it back, kept it tight in her throat and wiped them away with her sleeve and the back of her hand.

"What do you mean?"

"Sometimes," he said, "the hose just breaks."

She felt the break happen that night.

They walked together up the hill to the generator shed, the beams of their headlamps slicing the night, their footsteps crackling in the leaves. Sounds came from strange directions. Elsa was on the edge, alert to every noise.

Inside the generator shed Ethan inspected the fuel line. "Look at that," he said. "It's busted all right." He showed her where the hose had rubbed against the wheel of the alternator, how it wore through until it broke. "Probably it got bumped at some point," he said. "These things happen. Nothing's been cut."

He showed her how to splice in a new fuel hose—there was a bag of hose clamps already there in the shed, ordered just for that purpose. He walked her through the process and mended the line. She felt like a child, a useless idiot because the tears kept falling, and he said, "It's nothing to be ashamed of. You did the right thing in calling." His voice so patient and kind, so much like Silas, and she saw how like a father he must have been to her husband, and how like a father he was becoming to her, and she cracked, like one of the stubborn logs that wouldn't open.

Some inner resistance finally gave way, that hardness inside her let go, and she thought that, maybe, slowly, she could allow herself to change.

34

The first leaf fell during the second week of August. Already the ferns had yellowed. They huddled in the ditches as if panhandling for light, the black-eyed Susans shriveled and the asters fringing the fields. Ethan couldn't sleep. He felt the anniversary of the accident approaching like a weather front that gathered and rolled in the back of his head. He got up without waking his wife and went down the stairs.

He drank a glass of water. The kitchen clock displayed his birth date, 2:22. He often wondered if the fundamental differences between him and his brother came down to a question of birthdays, his deep in winter, Robby's at the height of summer. He finished his water, slipped on a jacket, and went outside.

A half-pie moon had risen over the whole of the farm and he walked between the rows with Maggie running a few noses behind. They had started bringing in the hay, wrapped and dropped the bales off the back of the baler with the help of Caleb, his new hired hand.

This time last year it was Silas who helped get the hay in. He'd made time for it even with everything he had going on, and there was never any question that he wouldn't be here, that he wouldn't give those precious weeks to the farm. The boy knew where he was needed, and though Ethan would never have insisted on it, Silas must have felt pressured, the weight of so many obligations, unable to prioritize because in his mind, everything held parity.

Ethan missed it, he supposed, because Silas had spent all of

October humming, whistling under his breath. That was his way of dealing with stress, and Ethan knew it, but had somehow forgotten. It crept up on him, the fact that they were rushing, and maybe it crept up on Silas, too. He had to get the well in before the ground froze, and he needed the money from that job. It wasn't like him to rush or hurry, and it wasn't like him to misread a tree.

Silas could read trees like most people read books. He scanned and measured with his eyes, how much light it got, which way it grew, how it would fall and why.

One time they had a real tangler, three trees cut but leaning, crisscrossed and hung up in each other's branches. A mistaken calculation by one of his men, what could potentially be a fatal problem because at any moment those trees could break and fall to the ground. Silas came over and studied the mess. He suited up in the harness and walked out along one of the leaners with his chain saw—just walked right up its trunk—and spent a good twenty minutes limbing off branches. There came a slow series of snaps and breaks that accelerated louder and faster as the trees began to fall, the whole mess moving toward the ground. And then came Silas down out of the canopy. He hustled along the moving trunk like an acrobat on a high wire, practically running he came, and as the trees fell and the branches broke, all that snapping and crackling and shifting masses of weight, he hopped off nimble and quick before it all came crashing down.

The boy oversaw the whole operation and on his own terms, in spite of the way that he, the foolish uncle, had sat him down and explained all the reasons why it wouldn't work, in this day and age, to harvest timber the slow way using draft horses and skids. Ethan used to watch his own uncle drain quarts of oil from the tractor right into the dirt, but not anymore. Silas had operated a green outfit. For every mechanized harvester, he employed twelve men. He had his standards, his ideals, and word spread. Silas got work. Ethan had been wrong about the business, he'd been wrong about that.

Ethan looked out with a sharp eye across his field. He'd been fooling himself, hadn't he? Dragging himself out of bed every morning as if dragging along the gravestones of the ones he'd lost, along with the weight of running the farm, keeping the animals safe. He'd always thought he would leave the farm to Silas because the boy belonged here, but he couldn't imagine Elsa doing the same, and it wasn't what he would want for Hester or Finn, the way the industry had changed. No, it wasn't what he would want for them at all.

Last winter when Elsa rejected them and said no to living with them, he'd gotten his feelings hurt. And he'd been feeling sorry for himself ever since.

That's why he missed it. Elsa wasn't doing okay. She'd been nearly out of her mind the night the fuel line broke. He'd thought she was fine. He told himself that she had things in hand with her new job and the well she had put in, but he saw it that night, how she was falling apart, breaking under the weight of it, the responsibility of running the place, keeping the children safe. He'd asked her, the two of them in the generator shed, their faces lit by the glow of the headlamps, he'd said, "Elsa, why are you still here?"

She'd held her face perfectly still, as if it were an egg about to crack. "I want him to be proud of me," she'd said. And a moan escaped her. "I made so many mistakes!"

"Now listen," he told her. "Look here. We all make mistakes. It's not about what we get wrong. If we dwell on that, we're not honoring their life. We got to remember the good times. Think of what we got right."

Across the field the moon shone down its cold hard light. Robby's face flashed before him, sharp and exact from his memory, that easy smile, that cake-eating grin. And Ethan knew it then—his brother would want him to be happy. Was it possible that he and Elsa were both guilty of the same foolishness? Both of them holding on to what made them miserable out of loyalty to the dead? Sacrificing their own health and perhaps even their sanity in the hope of some kind of pardon for the crime of still being alive?

Maggie came up behind him and nosed into the cup of his palm. She licked his fingers, pressing her body into his calves, and wagging her tail. Ethan reached down and gave her a scratch. It was hard to find fault with loyalty, but Elsa didn't know that she was asking of herself the impossible. He could see her mistake and the toll it was taking, see it clearly as he saw the stars. But how do you convince someone that the best they can do is walk away, move on, leave behind a good thing they've known and loved, when he'd been unwilling to do the same?

He came back in through the garage door into the kitchen and found his wife in her bathrobe slumped in a chair with her father's shotgun on her lap. When he closed the door, she jerked awake and raised her rifle.

"Hell's bells, Luvey."

"It's you!"

"Well, of course it's me. Who else were you expecting?" He had his hands up in the air and she launched herself from her chair and threw her arms around him. Surprised by the sudden display of emotion, he patted her back, slowly took the shotgun from her, clicked on the safety, and leaned it against the wall. "What's this now?" he said to her.

"I had a terrible dream," she mumbled into his shoulder. "I woke up, and you weren't here and I thought something might have happened and I started thinking about all kinds of terrible things." She pulled back, dug out a tissue from her robe pocket, and blew her nose. When she spoke again, she sounded more like herself. "Where the devil have you been?"

"I went for a walk."

"A walk? At this time of night? What were you doing, walking to town?"

"Now, why would I do that?"

"Well how should I know? Half the things you do, you just do them, and I don't know why or what got you there."

Sensing her distress, the dog nosed into her side. Luvera scratched behind its ears and took a seat at the kitchen table.

"I aim to make some coffee," he said. "Do you want some?"

"No." She fussed with the dog, patting its head. "I don't know. How should I know? When have I ever asked that question, *What do I want?* Nobody cares what I want. Young people nowadays ask that question all the time, it's all about what they want, and they expect to get exactly that delivered right to them on a silver platter, as if they had every right to it."

Ethan spooned the grounds into the percolator, lit the burner, and set the pot to flame.

"But that's not how I was raised." She defended herself, as if he had responded contrarily. "As a person of faith, I accept what comes and what doesn't come. When we couldn't get pregnant, I thought it wasn't meant to be. When I did get pregnant and then miscarried, I thought that was God's will. I don't ever remember deciding not to have kids. But now look at us. I look around here and I think, what's it all been for?"

Ethan leaned with his back against the counter confronted with one of the great mysteries of married life, how they had both gotten here to this point, from young fools to the old people he had once been taught to look up to, and how they had both landed on the same conundrum at the same time. His fondness for her leapt right out of his chest.

It had been for this.

"Tell me, Mrs. Arnasson, what do you want? I'd like to know."

He thought of that day out on Hawk Ridge when she'd handed

him the binoculars, shy, but a little forthright, as if he should have
known better than to come up there unprepared. He'd shown her
an osprey; she'd shown him a Cooper's hawk and a northern har-
rier. They'd been different people back then, but also the same.

In the long silence the coffee rose to a gurgle and he let it boil
on for as long as he could before pulling it away. The question had
quieted her. She lowered her eyes, soft and brown as a wren. He
snapped off the flame and took down two mugs. Behind him came
her voice.

"The Bible says, 'Ask and ye shall receive.' Do you suppose that
maybe we didn't ask for enough?"

He brought her a coffee and she wrapped both hands around
her mug.

"We never tried any modern methods, in vitro or artificial in-
semination, never even looked into it because it felt too much like
meddling, but now I wonder. And adoption, what would you have
thought about that?"

"I think you would have been a good mother," he said. "I know
that."

"And you as well."

"I know."

"Not a mother, but a father."

"I figured."

"But we're too old now."

"Are we?"

Fishing around in her robe for another tissue, she blew her nose.
"I was so worried about you. Pictured all kinds of horrible things.
I thought you had gotten lost out there."

"Lost? On my own farm?"

"Confused. Turned around. I pictured you walking alone down
the road. You've gotten so skinny, and you haven't been yourself.
I really wish you would go see Dr. Olson. I'll make the appointment. I know he'd be happy to see you."

The morning light brushed timidly at the kitchen window. That moment just before the crack, Silas working across from him in the woods, it came back to him more vivid than he'd remembered before. That root had snapped. Ethan had felt it beneath his feet, that pop underground and the shift of soil, without knowing what it was. But he'd felt a sense of foreboding, knew that something was about to go wrong.

"All right," he said. "I'll go."

She looked at him.

"Make the appointment for after we get the hay in."

"Thank you, Ethan."

"Well, I'm not doing it for you."

"I know."

"Yuh, okay." He drummed his fingers on the table. "Maybe what we all need is a vacation."

"A vacation," she huffed. "I wouldn't even know what one is."

"Yuh," he said. "Sometimes I wonder"—he was testing the idea—"who would we be without this place?"

She took him seriously, a good sign. "Those kids need us."

"I know it. But what does she need?"

"Elsa? She's just taking it one day at a time."

"Maybe that's all she can do."

"But she could go anywhere." Luvera looked into her cup. "I've never been anywhere. Never even left the state. If you asked me where I wanted to go, I wouldn't even know what to say."

He took the bait. "Where do you want to go, Mrs. Arnasson?"

"Oh, well I don't know." She brushed away imaginary crumbs from her spotless table. "If I had to give an answer, I'd probably say Florida."

"Florida?"

"I hear it's a nice place. They have palm trees. I've never seen a palm tree."

Sitting back in his chair, Ethan turned his head to the kitchen window. He'd had a bad feeling all summer, a sense of foreboding only prolonged. Luvera fussed with the dog. He drummed his fingers again on the table.

"Do you think," he said, "that if we left, she might leave, too?"

"Who, Elsa?" She stopped petting the dog, sifted out fur from her hand. "You mean, like for a vacation?"

"No. No, I'm thinking about something more permanent."

Luvera studied him for a moment, sitting back in her chair. "I see what you're getting at. I think that I do." She pressed her lips together and tipped her head. "I don't know, though. I can't picture it. Where would we go? What would we do?"

"Maybe we ought to think about it," he said, seeing in her the hint of wonder. At heart, she was still that girl watching the birds up at Hawk Ridge. "Maybe you and I should try a little meddling together. See where that gets us."

35

The day of the shower arrived with a parade of clouds. It started raining after she hung up the clothes on the clothesline and then it picked up as she pulled out of the driveway, a hard rain with large heavy drops. They battered the trees all along the road, splatted along her windshield, and pattered on the roof of the car. Then they were gone. The road that had baked all morning in the sun released its steam like the resurrection of run-down souls.

The parking lot was crowded. A good turnout for the shower, the Kroplins a popular family, she thought. And there in the parking lot across from them was Tommy Kroplin's wife, unfolding a stroller. Both her son and daughter were with her, but not Tommy, and it was a large stroller, cumbersome with a front and back seat, and she would have trouble maneuvering it through the front entrance, Elsa knew. She hurried ahead to hold open the inner door while Hester held open the screen, and when a small baby toy bounced out from the stroller, Elsa retrieved it.

"Oops, don't want to lose this," she said. It was a stuffed lamb. She handed it to Cherice.

"Oh, thanks." On her face—relief, to have finally arrived, to have all three kids washed and fed and dressed. Nothing more, and that was good. Cherice moved away into her circle of friends.

The tables in the Den were all filled with young mothers and boisterous children. Hester and Finn ran over to the shelves with all the toys and puzzles and settled in with the other kids. Dee stood and waved her hand. "Elsa!" she called her name from across the room. "I saved you a seat!" Elsa's heart swelled—someone had saved her a seat. She moved across the room with a place to go, every table decorated, every color pastel with baby feet and frills. When she sat she noticed—no sign of Al and his daughter. They weren't there.

The shower was beautiful. Baby Gwendolyn was passed around. When it was her turn, Elsa stood with the infant in her arms and excused herself from the table. It was the way her back rounded in a hump and the way her head lay in the crook between her shoulder and neck. It was the smell of the top of her head—Luvera had told her about that, the smell of a baby's head when she'd first had Hester, and how had Luvera known? And the sounds—she'd forgotten how they cooed and squeaked. Elsa stood alone by the windows, apart from the others, and rubbed little Gwendolyn's back. She thought about what Ethan had said. Of course, it was true. They had gotten so many things right, she and Silas. She had so many good memories of so many good times.

"Is she sleeping again?"

Elsa turned. Tommy was there, his wide shoulders and quiet air, his flannel shirt rolled up to reveal the muscle of his forearms. Sawdust and wood chips creased in the folds of his pants just like they did when Silas came home after work.

"I can take her," he said. "If you want to get back to the party."

She handed the baby over, not because she wanted to let her go, but because she saw that Tommy needed to hold her. Gwendolyn seemed to shrink in his arms. She squirmed and squeaked and resettled.

"Congratulations," Elsa said. "She is really beautiful."

"Yeah, thanks." He avoided her eyes. "Ain't she something?"

He still had that same heavy air, but when he looked down at his daughter, he smiled. And she thought of what Silas had once said about neighboring trees, how they never overreach.

"Goodbye, Tommy," she said, leaving him to his own patch of light.

Elsa was back at the table with Dee and Cherice and the other mothers. All the presents had been opened, the children were getting cranky, and the parents too tired to move. She sat with Finn on her lap while Hester next to him kept him entertained. They were playing with the clumps of curling ribbons from the opened packages, Hester moving them around while Finn swatted at them with his quick hands. Lunging forward, he knocked over a forgotten cup of coffee, spilling its liquid out.

"Oh Finn!" Hester leapt up in a panic, her voice loud and frantic. "What did you do!"

They pushed back their chairs, lifting presents off the table. Dee left to go get some towels while Finn cried on her lap. Hester reacted as though the spill were a fire and her brother in its path. She put herself between Finn and the trail of liquid, tugging frantically at the napkins in the dispenser.

"Hester, it's all right." Elsa stood to help, but Hester wouldn't look at her. "It's all right, honey," she said again, but Hester pushed her away.

"No, this is my responsibility." And the look on her face. Elsa sat down.

Her daughter, wadding up napkins, wiping the table, rubbing at her brother's clothes—her daughter so worried about the stains to her brother's clothes, because of how hard the laundry was to do, she thought. Hester a young girl of seven, anxious and overwhelmed.

Elsa saw it, although Hester wouldn't look at her, she saw what she had missed before, how much her daughter had changed.

They were driving home from the café, it was after five o'clock, the children tired, worn out from the big day. The boy slept in his car seat with his arms around his toy truck; her daughter sat facing the window.

"Hester?" She called to her softly in the quiet hum of the car. "Are you happy here?"

Hester didn't answer right away. She turned her head slowly and their eyes met in the rearview mirror.

"Do you like living here?" Elsa asked. "In our house in the woods?"

"Yes." Hester yawned and turned back to the window. They went by the brave tree out in the clearing and she lifted a hand. It was still standing, although tipped, and patches of its needles had turned brown.

"The reason I'm asking is because I've been relying on you to take care of Finn an awful lot. And you're doing such a good job. But honey . . ." She paused. Hester kept her face turned away. Elsa flexed her hands, squeezed the wheel. "You're just a kid, and I've been asking too much. It's made me realize that I've been unrealistic, thinking we could stay here, much as I want to. This place is too much for us to take care of without Papa."

"What do you mean?" Hester turned her head. "You want to leave?"

"No, I don't want to go." Gravel pinged under her tires as the bones of her face buzzed. They drove up the long driveway lined by the trees they had planted together as a family. The tires dipped in and out of the pitted ruts, and branches clattered along the car.

"We can't leave," Hester said. "I'll help you more. I don't mind taking care of Finn. Please, we have to stay."

Elsa parked under the red pine that dropped sticky resin all over the car. "I know this is upsetting to think about. I'm having a hard time, too. But we have to talk about what would be best for you and—"

"No!" Hester popped open the latch on her door. "You can't make me leave, and if you do, I'll just run away!" She scrambled out of the car before the engine was off. Up the hill past the porch she disappeared to her hiding place on the unfinished second story of the house.

Elsa let her go. She pulled Finn out of his car seat and carried him up to the house. He woke happy to see her, his cheeks warm and flushed. Heating up dinner, she fed him, while above her on the ceiling she heard the sound of Hester's footsteps, light and fleeting.

Later, outside in front of the house, a swarm of dragonflies worried the shelf of air above her head. A late-day stillness settled over the land. Never was a place more beautiful than when she knew she had to leave.

In the room that had been planned for her daughter, she found Hester hunched up and alone. Elsa lowered herself next to her. The girl tightened, turned away. She sat with her back against a beam wrapped in plastic, legs pressed together up to her chest, the pose of a mini mountain.

"Hester? I'm here. Please talk to me," she said. "I don't want you to run away." A sheet of Tyvek crinkled and the air smelled faintly of sawdust and plastic fumes. She waited, but the little mountain didn't move. "Please, tell me how you're feeling. I'm listening now. You have all of my attention."

Her voice came muffled from behind her knees. "Where's Finn?"

"He's watching a movie on my laptop."

"What movie?"

"*The Little Engine That Could.*"

Hester lifted her chin up on her knees. "I hate that poopy movie." Her face was streaked with dirty water lines like the plastic sheets.

"Wouldn't it be nice for you to have some friends your own age?"

"You don't want me to have friends."

"That's not true. Why would you say that?"

"You won't let me have Anya over."

Elsa bowed her head. "I'm sorry, Hester. I'm just not comfortable with Anya and her father. I don't like the way they left you and Finn that day."

"Papa left us."

The wind swelled in the plastic wrap around the wooden beams and the house breathed, taking in and expelling air. Elsa put an arm around her daughter. Hester didn't move. Her back felt different, stronger and wider than she'd remembered. The sky glowed purple around them, bruised and hushed.

"Hester, what did you want to ask me about hell?"

The wind lifted the plastic, filled it like a sail and then set it back down.

"Aunt Luvera said that some people go to hell. That when they die, they go there and burn forever in a great big roaring pit of fire. Is that true? Is hell real?"

"I don't know."

"I want you to tell me yes or no."

"I can only tell you what I think."

"Okay. What do you think?"

Through a rip in the plastic sheeting, Elsa noticed in the small clearing behind the house the press of cloven hooves. They were everywhere in the soft earth, deer tracks, dozens of them. For one breathless minute she imagined them back there, grazing at dusk.

Did they go up onto the second story of the house, too? Nose into the corners, looking for food?

"I had an art teacher once who taught me how to see. What I learned from him was that sometimes, we don't see what's actually here, we see what we think." She felt the bones of her face start to buzz. "I used to think that hell was a real place. But now, I think it's a state of mind. Do you know what that is?"

"No."

"What you're thinking about. So, if you are thinking about how mad you are at someone, like yourself, for example, then you will be in a kind of hell because you will be stuck thinking about all this stuff that makes you feel bad. And what that does, it makes everything around you look bad. And you start to think, what the hell, and so you start making bad choices. And you can get stuck, looking at life this way, expecting bad things to happen, doing bad things, and your life becomes a kind of living hell. I mean, it can. If you let it."

Elsa looked out across the unfinished rooms and in the flash of an instant Silas was there, kneeling in his work pants, wearing his tool belt. It was just her imagination, she knew, but she could see him so clearly—his exact posture and the look on his face. He smiled at her and was gone. The greatest love of her life, and she'd reciprocated that love too late. As an adolescent, she'd always hoped to find such a love. As a young woman, she worried that the love she found wouldn't love her back. Now, as a mother, her greatest fear was that she hadn't loved enough.

She reached for her daughter's hand. It was warm and larger than she would have thought, and Hester let her hold it, and she gave it a squeeze. Her daughter still wore Silas's old wrist brace, it was peeking out from under the sleeve of her sweatshirt, the sleeves riding up past her wrist.

"Papa didn't mean to leave us," she said.

"I know."

"It was an accident. It wasn't anybody's fault." She turned to Hester, and she wanted to give her something, a recipe to follow, a pearl of wisdom to hold. But she hadn't yet found that for herself. "I want you to go back to school," she said instead. "I do want you to have friends, and I think it would be good for you to be around people your own age."

"I don't want to go back to school."

That surprised her. "Don't you want to see your friends? It's not too late to get registered. You can start out the first day just like everyone else."

Hester let go of her hand. "They aren't my friends anymore," she said. "But I'll go if we can stay here." She got up and walked away, stepping off the unfinished second story of the house and walking out into the clearing. She stopped and stood the way her father had always stood, as if perusing their land, her back to the house in the twilight, wearing her sweatshirt with its pine-green hood.

A butterfly landed on her back. An orange butterfly, its wings unfolded. Another butterfly landed on her wrist. Hester noticed and held out her hand. The butterfly opened and closed its wings, and another one joined it, landing on her sleeve. It was late in the season for butterflies, but soon they were all along both arms, orange butterflies with stained-glass wings, eight, nine, ten or more. Two butterflies volleyed in the space above her head. She looked up—and all at once the butterflies rose in unison and lifted away.

FALL

36

On the first Monday in September they left from the farm-house and drove along the quiet county road past open fields of cows and horses that curved up hills. At the corner of Bugsy's Bar they turned left onto Highway 53. Coming from this way, they didn't pass the brave tree, but Hester thought about it. She thought how it was still out there on its own, standing its ground. At the front entrance of the school, she hefted her backpack and the two store bags filled with new notebooks and markers and big boxes of Kleenex and ziplock bags.

"Do you want me to come in with you?" Aunt Luvera said. "I can, you know. I don't mind."

"No thank you." Hester scooted out the door. "I've been here before." Her feet hit the sidewalk and being out of the car she felt unmoored, alone. She wore a brown dress with blue flowers over her denim jeans, a dress her mom had bought for her, but Aunt Luvera had made her take off her father's wrist brace that morning.

"You can't wear that thing to school," she'd said. "The nurse will want to know what's wrong with your arm."

She felt weird without the brace on, her arm lighter and unpro-tected like it might float away. She kept moving, walked through the entrance doors held open by the volunteer grandpa who smiled and said, "Have a nice day." That gave her a small burst as she moved into the hallway filled with bobbing kids who took things out of new backpacks and put new shoes in cubbies outside class-room doors. Ben and Owen were there, joking around. People when they saw her either looked away or gave her an "Oh, I'm sorry" smile. Last year when she stopped coming to school, everyone from her class wrote her a card to say that they were sorry her father had died. The cards arrived in a big yellow envelope with her name on it, and when she opened it, they dumped out and sat there on the kitchen table, great big piles of sorry.

"Hi Hester." It was Brianna, wearing a pink ruffled dress, white tights, and a matching purse. Her blond hair was brushed and curled, and she looked happy to see Hester; not because they were close friends, but because she wanted to show her the heart-shaped pendant she wore. "I also got my nails done." She showed off her fingers. They had bright stickers on their polished tips, tiny birds, red hearts.

"You look like you're ready for school," Hester said.

Brianna hopped up on her toes, twirled around, and hopped up on her toes again. Next to her, Brianna's dad laughed, and next to him Brianna's mom wore a skirt and tall boots just like her own mother used to wear but didn't anymore. Now, she wore her papa's flannel shirts.

"What teacher do you have?" Brianna asked. "My classroom is right here. I have Mrs. Conner." They looked together inside the room filled with low tables in clusters, the chairs all different colors and tucked in. Hester said she was in the other second-grade room, and they separated and went their own ways. It felt right that they would be apart now, and Hester felt again that ache; it hurt, but also, she knew that it was somehow good.

She entered her new classroom. Walking in for the first time felt kind of like walking into church: it was clean and hushed and she wondered at first if she really belonged. Light slanted in through the side windows and landed in patches on the floor. Hester moved with awkward reverence up one of the aisles between the individual desks lined up in columns.

"You may put your supplies in your desk," the teacher said.

"This desk will be yours for the entire year, and it's your responsibility to keep it neat and clean. Just find the one with your name."

"We have desks?"

"We're one of the lucky classrooms this year." Her teacher, Mrs. Dolson, had a face like a cookie, round and sweet-looking, with only small wrinkles that belonged like cracks in a biscuit.

Hester found her name written on a laminated card. The desk had a chair attached and Hester slid into the seat, opened the lid, and inspected. She never had her own desk before, and it felt grown-up and remarkably private. Around her the classroom filled up with noise and kids, but Hester stayed anchored to her desk like a ship in a great heaving sea.

A girl appeared in the doorway. She was interesting for three reasons: One, no one had ever seen her before, Hester could tell by the way the other children stared, and it was a small school where everyone knew everyone. Two, she arrived not with a mom or dad, but with an old man who had a bushy white beard and denim overalls that gave his big belly lots of room. He might even have been Santa Claus. And three, the girl was stringy. Her brown hair hung in oily strands not curled or brushed, and she didn't wear anything pretty, just jeans and a T-shirt with sneakers that had laces, not Velcro.

During recess Hester found the girl, whose name was Karlie, sitting alone at the swing set. Her back slumped as she sat on the black band of the swing, poking her toe into the sand. Karlie didn't have new shoes. Hers were red and dirty, with gray laces.

"Hello," Hester said. "Do you like swings?"

Karlie looked at her, wrinkled her nose. "They're okay."

"Did they have swings at your old school?"

"Yeah. I guess. I didn't really play on them though."

"What did you do?"

"I ran around with my cousins. Played freeze tag and stuff."

A boy ran up and crashed into the swing next to her. He stood up in the seat, twisted the chains, and spun around. When they unwound, he hopped off and said to Karlie, "Are you jelly?"

Karlie squinted. "Huh?"

"Are you jelly of my butt chin?" He squeezed his chin together with his two fingers so that it looked like a naked butt. Then he cracked up laughing.

Karlie looked at Hester, hopped off her swing, and lunged at the boy.

"You're it!" she said, and tore off across the baseball field.

"Wait for me!" Hester shouted, and took off following at a run.

One week later during morning library time, the school counselor, Mrs. Seeley—which rhymed with "feely," because she was the person who talked about feelings—showed up in the doorway of their classroom. She asked for Hester and Karlie to come with her. The two girls followed Mrs. Seeley down the hall and into the teachers' lounge, where kids weren't usually allowed to go.

"What are we doing here?" Hester asked. On the counter was a coffeemaker with a pot freshly brewed. The tables were clean and white with lots of chairs pulled around. Country knickknacks decorated the walls, and a corkboard pinned with notes had a piece of paper on it that said, "Here is your smile for the day!" Fringes of tear-off tabs hung down with smiley faces drawn on them.

"We're just going to have some girl time," Mrs. Seeley said, taking a basket from a top shelf. "Go ahead and have a seat." She slid the basket in front of them and Hester leaned over her arms to peer inside. The basket was filled with nail polish, all different kinds. "Who wants to go first?"

Hester looked to Karlie, who also peered into the basket, her brown hair frayed and netted up like she had slept on it and just woken up. "You go first," Hester said.

"Pick out your color." Mrs. Seeley opened up a new hairbrush from a package and went around behind Karlie to brush out her hair. "And Hester, you can rub your hands in that lotion, if you want. It smells just like peaches."

"I don't like peaches," Karlie said, picking through the bottles of polish, her head getting jerked around from the brush. "They're too drippy."

"Oh, I like them," said Mrs. Seeley. "Nice and juicy, and their skin has a nice soft fuzz. Delicious. What do you think, Hester?"

"They're okay, I guess."

"My grandpa makes me eat canned peaches." Karlie handed Mrs. Seeley a shade of electric blue. "He said that they will put hair on my chest."

Mrs. Seeley laughed and shook the bottle. It made a clicking sound and when Hester asked why, Mrs. Seeley explained that it was because of a little ball inside that mixed up the paint. The counselor sat at the table across from Karlie and painted her nails with a tiny black brush. She stayed perfectly inside the lines of her fingernails and didn't get any paint on Karlie's skin.

Later, when their nails were dry, the girls walked back down the hall to their classroom, and Hester could feel the weight of the paint on each fingertip. "My mom doesn't wear nail polish anymore," she said to Karlie. "Does your mom?"

"No," said Karlie. "My mom is at the bottom of Lake Superior. She got eaten by the alligators when her car went off the bridge."

Hester stopped walking. It felt like a little ball inside of her just dropped to the bottom of her stomach.

After school at the farmhouse she told Aunt Luvera about Karlie's mom who got eaten by the alligators at the bottom of Lake Superior. Aunt Luvera said, "There aren't any alligators in Lake Superior."

"Are you sure?"

"Yes, I'm sure, hon. It's too cold. The lake freezes during winter."

"I wondered about that." Hester looked at her fingernails. "But why did she lie?"

"Oh, sometimes things are just too sad to talk about. Maybe Karlie's mother was in a bad car accident and it's easier for her to say that it was alligators."

A few days later Hester went again with Karlie to the teachers' lounge, and they each picked out new colors of nail polish and put lotion on their hands. When Mrs. Seeley had to pop out of the room for a few minutes, she told the girls to shake up their bottles and they did. Hester made the little silver ball in her glass bottle tick around, and she said to Karlie, "My father got trapped by a giant tree."

"What kind of tree?"

"A white pine."

Karlie didn't say anything.

"The tree crushed the butterfly wings inside his spine so he couldn't walk or talk or breathe and that's why he died."

Karlie stopped shaking her bottle and leaned forward on her elbows. "When the alligators ate my mom," she said, "they crushed her skull."

37

The kettle on the stove rose to a whistle just as the car pulled into the driveway. Luvera hopped up from the kitchen table. "Perfect timing," she congratulated herself, and poured the water for tea. Elsa hadn't been feeling well all week, probably the change in the season and the start of school, and she thought a little tea with honey might be nice. Maggie trotted over to the back door that led out to the garage and wagged her entire body. When the door opened, she insisted on getting all the attention before Elsa could even come through.

"Somebody is happy to see you," Luvera said. "I have your tea right here. Why don't you have a seat."

"Tea?" Elsa closed the door and looked warily at Ethan, sitting there at the kitchen table in the middle of the day. "What's going on?" she said. "Where are the kids?"

"Oh, they're in the office," Luvera said. "They're playing on my 'pewter'—that's Finn's word for computer. Isn't that precious?"

"Is everything all right?"

"Everything's fine. Hester had a good week at school. She made a new friend and learned about an educational website where they can play math games. I told them they could take their snack and play in there." Luvera set down the two steaming mugs and they both took a chair. She nudged Ethan with her elbow. He cleared his throat.

"We have some things we'd like to talk over with you. I made a list here." He slid a piece of paper across the table to Elsa.

"What's this?"

"All the things you'll want to see to before the snow flies." He looked to Luvera, who nodded and said, for clarification:

"What needs to be done before winter, hon."

Elsa pulled in the list with her fingertips.

"You'll want to check the water level on the batteries in the generator shed and get them filled," Ethan said. "You don't want to be hauling water up there when it's freezing out. And the gas tanks, there's six or seven of them, I'm not sure which ones Silas bought outright and which ones he's renting, but if you want to avoid paying the rental fee, you'll have to fill them, or at least put a few hundred bucks in."

Elsa looked up, confused.

"He means the gas tanks on your property, honey. They hold the diesel, what you need to run your generator, and the propane to run your refrigerator and the gas range."

"Oh. Those."

"They need to be filled," Ethan said. "You'll want to address that before the snow comes because once it does the trucks can't get back there to fill them."

"I see."

"I checked the meter on the one by the house this spring and it was at twenty percent."

"What does that mean?"

"It means you want to get the tank filled. If it runs out, air gets in the line, and they have to reset the appliances. October is just around the corner. We've had early snow before."

Luvera lifted the string on her tea bag and dunked it a few times. "Before we got the snowblower, I used to keep three weeks' worth of meals stored in the deep freeze. You might want to do the same. In case you can't get out."

"Can't get out?"

"If you get snowed in. Ethan might not always be around to plow, you know." She casually sipped her tea. "What size tank is up by the house? Do you know, Mr. Arnasson?"

"Oh, it's a thousand-gallon tank. At the going rate, it'll be around seventeen, eighteen hundred to fill it, Mrs. Arnasson." Then he said, "The diesel tanks are smaller."

"But diesel is high right now," she said. "Isn't it? Higher than unleaded?"

"That's right." Ethan nodded and said to Elsa, "But you don't have to fill the tanks. You can just tell them the amount you want them to put in, and that's what they'll do."

"There might be a minimum though," Luvera added, "with the rentals."

"That's right. Usually a few hundred bucks."

"For each tank. You have to at least put that in for each tank. It'll add up."

"I have some savings." Elsa folded over the list.

"Never spend it all," Ethan said. "That's the only way to keep the wolf from knocking down your door."

Maggie from under the table thumped her tail on the floor. The Organic Valley truck pulled up, early that day. Ethan stood, all too eager to get up and go. Luvera asked him, "Do you need the iPad?"

"No, I already got it out in the barn." He zipped his jacket, paused at the back door. "You two finish up and let me know what you decide." He looked to Elsa. "I think you should consider a wood splitter if you're going to stay." He looked to Luvera. "Make sure you tell her about that."

"A wood splitter?" Elsa said after Ethan had left. "He wants me to buy a wood splitter? How am I supposed to do that and fill up the tanks and save for the property taxes and buy the groceries and pay the hospital bill when the greenhouse is about to close?"

"I know, it's a lot."

"You have no idea!" She pressed her fingers to her eyes, and Luvera slid over the tissue box. She'd known Elsa would be too proud to fall apart in front of Ethan.

"I'm sorry, Elsa, but Ethan and I just want you to be prepared. We might not always be here, and so there's certain things we want to make sure that you're aware of."

"What do you mean, you might not always be here?"

Luvera pulled her hands off the table and sat with them in her lap.

Elsa straightened and her tears halted right there in her eyes. "What's going on?"

"Ethan hasn't been himself lately. I didn't want to tell you because I know you've got an awful lot on your plate, but he went to the doctor, and it turns out he's got the depression." This hadn't been part of the plan; it just came out.

"Oh, Luvera. I'm so sorry. I don't know what to say."

"That's all right. It's probably best not to say anything at all. He's ashamed, had a hard enough time just telling me, though truthfully, I was so relieved." She brought a hand to her neck, rubbed her cross, and turned the clasp. From the living room Charlie started chirping in his cage. He always knew when she was upset, he started singing, and leave it to Ethan to find a bird like that. "Oh for goodness' sake," she said, fanning her face with her hand. "Really, it's fine. I was just so worried, that's all. I thought it was Alzheimer's, the way he was acting, I thought he was losing his mind." She grabbed a tissue, laughed. She'd really been convinced, had even told her prayer group that's what it was, and they'd all sat in their circle and prayed. But she'd been wrong, or maybe the prayer had worked. "It's situational depression, nothing severe." She blew her nose, wiped her eyes. "He's got the little blue pills. He won't take them forever. It's just for now to get over the hump." The hump being this time of year with the anniversary of the accident, and when they had also lost the baby, all those years ago. "So, yuh," she said, pulling in her tea, shaking her head, her voice sounding oddly deep. *Hells bells, Luvey,* she could hear him inside her head, *what did you have to go and tell her all that for?*

"I'm sorry," she said, both to Elsa and the imaginary Ethan inside her head. But she could breathe now without that lump of emotion in her chest. "There's a lot going on, and it's a lot of work to take care of a place like this, and we're not getting any younger. Even with the hired hand, it all falls to Ethan. So yes, Elsa, we're thinking about selling the farm."

Elsa sat back in her seat, her face white as a sheet, even her hands, her veins the only color left, thin and blue as arctic creeks. Her fingers walked up her throat to close the collar of her shirt, as though she'd taken a chill.

"It won't happen right away," Luvera clarified, balling up her tissue and moving the box over to Elsa. "We'll lease it out for a while most likely. Ethan moves pretty slow on things, he's always been cautious. But one immediate thing we talked about that involves you is the logging business. We thought that with your hours getting cut during the off-season, you might consider finally selling, and that would help us out quite a bit."

"Selling what?"

"All that logging equipment being stored in the barn. The greenhouse where you work holds an annual Fall Fest at the end of October with vendors and an auctioneer who comes up from Iowa. Buyers come in from miles around, it's a three-day event." She squeezed the tissue in her hand. "Some of those skids are antiques, you know, what Silas inherited from his uncles. They've been in the family for generations. One of the carts even has wooden wheels. You don't see those anymore. Might be surprised what people are willing to pay for them."

"Oh no," Elsa said. "No, I can't do that. He would never want me to sell them. He was so proud of them."

"Of course Silas wouldn't want you to sell them, but he isn't here now, Elsa. You have to make decisions based on what's best for you and the kids, and he would most certainly want that. Ethan agrees. But the equipment is yours," she said, gently, "to do with as you see fit."

Elsa nodded and looked away, tears spilling down her face. She turned toward the window, the red semitruck parked by the barn.

Luvera saw it then, Elsa's face bathed in the stark slash of sunlight coming through the window. She saw why Silas had chosen her, why this girl above them all. It was an ethereal quality to her beauty, what shone from within. Elsa was a creature of the air. She never did have her feet all the way on the ground, but her heart was here, her heart had always been here, and that was why she needed him, why she needed them all.

"I know it's difficult, honey," she said. "And I know it often seems like I'm tough on you, but it's only because I learned the hard way that if you don't make a decision, then life makes one for you. And you might not like what life decides."

"I know we have to leave." Tears flowed unguarded down Elsa's face. "I've known for some time. But I don't know how to do it. I don't know how to go on without him." And it was the truest thing she had ever said.

"None of us do, hon. We're all just hanging on."

"But the house," she said. "I don't know what to do about the house."

"It is a lot," Luvera said. "What you're doing is a lot. A lesser woman would have given up a long time ago."

This broke her, all the way. Elsa's shoulders fell and she shuddered with great heaving sobs, and for the first time, for the first time in a year, she let it all come down.

Luvera stood and went over to this girl—she was suddenly a girl, so young and motherless and hurting—and she held her, folding her head into her chest with her arms. "There there, dear," she said. "Let it all come out now. Let it all come out."

And she did. And they did. Together they wept for the man they had both loved.

38

In the past Elsa marked the changes of seasons by certain signs—the first snow equaled winter, when the leaves turned that was fall, and when they returned to the trees again in canopies of bright limey green, that was spring.

Now, she understood that change happened slowly, months before the outer signs. The changes internal and unseen, the forces turning in the earth. A blunt chill filled the air, it receded, advanced, pulled back again, leaving more and more of the cold behind—that was how winter came. Spring deposited its warmth in the same kind of increments, and the heat of summer could be felt in the winds of March. Gradually and in stages—the way nature changed was the way changing forces went to work inside of her.

Over the course of the next four weeks she was carried by a momentum. She rose in the morning and stepped into the stream of life—what always seemed to be moving even while she slept. She went to work and came home and stayed up late every night, going through her husband's things—his tools, his notebooks, the dress shoes he only wore once. A reverie, a nostalgic dance, she lifted, folded, touched each and every thing.

The anniversary of the accident arrived. She stepped into it like someone boarding a ship and sailed through as if in a dream, removed, watching back from the shore of herself. She saw who she was one year ago on a Tuesday when she stood out in their field, wearing their son in a backpack carrier, watching a puffball. Never had she been so happy, or so at peace.

Who she was and who she was becoming, this place and how it had changed her—it wasn't just the house that was unfinished; it was her.

Sometimes the wind shuffled the leaves far back in the forest and the white sunlight scattered among them would take the shape of Silas. She would see him back there, moving around. Sometimes he would come toward her, smiling the way he used to, eager to tell her about some new thing.

Her mom once told her she'd never be the kind of artist or even the kind of person she wanted to become unless she learned how to see with her heart. And that was what this place had taught her. How to see with the part of herself that had nothing to believe, not about anyone, not even herself, and so every day, every minute, she came stumbling into all this beauty.

And that was how she knew it was the right time to go. In her heart she no longer wanted to leave.

Elsa dragged two industrial garbage pails out through the back door of the café and onto the paved area alongside two dumpsters. The sky cast a leaden hue in the air marked by an occasional leaf. They'd been watching a weather front from Alberta all week, a storm system moving through Saskatchewan and down into the central plains, Montana and North Dakota already reporting eighteen inches of snow. The storm was due to arrive early tomorrow, on Hester's birthday, the day before the auction. But now it was Thursday, and she had to clean out two pails before going home.

She'd helped Ethan clean up the skid carts, and the portable bandsaw; learned how to sharpen the blades. Ethan and Luvera suggested she wait until spring to sell the house. They had room at the farmhouse, they said, if she wanted to stay with them during the winter. This time she accepted and said yes. She would drain the water from the pipes and close down the house; she'd already started packing up their things.

Kicking aside a pile of soggy cardboard, Elsa yanked out the hose. The garbage pails were empty but crusted with mildewed vegetable peelings and slimy coffee grounds. Her sinuses were stuffed up, and her forehead was clammy. All week she'd been feeling lousy, but she couldn't take time off from work when they were closing at the end of the month. She gripped the squeeze trigger and turned on the spigot. A blast of water shot out, knocking over both pails and splashing her with back spray. The pails tumbled and rolled down the hill toward the parking lot. Dropping the hose, she turned off the water, and in her splotched and spotted apron jogged down after them.

She hadn't told Hester about leaving. She thought she would wait until after her daughter's birthday, after the Fall Fest when the café would be closed, and they could sit down and talk about it without distraction. They needed whatever money they got from the auction to live on, and to start their new life would require the proceeds from the house. Money had always come easily to her growing up; she thought it would always come easily and that she would never have to compromise what she wanted to do for what she had to do, even thought that people who did were lazy or weak-willed or both. That thought embarrassed her now. How careless she'd been with the advantages her parents gave her. She thought of her father and wondered, not for the first time, if growing up wasn't just one long painful process of realizing that everything your parents tried to tell you was right.

At the bottom of the hill by the edge of the parking lot, she caught up to her rolling garbage pails. She dug around in her apron pocket for a tissue, her nose runny, her eyes threaded red from staying up late packing every night.

A few flakes of snow fell aimlessly through the bare branches of the trees. Change happened slowly, and then all at once it made itself known. Behind her rib bones, up under her sternum, that dark quickening stirred. She'd hoped to be out of the house before it snowed. She lifted the garbage pails and headed back up the hill.

A navy-blue sedan pulled in riding low to the ground. Its engine rumbled as it parked in front of the café. The driver's-side door popped open. A large man with impudent black hair pushed out, wearing sweatpants and a kelly-green tee. He held open the door for his dog on its harnessed lead and together they lumbered to the front entrance, and what was Al doing here on a Thursday? And without his daughter?

A wind moved in from a distance and disturbed the trees, branches creaked and swayed. From behind the dumpsters she watched him disappear inside and wondered again why he'd been so interested in her kids. What would have happened that day back in the woods when he gave Finn that candy, had they accepted a ride in his car?

She bungled both garbage pails through the back door and into the kitchen and lugged them over to the tiled standing sink. She lined them with fresh garbage bags as the Hobart hummed behind her, washing its dishes. The sound of voices drifted from the front of the café, mingled with the chink of coins dropping into the register till. Why was it so easy to believe bad things about what you thought you knew, and so much harder to believe good things about what you couldn't know for sure?

Elsa dropped the bin liners and moved out into the café.

"Where is he?"

Dee looked up from where she was counting the day's sales. "Who?"

"Al. I just saw him drive up." She didn't wait for an answer. She moved past the tables and chairs and out into the hallway past the bathroom doors painted with cows. There was no reason she couldn't talk to him once and for all, find out what, if anything, was going on.

The Den this time of day was quiet and dim, with a waning light coming in through the low windows. Three elderly ladies sat on the couches playing cards; a greenhouse employee in one of the armchairs pecked at her phone. Other than that, the room was empty.

Al was gone.

39

Hester lay on the floorboards of the unfinished second story while the snow fell down around her in the dark. She could feel her mother moving around inside the house, building a fire, getting her brother dressed. Her mother sang "Happy Birthday" to her when she woke her up, brought a muffin into her bedroom with a birthday candle in it. All month she had been acting different. Hester watched her pack up the boxes of her father's things—his papers and books and awards from high school. Her mother would ask, "Do you want this?" And she would hold up a compass or a book. Or she might leave an item on her desk: a magnifying glass, a special rock. Boxes and boxes, piling up inside their house. Some of the boxes had baby clothes in them, and not just her father's things.

Hester pressed her face to her arm and curled up tight in a ball. She closed her eyes and pretended what she always pretended: that her bedroom was already built and finished with skylights and a yellow bedspread, her papa next to her reading a book. But something felt wrong. The plastic sheeting hung in strips, and her mother didn't fix it like she said she would, to get ready for winter. At night when she fell asleep, she no longer heard the thud of her mother's ax.

Karlie wasn't at school anymore. One day she just stopped coming. Hester thought it was because she was sick, but then she didn't come for an entire week, and Hester finally asked her teacher at the start of recess, when all the other kids were outside playing happily with their friends, "When is Karlie coming back?"

"Oh, honey." Mrs. Dolson made a sad face. "Karlie isn't coming back. She's gone to live with her grandma in San Antonio."

San Antonio was in Texas and very far away, and there wasn't even an address where she could write. They never got to say good-bye, and it wasn't fair when people left without first letting you say goodbye. Now she wasn't Hester, Karlie's friend, or Hester, Brianna's friend. She wasn't even Hester Pester. She was just the girl whose father had died and the girl people looked at and felt sad.

Rolling over onto her back, Hester looked up at the damp rafters that smelled of wood and sand. They were giving away Papa's things. They were going to a big sale where other people would buy his special collections. At first, she'd shouted at her mother, "We can't get rid of Papa!" And she'd felt embarrassed for her tears, but her mother said she understood—it felt like they were losing him all over again.

The brave tree stood out there all alone in the clearing and a rust brown had crept into its needled boughs. She worried that it wouldn't make it another winter, getting piled on by snow, but her mother said that injured trees can receive help in ways we can't always see.

The snow hissed and she listened to that, to the faint sound of it tapping against the plastic and landing on wrinkled leaves. She wasn't cold. Aunt Luvera had made her a red coat for her birthday, dark red wool lined with warm vanilla fleece. She could sleep here, while the sun came up, in the peaceful dark with the snow falling gently all around.

With her eyes closed she could be the snow, a lone flake dropping in a clean white space.

In dreams she looked for him—how she was always looking, and would she never stop her looking? He lived at the edge of her mind, her papa, a lone figure in the distance. He moved the way he always moved, tall and relaxed as the sky. If she could just be patient and not get distracted, he would turn and see her waiting for him there at the edge of the white space, he would come like he used to come in her dreams, and she would wake feeling certain that he was with her and all around.

A sound tugged on the corners of her mind, faint but crisp, *clomp, clomp.* She had her eyes closed but he was not coming closer, *clomp, clomp,* her papa, *clomp, clomp,* a gray smudge slipping further away. She called to him but he was fading into the distance, the space still and brightly lit as winter air.

The sound came again, this time much closer, *clomp, clomp, clomp.* She sensed the warmth of her own breath and the vibration of the floorboards under her coat, and then she felt quite distinctly the wet kiss of snow. Snow, falling gently on her face even though she was under the roof.

She opened her eyes.

A white deer, big as an elk, stood above her, lit by the eerie glow of snowlight at dawn. It stood over her just under cover of the roof, its eyes pale and rimmed in mauve. A giant white deer, its nose and antlers fuzzed in pink. Its nostrils flared; moist air snorted out in sawdust curls. It lifted a hoof, then set it down. Antlers curved around like the great branches of a spiraling tree, and she wondered how he did it, holding it all up, how he turned his head or moved, and then he did move, shaking his head, and snow fell down from his antlers and showered her in a spray of silvery stars.

Papa? she called to him in her mind. She knew that he was still here; he'd always been here. He was in this deer, but also, he was everywhere.

The floorboards beneath her shuddered when the front door of the house opened and closed. The deer turned the cup of one ear out toward the sound. Her mother's voice called out, "Hester? Are you up there? It's time to go."

Hester looked away only for a second, turning her head toward her mother's voice, and when she looked back, the deer was gone.

"Hester?" her mother called again. "We have to go!"

She sat up. Understanding came cold and she swallowed it whole: they were leaving, not just for the day, but forever. Her mother was packing them up. They wouldn't be staying in the house for the winter. They had to go.

Hester rose to her feet and went to the edge of the house. She could smell him, the white deer, the thick winter fur, damp in the pearly air. It was the same deer, she felt certain, the one they had almost hit with their car.

Why had it come back here? Had it come looking, for her? Maybe he didn't want them to go. Maybe Papa's spirit didn't want to be alone.

She hadn't dreamed it. There were footprints. There in the new-fallen snow was the path he had left for her to follow, the crescent-moon arcs of twin cloven tracks.

40

With the last box of his things, Elsa hurried out to the car, apron tucked under one arm, Finn toddling a few steps behind. The snowflakes tumbled through the air and she called up to the house, "Hester, come on! We're leaving, it's time to go!" She'd heard her daughter's footsteps on the ceiling earlier and knew she was up there brooding. Something had happened that week at school, something to do with her new friend, but she'd been so busy all week, bringing the skids to the greenhouse, where they now stood in rows on the rubber-mat flooring among the other items, lotted and listed and tagged.

She loaded in the final box and Finn climbed into the back. She buckled him into his car seat and turned over the engine to warm up the car. A few minutes passed and still no sign of Hester. Elsa unbuckled her seat belt. "Finn, you're going to have to wait here while I get your sister. Stay here. I'll be right back."

They'd gotten about six inches of snow, but she wasn't cold, her warmth from the tension inside her that wouldn't release. She was anxious about the auction, about selling the skids; she wanted to get that over and done with, and hoped people would turn out despite the storm, but most of all, she was worried about her daughter.

"Hester? Where are you?" She stepped up onto the unfinished second story. Usually, her daughter hid in the far-right corner where her bedroom was supposed to be, where it would now never be. "Hester?" The house breathed, wrapped in its plastic shroud.

Hester wasn't there.

Elsa stepped down off the back of the house where it met the earth, and that was when she saw the tracks, the zigzag press of her daughter's boots. Tracks roughing up the snow, and the path that disappeared into the snow-filled woods.

All during her childhood and adolescence, years before her mother got sick and especially after, Elsa was plagued by a recurring dream. In the dream she was holding on to the end of a rope being spun by some invisible hand. And every time that hand let go. She would be cast off, falling through an endless dark. She would wake with that panic certain inside her, as though some part of her continued to fall into nothing, with no one to catch her, not one connection; she would continue to free-fall, not connected to anything at all.

It was that panic which filled her now, a rapid churning in her chest. She hadn't felt it since that Tuesday when she saw Silas lying there, the man who understood her and saw her above all others, the one person she could trust never to let go.

She followed Hester's trail through the woods—her daughter was wearing her new red coat and would be easy to spot. But there was no movement in front of her, no sound of any kind, and no color at all. Only a white cushion of shimmering air. She called Hester's name, conscious of how long Finn had been waiting alone in the car. But there was no sign of her other than the footsteps that disappeared into the woods for as far as she could see. The snow continued to fall, the treetops rocked in the wind.

Her daughter knew, she thought. Hester knew they were leaving the land and she had run away. This time, it was her daughter who was afraid and hurting, her daughter who was holding on to the end of her rope, alone and spinning in the dark.

Turning back, bringing Finn up from the car, she phoned Ethan and Luvera from inside the house. Pulling on snow pants and tugging on a sweater, she found Hester's mittens and tucked those inside the pockets of her coat. Ethan's truck pulled up, Luvera next to him in the front seat, their headlights slicing through the snow-crammed air.

She passed Finn to Luvera and he watched his mother but did not cry. He looked over Luvera's shoulder as they separated and moved apart, his arms puffy and stiff in his snowsuit, his cheeks two circles of red.

Behind the house with Ethan she showed him the tracks left by Hester's boots and together they followed her trail into the woods. Ethan led, and they called out Hester's name while the snow continued to fall.

After some time they came to the edge of a clearing where the county had logged off its trees last winter, a vast terrain of ruined ground with shorn limbs and branches and tree trunks buried under the snow. They stopped and looked out. Wind roared and gusted across the ragged plain, picking up and blowing snow in great whirling cones.

The trail ended. Hester's tracks—gone. They walked back and forth, boots slipping over the hidden crevices and debris. Ethan thought Hester must have gone across the clearing, but everything looked like a footprint out there in the blowing snow with the divots and branches beneath.

"I think she was following a deer," Ethan said. "I noticed hoof-prints back there, but I don't see them now." There were no other tracks to follow. Maybe the wind had driven snow over them, or fresh snow had covered them. Over and over they called her name.

He had a map and held it out; they stood in the lee of a tree out of the wind in the woods near the clearing. Ethan in his wool coat and hat, his cheeks ruddy, the exposed skin of his face gray and wet as unset cement. The snow pelted and melted and the worry carved deep grooves in the lines of his face. He showed her with a gloved hand where they stood on the map, and how out across the clearing there was a road, but she couldn't see the road, couldn't

slow her mind enough to orient herself to the map. He said the
name of the road. They would split up to cover more ground and
meet at the end of Yarrow Road.

"Elsa?"

Blood roared in her ears.

"Did you hear what I said?"

She felt out of her body. "I have to go down that road." She
stepped out from the tree cover, and the biting wind struck her
face. She stopped, looked back. "Hester knows somebody who
lives there," she said to Ethan. "I think she might have gone there."

"Okay, all right." He folded up the map. "I'll go with you."

"No," she said. "No, we should split up. I might be wrong."

He pointed out where the woods continued on the other side of
the road, and they agreed on a time and a place to meet up. Then
they headed out across the clearing, first Elsa and then Ethan,
pressing their bodies against a wind that drilled them with pellets
of snow. When they got to the road—a single gravel spit plunging
into a tunnel of more woods—they split up, he to the south and
she to the east. She marched down the center of the road following
the faint twin lines left by tire tracks under a skein of snow.

Al's trailer home sat on cinder blocks, and a stovepipe fit through
the roof hurtled out smoke. A child's picnic table sat up against
the trailer, for Anya, she thought. Elsa stood in the middle of the
road. The dark shelf of a sedan protruded out from under the
snow in the driveway, and from somewhere back in the woods a
generator droned. Racks of antlers were hung up around the front
door, and all along the body of the trailer were nailed the hides of
squirrel, skunk, and deer.

Her boots pressed through the heavy slush on the gravel and
waded into the blanket of snow draped over the yard. She passed
under the tall rod of an outdoor light that shined down over wasps

of buzzing snow. From out of the woods to her right a large animal lunged. Elsa stumbled back and fell in the snow. Fish stood over her, teeth bared, gums black; he barked and snarled and wore no chain, no harness. On her back in the snow she tried not to appear threatening while shielding her face.

"Stop that barking! Cut that out!" Al's voice in the doorway. "I said stop that! You cut that out now!"

Al labored down the cinder-block steps and called out until Fish backed away and came to his side, but still the dog kept up his hacking bark. Al shuffled through the snow in front of his trailer in sweatpants and a T-shirt, no coat or jacket. He clipped a chain to Fish's collar. Shaking, Elsa got to her feet.

"It's Elsa," she called out, "from the Den."

"I know who you are," Al said. "Don't let the dog bother you none. He's just looking out for me." He turned back to his trailer, the dog still barking. "You'd better come on in," he said. "He won't give us a moment's peace until you do." Al pulled open the door and went in as though not at all surprised to see her.

She brushed the snow off her coat, approached the trailer. Fish wheeled up, pulled on his chain, barked and snarled. The dog wasn't more than three feet away, but Elsa took the cinder-block steps and went inside. Behind her the door fell closed.

"You can have a seat here." Al moved stacks of catalogs off a padded metal chair. In the living room to her left a TV blared and computer parts sat out on the floor against the walls. In front of her a kitchen no bigger than a bathroom was strewn with power tools and cupboard doors piled up in stacks. A circular saw sat on the stove, its arm raised, silver teeth and rust stains. In the drainboard instead of dishes, a power drill spilled out its orange cord.

"I'm looking for Hester." Elsa stood in her boots on a plastic floor mat and held herself together. "Is she here?"

Al turned off the television. The room fell into a sticky quiet.

"I need to know if you've seen Hester or if she's been here." Her legs shook and her chin quivered. Inside her core she clenched, her bones shot through with cold, and she couldn't shake it, the terrible chanting that rose up from that dark place, *What should I do, what should I do, what should I do?* For one long moment in the silence Al stood in front of her and said nothing. One eye pointed sideways but his good eye looked back into hers. Behind him in the small room the wind tunneled down through the stovepipe and fluttered the aluminum cuffs of its chimney.

"When did this happen?" he finally said.

"Six o'clock this morning. She ran off."

"That's no good."

"Is she here?"

"Why don't you sit down."

"Is she here?"

"No, no I haven't seen her." He was moving in that slow way of his into the kitchen, opening up a small refrigerator, pulling things out. The heat in the trailer cloying with its smell of cooked onions and something else, some unfamiliar spice, and in the living room a bedsheet tacked over one window blocked out the light. She saw the dark doors then, two of them leading into other rooms. A manifestation of all her fears culminating here in this greasy box and she was nauseous and shivering and flicking on the light.

Bathroom towels lay on the floor next to a fake plastic plant and stacks of magazines. The back lid of the toilet tank had been removed and a rusty coat hanger led down into the water inside. Adrenaline pumped through her and blood rushed into her head.

"If you need to use the bathroom, just ask."

Al stood in the doorway behind her, blocking her way out. He outweighed her by a good hundred pounds and his breath rattled and his hair sprung oily from a thick sweating neck.

"Let me pass." Her voice not her own, graveled and deep. Her teeth vibrated from the cold and the fear as he stepped aside and she went into the doorway of the second room.

She got there, and everything halted and folded down as though a glass dome clamped over her head. She understood, then, how all this time she had been rushing, even in her mind, rushing, and only now had she gone still. There was nothing alive in this room. It held only objects. She accounted them: a waterbed, low and sitting on the floor; a Mr. Potato Head cocked to its side, one eye staring up; blankets and bedsheets twisted across the mattress; and a trail of scattered coins—she had to name each item, what she saw, because even as she saw these things, she couldn't make sense of it. These things were not what she had expected them to be, what she had thought they would be, her daughter, Hester, lying on the bed. Hester was not there.

"My daughter," Al said from behind, still standing by the bathroom door. "She used to sleep in there. I let her have my room. But she ain't here no more."

Built-in dresser drawers against the far wall pulled open, clothes spilling out. A single window hung with a sheet. Pennies, quarters, dimes.

Al shuffled back into the kitchen. She heard him drop like a sack into his chair, and the television came back on, its volume on low. The sound of it droned in her head with the empty lines and colors that cut through her because even though she was looking, she still could not believe that Hester was not here.

If she wasn't here, then where was she?

Moving back into the kitchen she didn't know what to do. A sickening flooded her, swelled and filled all the spaces in her head. The spinning started up with a violence that threatened to tip her upside down, and she was alone again in the dark, falling, untethered, with nothing and no one to catch her.

She stumbled into a chair, reached out for the door, and fell.

Al caught her, offered a chair.

"No," she said. "No, I have to go."

"Maybe you should sit down first."

She sat and the room returned. With it came her embarrass-
ment for having come here, for pushing into his private rooms, and
accusing him of taking Hester. She covered her face and it blazed
hot under her cold hands.

Al had gotten out a new water bottle for her and told her to
drink. She realized how thirsty she was, all morning out calling
and searching in the snow. The water put her back in her body. She
drank and drank some more.

Across from her Al sat at the table and fumbled with some
kind of foil packet. It crinkled and flopped. His own water bottle
dented and with a torn label, clearly used. His T-shirt had worn
through so thin, his skin showed through the fabric even where
there weren't any holes.

"Satisfied?" he said.

The water slid cool down her throat. She'd been out searching
for two hours, she realized, the clock above the stove. She noticed
everything, all the colors sharp and exact, as if she were just coming out from a fog.

"I'm sorry, Al. I owe you an apology."

He fiddled with the packet, still trying to get it opened. "Why
did you come in here like that?"

"I . . ." She took another drink of the water, screwed on the cap.
"I thought my daughter was here."

"Why would she be here?"

She left the water bottle in the middle of the table and pulled
her hands into her lap. "I don't know, Al. You scared me, and your
dog scared me. That day you found my kids in the woods, you
offered them candy and a ride in your car." She wiped at her face
with the backs of her hands. "And that day at the café when you
left them like that, you said you would watch them, and I know

it's not your job to watch them, but you said that you would, and then you left them, and it upset me. It upset them." She inhaled, exhaled, held on to her tears. "I don't know why you did that."

He looked away. He scratched the back of his head. "I don't know about that," he said. "Probably Anya had to leave. She gets anxious around too many people, she gots sensory issues."

"I didn't know that."

"She's not a normal kid."

"I'm sorry, Al. I didn't know."

"And the chocolate bar is from Harry Potter."

"Excuse me?"

"I always keep a chocolate bar in my first aid kit, you know, from the Harry Potter series. Your little one got hurt, and pain takes away your hope. Chocolate brings it back."

She almost laughed. The snow pinged against the windows and the wind fluttered in the stovepipe. The plastic of his water bottle crinkled.

"I didn't mean no harm by it," he said.

"No, I see that now. I'm sorry. It's a nice idea."

"No, no I see it now, too," he said. "I understand."

He looked to her with his one good eye, and she saw herself in him; she saw how much they were the same.

"I have to get back outside." She stood and pushed in her chair. Her eyes filled and roved and dried up as she looked around the room. "I don't know where to go."

Al was trying again to open the foil packet and, unsuccessful, he tossed it onto the table.

"Can't never get them things open," he said. "It's for my breakfast."

She reached for the packet. It contained a strawberry-flavored protein powder. She tore it open easily with her nimble fingers and Al lifted his battered water bottle. Carefully, working to keep her hands steady, she poured the powder in through the small opening. He nodded thanks, screwed the cap down on his bottle, and rocked it back and forth. "I have a map here somewhere," he said, "and some chocolate powder if you want one." He stood with some effort, leaned against the counter, and pulled down a stack of papers from one of the doorless cupboards. "Anya and me used to have these for breakfast and I got the chocolate ones for her." He tossed out a foil packet and laid down a map.

She studied the map, her mind calmer now. She picked out the dirt road her house sat on and its driveway long and winding and where Hester had walked off. She saw Yarrow Road and the space between where they'd logged off. She turned the map around and showed him the place where Hester's trail had ended.

Al nodded, picked up a pen. He drew the shape of a hatchet. "It looks different now they got it logged off," he said. "Makes things confusing." He drew the clearing; it was shaped like an ax with the handle of it long and falling alongside their entire back forty and beyond. "This is where I found them last spring," he said, pointing to the map. "They was back here when the wagon got busted and then they went running up that hill." He drew the hill and the road at the bottom of it, marked an X for his trailer, and squared off the two twenty-acre parcels of land across from it. Then he turned the map back toward her. "Does that help?"

She studied it, was able to orient herself, to see where she and Ethan had gone, and where they had not.

"Yes, it does," she said. "Thank you."

"You're welcome." He drank from his bottle. "Your girl was good to Anya. Not like some of them other kids with their smart mouths and attitudes," he said. "I can go out there and help youse look if you want. I'll take Fish with me. We'll cover the north ground."

"Thank you, Al. I would really appreciate your help."

"You're welcome," he said. He screwed the cap down on his bottle and went to get his coat. He had his back to her. "Anya's mom come by and picked her up last month," he said. "It's just temporary, her staying with me, only for the summer."

"That's hard." Elsa said. "You must miss her."

"I do." He turned back around. "Without her next to me, the world ain't so kind."

Al gave her the map and she left before he did, anxious to get back outside. Fish barked at her as she marched out through the snow to the end of the yard and turned left. Al would go to the right, where the road ended in a culvert; she headed west across the road and plunged into the woods on the other side.

She called Hester's name, moving through the trees. After a time the woods ended and all around her the land opened out into the clearing. She held out the map as the wind whipped and teared her eyes, but she didn't see any sign of her daughter in her red coat. The snow lifted in bands that arced and writhed across the ruined ground. She didn't want to go back out there, didn't want to pick her way across the remains of fallen trees like she was walking across a graveyard, and she didn't think Hester would want to do that, either. But the tracks had ended at the edge of the woods and Ethan had thought that her girl had walked on.

Elsa turned back around and plowed through a different section of woods until she came again to the road. She headed down it a little ways until she got to a new patch of woods on the north side of the clearing, these woods directly across from their land. She found a game trail, headed in.

The snow continued to fall and the branches above her rocked in the wind. She walked, calling out Hester's name until the spinning blackness inside her became overwhelming. With her arms outstretched she reached for the trees, pressing her hand against one and then another trunk. She held herself there with her head bowed and listened to the trees.

The quiet filled her, a deep and abiding silence all around. She found the point inside herself where she met what was there, what was actually occurring, where the wind blew and the snow fell and she was part of it, this rolling land, this rousing air.

Elsa walked on. She was open to the sounds and movements in the woods, as though in meditation, not slow, but alert, neither harried nor rushed.

A branch cracked to her left. She stopped, looked out. There through the woods a pair of eyes. Silent and watchful, sentient but not human. A deer, two deer, three of them in all, a small band not fifty feet away. She thought about what Ethan had said, how Hester had followed a deer, and these were difficult to see, their fur white as the snow that filled the air. They flicked their ears, eyes rimmed in mauve and fur iridescent in the shimmering air.

One of them studied her, the largest one, a mother, Elsa thought, because it was watchful and wary. Elsa did not move. The space between them filled only with snow sifting down and the creak of boughs overhead, and the two smaller deer moved away, unconcerned. But this mother deer did not move. It watched her, neither blinking nor turning away. Its face quiet, serene in the pearly air.

Elsa took a step forward off the trail, toward this mother deer, and the deer did not flinch or move away. Elsa's foot snapped a branch; the deer flicked its ear but stayed. Elsa closed the space and the mother deer turned and walked away. It did not run; it walked, then stopped, looking back. Elsa followed, the deer graceful as it wound in and out through the snow-filled wood.

She followed them, these ghosts of the forest, until the trees ended and the land opened out. This time they were on the edge of an even bigger clearing that faced north. She thought about Al's map and imagined they were in the handle of the ax. The mother deer stepped out, then looked back. Beyond her the ruined ground opened out and the wind rolled down and the snow gathered and twisted into great whirling cones.

With a flicker of movement, the mother deer was gone. All the deer were running now, leaping out and springing across the clearing through the snow. A fourth deer stood farther off on a rise that overlooked the clearing. The father, Elsa thought, its neck muscled and thick with a rack of antlers that rose immense above its head. It stood watching them, the other deer coming toward it through the snow, and it watched her. It stood proud out there on that ridge in the snow, it stood there like it belonged. Then it turned with the others and ran, their tails springing up and away through the snow-filled air.

Behind her a cry rippled out, a mere ruffle in the wind.

Elsa turned. Her daughter—there. Small and huddled beneath a snow-covered pine. Knees drawn to her chest, face hidden beneath the hood of her coat, the red of it draped and muted by a skein of snow.

She went to her daughter, approaching gently as though Hester might scare away, and kneeling before her she called her name.

"Hester?"

The girl raised her face. She lifted both arms and reached out, slowly, pitifully. "Mama," she said.

Elsa pulled her in, wrapping her tight with both arms, and Hester fell willingly, meltingly into her chest. They wept. It was a time and a spell under which she had no impression of clock time or thoughts passing, only the largeness of how much she could hold, the heart so capable, it could hold so much, the light and the dark, the fear and the love, all of it, and the loss of what they had both shared.

Eventually, the moment passed, and Elsa lifted her daughter into her arms and stood. Snowflakes hit her face, mixing with the salt of her tears.

Hester molded herself to her mother, wrapping her legs tight around her waist, and with her arms around her neck, laid her head in the crook of her shoulder.

Elsa carried her through the woods, feeling capable and strong, and in the space that had been cleared inside of her she knew what she could give her daughter, what she could teach Finn and what they could all hold on to. What Silas had tried to show her in those dreams but what she hadn't understood: He was here. Not on the land but inside of them. He was their heartwood. What she would carry with her for all the days of her life, wherever she went, in everything she did, in what she said, and in the ways that she thought and in the actions she took. Because he was in her, he was in them all. It was the heartwood that kept the tree strong and the heartwood without which they would fall.

She wrapped her arms tighter around her daughter as they came out onto the road and walked along the median. The wall of woods to her right fell away and opened out to the clearing directly across their land. The trees at the edge rocked and swayed, a whole line of them, pulling apart from each other in the snow-filled wind. They clattered like giant rakes against the sky. And it came to her then with a flash of clarity—the dead bolt slid out of place and the pin dropped down through the locking mechanism of her mind—she saw it!, what had been taking down her clothes-line all this time, her clothesline that was tied to the trunks of the trees. Elsa tipped her head back and laughed.

Hester lifted her head off her mother's neck. "What it is, Mama?"

"Oh, it's nothing," she said. "I just figured something out."

"What?"

"I'll tell you later." She kissed the top of her daughter's head. "I will tell you it all." And then she whispered, "It's the trees. It's only ever been about the trees."

SPRING

E than Arnasson sat behind the wheel of his truck and followed
Elsa's car in front of him. His wife in the front passenger seat
beside her was going on about something—he saw gestures in silhouette, along with the hump of chirping Charlie's birdcage in the
back seat, and the two little heads of the kids bobbing gently along.
They came up over a rise on the county road that looked out over
acres of young budding trees.

He pulled the U-Haul trailer they had just picked up in town,
the dog in the front seat next to him. Maggie pushed her snout out
through the window he'd rolled down a crack, inhaling the fresh
forest funk. Heavy clouds brooded in the distance and thunder
rumbled along the horizon. In her fur, he smelled rain.

They had found a buyer for the unfinished house, a school-
teacher from Madison willing to take on the property as is. He
and his partner and two dogs would live there once they settled
in. Elsa and the kids had lived at the farmhouse all winter. Hester
went to school and Elsa applied to colleges while helping out with
the farm chores, he and Luvera got their house packed up and
somehow, everything got done.

The brake lights in front of him lit up. Elsa slowed her car in the
middle of the road. In silhouette, he saw all three of them turn their
heads—Elsa, Hester, little Finn—they all lifted their hands in unison and waved to the forlorn pine left scraggly and alone out in a
clear-cut field. A moment later, he saw his wife give the tree a wave,
too. Then Elsa took her foot off the brake and the car rolled on.

A few miles later they turned onto the dirt road and wound up the driveway past the spruce and balsam firs as gravel popped beneath their tires. The house came into view tucked up there in the side of the hill. Everything inside already packed into boxes—Elsa had been working on it all spring. The skid carts and logging equipment had sold, and the draft horses had been given new homes. Elsa had been accepted to a university in North Carolina, and they had surprised her when he announced, "We're coming with you. Wherever it is you need to go, we'll follow, if you'll have us." The look on her face, and she'd about knocked him over with the force of her hug. They had leased out the farm to the new hired hand, so while Elsa finished her education, they would be neighbors. The coastal town even had palm trees. Their furniture was already loaded on a moving truck and on its way because, as he told Luvera, they were a family now. Maybe not the family they set out to have, the family they'd always envisioned, but a family nonetheless.

A few raindrops fell from a featureless sky, and if they wanted to get to Madison by nightfall, they would have to hurry to load in the boxes. Ethan backed up the U-Haul across the field and parked close to the house so it was easy to load. He pushed the dolly back and forth from the house to the truck, while Hester and Finn ran around with Maggie under the Scotch pines. In the open door of the trailer his wife stooped and moved the boxes around, making room.

"Elsa took her ax and left," Luvera reported. "Just left me here to finish all this." She took a box from his stack and loaded it into the trailer.

"Where'd she go?" He hefted another box and heard the thud of the ax. Peering around the U-Haul, he found Elsa down at the woodpile at the bottom of the hill.

"I told her the new owners can split their own firewood," Luvera said. "But she's worried about the logs being left out on the ground in the rain. Said she doesn't want the wood to rot." She took another box and pushed it in, wrangled with the rake and the hoe. "You know how she is once she gets something in her head."

"I do know." Ethan hefted another box. "I know somebody else like that, too."

"And who would that be, Mr. Arnasson?"

"Oh, I'm not complaining, Mrs. Arnasson. It's a lucky man who finds himself surrounded by strong women."

"Muleheaded, you mean."

"You said it, not me."

They got everything loaded, and he pulled down the sliding door of the trailer and latched it closed. The rain held off, but he could smell it in the air now. Taking out his handkerchief, he wiped the sweat and dust from his brow. From the bottom of the hill came the hollow thuds of Elsa's ax.

"We should get the kids loaded into the truck," he said. "It's about to rain."

"You go grab Maggie," Luvera said. "I'll get the little ones."

They'd already said their goodbyes to the little house in the woods, had a kind of ceremony outside with a campfire once the snow had melted and the ground had thawed; they'd even invited over the new owner. He told them about his plans for the house, and Ethan felt satisfied that they would take care of the place, but they wouldn't be finishing the second story. He was taking it down, he said, the skeleton walls, the unfinished roof, he would turn the space into an attic for a single story. The floor joists that Silas had milled from trees that he had known and felled by hand would remain. Those beams would lie in the dark of an attic, one man's dream to raise a roof, raise a family, his intention to build a life. They would hold their vigor and lie in wait for some new family, some other time, because this dream just wasn't meant to be.

The kids clambered into the back seat of the cab with Maggie between them, and Luvera slid next to him in the front. The first of the rain splatted down against the windshield with giant liquid paws. Their breath steamed up the windows, and Ethan turned over the engine and ran the heat.

"How long is she going to be?" Luvera asked. "We don't have all day." The rain wasn't falling hard, it came in intermittent drops out of the soft, white sky. He took the truck out of park and rolled it down the hill slowly across the field to park it again at the top of the drive next to Elsa's car. Luvera unbuckled her seat belt and made to leave.

"Wait a minute," Ethan said. "Look at what she's done."

The woodpile stood chest high on wooden rails, several rows deep. Elsa had learned how to run a chain saw. She'd sawed up the spruce that had fallen in a winter storm, then later she'd taken down her first tree, a birch that had lost a limb. She held the ax lightly by its handle and bent and tossed and stacked the splits. She stacked them the way Silas had always done, the way Robby had taught him when he was a boy.

"The Elsa we knew a year ago wouldn't have been able to do that." The air so still, he could hear the chink of gravel when she set her blade down and the rustle of the tarp as she worked to cover everything up. In the distance the thunderheads rumbled and growled.

"It wouldn't even have occurred to her," Luvera said.

"But it occurs to her now."

A smatter of raindrops darkened the dirt.

"If Silas were here," he said, "that's exactly what he would have done."

Luvera reached out for his hand. He took it, and they threaded their fingers together. The rain pattered as it fell against the car and stained the earth, a soft rain, warm and cleansing. They both watched from inside the car as Elsa covered the woodpile that would see the new owners through the next winter. They watched with a kind of pride as if she were their own daughter, and in all the important ways, she was.

Acknowledgments

First and foremost, I am grateful to my family for casting such a wide net under my feet:

My parents, Richard and Lorraine, for love I can count on; my two sisters, Theresa and Kimberly, my always friends; and Carol Kramer, my second mom, and her wife, Nancy Shoop, for encouragement from this world and beyond.

To Bob Dunbar for giving me his old laptop so that I could write when my babies were sleeping without firing up the generator; to Vivian for inspiration, Robin for challenging me to go "parkour," and Joni for helping me edit "to the bone." To Ansley of Narrative HiFi for the most incredible book trailer known to man and trees.

Huge thanks to the Madeline Island School for the Arts (MISA) for granting me a scholarship to study under Paulette Bates Alden, that rare writer who is both teacher and artist, and to my fellow students for giving me a hand up in the dark: Mae Sylvester, Welcome Jerde, Dianna Granger, Diane Rock, and Rita Sharp.

To the members and writers of Lake Superior Writers for decades of encouragement, classes, and fellowship—I wouldn't have made it here without you.

Special thanks to Jim Perlman of Holy Cow! Press, my literary lifeline, and to my readers: Felicia Schneiderhan, Avesa Rockwell, Tina Higgins-Wussow, Luci Admundsen, Jena McKenzie, James Phillips, and Gail Towbridge. To Juli Patty for reading more drafts than anyone else—you were right about the two books. To my medical experts, Dr. Steve Laxdal and nurse Christine Houlton, thank you for fielding my endless questions with such encouragement and care. And thank you, Debra Raye King, my last-minute dairy farm expert. To Patti Lindelof, former principal of Four Corners Elementary, for the art room to write in. To all my early readers, my sincerest apologies and thanks: Michelle Greene, Angela Skinner, Ron Menzel, Mary Strom, and Theresa Baelin, who left a message on my answering machine, "It's going to be a bestseller, dahling."

To the David R. Collins Writers' Conference, thank you for the classes, teachers, and community of generous writers, notably Kali (VanBaale) White, Lucy Tan, Lyz Lenz, and Luis Alberto Urrea. Thank you to Julie Carrick Dalton, Pamela Klinger-Horn, Glendy Vanderah, and Julie Buckles for your kindness and for championing this book.

To my agent, Abby Saul of The Lark Group, thank you for your heart and integrity and for being by my side every step of the way. To my editor, Robert Davis, thank you for the keys that unlocked a better draft and for asking all the right questions. To the team of professionals working behind the scenes at Forge, thank you for your care and attention: Russell Trakhtenberg, Terry McGarry, Jessica Katz, Jennifer McClelland-Smith, Ashley Spruill, Jacqueline Huber-Rodriguez, NaNá Stoelzle, and Karen Richardson.

Lastly, to my children, Rae and Sawyer, who have been a part of this book since they came into this world—thank you for the privilege of being your mom. To my husband, Daniel Dunbar, for creating the "Books don't get written by" list, for giving me the title for this book, and for everything, everything.